EVERYTHING IS BROKEN

ANTHONY DECASTRO

Palmetto *Pulp Mill*

Cover illustration by Timmy Ryu

ISBN-13: 978-0-578-40145-4

Published by Palmetto Pulp Mill, Greenville, SC USA

www.palmettopulpmill.com

For Jill, with love.

B illy "Sample" Smith was a low-level dealer of weed and pills, who stayed out of trouble with the law by simply lacking any ambition. He spent his days playing video games at wherever he was shacking for free, and his nights selling dime bags to rich kids wandering around Ocean Boulevard in Myrtle Beach.

I didn't like Billy, but I had when we were younger. Back when he had earned his nickname.

It was a night in college, sophomore year, at one of the many strip clubs that flourished in the Strand. Billy escorted one of the girls to the Champagne Room. When she came back down twenty minutes later with a sodden Billy holding her hand like a little boy, she said, "Okay, I've had my free sample. Now I'm ready for the full dish. Who's next?"

Billy stood about five-three and weighed maybe 120 pounds after a full meal. The stripper could have referred to his stature, but a bunch of college guys would never come to that conclusion. So Billy spent the rest of his college days fending off teases about the size of his manhood. College only lasted a few more months for Billy. But the name, "Sample", stuck to this day.

Like I said, I didn't like Sample, but in my business it helps to have a conduit to the seedy side of the Beach. And he'd done me a solid in that regard many times. So when he texted me saying he had work for me and asked me to meet him at the Second Avenue Fishing Pier, I didn't stop to think whether I wanted to work for dirty money, or ask whether the work would involve me breaking any laws. I just agreed to meet him at 10 p.m. at the end of the Pier. Legality, prison time, or a knifing by rival dealers, I pondered on the ride over.

It was the Tuesday before Thanksgiving, and a light chill rode shotgun on the breeze coming off the Atlantic. I played the part of a beach bum put out by the cold, wearing a light nylon windbreaker, threadbare khakis, and white canvas boat shoes. I stopped at the pier's bait shop and paid a dollar walker's fee to a heavy-set, bald clerk. He looked annoyed that he had to lean forward to ring up my sale on the register.

"Ya know we close up at eleven, right? No excuses. Gotta be outta here by eleven."

I didn't point out that his breath smelled worse than the bait he was peddling, or how I doubted he would make the effort to walk down to the end of the pier and escort me out, if I rebelled and stuck around longer than eleven. I just nodded and stuffed the little orange ticket stub he handed me into the front pocket of my slacks.

Stepping out of the shop, I hunched my shoulders against the cold. Somehow, the smell of the salt, the fish guts, and seaweed was more potent on this side of the bait shop. Flickering, halogen lights hung from rickety posts illuminating a dim path down the pier. The boards of the pier creaked and sagged under my steps as they always had. It was a wonder that the thing hadn't collapsed. Especially during the summer months, when tourists lined the pier elbow to elbow, reeling in pinfish and toadfish and other useless game.

Tonight it was mostly empty, there were only a handful of old salts down near the end. They slouched, elbows resting on the rails, rods in their hands. They dropped their lines beside the pier's pilings hoping to lure sheepshead to the live shrimp or fiddler crabs or oysters, which baited their hooks.

I found Sample on hands and knees at the far end of the El shaped terminus, sawing the dorsal fin off an 18-inch, baby, black-tip shark. A light, spinning rod laid beside the shark, and I could see a circle hook set into the crook of the shark's mouth. Its tail swiped back and forth, painting the boards of the pier with its own blood.

"What the hell are you doing, Sample?"

He jolted, bolt upright. "Jesus, Fuzzy. You almost gave me a heart attack." He dropped the knife and stood wiping a bloody hand on the front of his jeans. He was naked to the waist, and his concave chest was as hairless as his bald pate.

I shook his callused hand. It was sticky with fish blood.

"With a grip like that Fuzzy, you'd think you was a dairy farmer, not someone who throws a ball for a living." He pointed to the impotent shark, flopping at his feet, its dorsal fin hanging by a flap of skin. "Best bait in the world there is for shark."

"Huh?"

"No lie," he said. "Wounded baby shark draws the big ones like flies to shit."

"Isn't there a size limit on what you can keep?"

"I'm using it for bait," he said. "I ain't keepin' it."

"I don't think it matters, Samp. And, didn't I see a sign prohibiting shark fishing from the pier?"

3

The crescent moon flashed upon his golden bridgework. "I ain't always exactly been what you'd call legal."

He had me there.

"Yeah, well, you asked me to come and I'm here. So, what's up?"

"Let me get this baby baited up and wet again. Then we can talk," He stepped down on the shark's head, bent over and yanked the fin from the fish's back. "There's beer in that styrofoam cooler. Help yourself to one."

Busch Light was stacked in neat rows in the iceless cooler. I grabbed a can, popped one open, and took a short pull of warm, cheap beer.

Sample worked on the shark's pectoral fins now.

"What's the deal with chopping off the fins? Isn't a lively bait, the better bait?"

"Sure, if you're hunting smart fish. Sharks ain't exactly smart, and they ain't discerning about what they eat, either." He mulled that over for a second. "Come to think of it they's kinda like me in that way. Anyway, a shark is drawn to an easy meal. I don't want this beauty dead when I toss it down there, but I want it hurtin'. Stick around. I'll be here all night. I bet I pull in a big'un."

Mr. Out-by-eleven would love that.

"Don't be so quick to laugh, Fuzzy. Just last weekend I pulled in a seven foot hammerhead. Doin' just like this."

"I wasn't laughing at you, Samp. A thought just crossed my mind. But do me a favor, get that thing on a line and back in the water, so I don't have to watch it die, while you're telling fish stories."

I watched in admiration of his efficiency when he set about the task. The person passionate about his work or hobby, even a person like Billy Smith, is a person not prone to wasted effort or bullshit. The bait remained hooked to his spinning rod, as he hurried to a boat rod as thick as a broom's handle, leaning in the crook formed by the corner of the pier. He slid free a 5″ stainless steel J-hook from where it was fastened to a huge 9/0 bait-caster reel. Flipping the drag on the side of the reel, he pulled six feet of monofilament line free, giving him enough slack to hurry back to the shark. He slid on his knees, and skidded to a stop right before the shark's snout, safely out of reach of its dangerous bite. He grabbed the shark behind its head, jamming his thumb and middle finger into gills on either side. Then he threaded the giant hook into one nostril and out the other. With the bait now hooked, he reached into his back pocket, produced a pair of needle-nosed pliers, and pulled loose the circle hook from the fish's mouth.

He exhaled a blast of breath and peered up at me. "I never feel real good about this until I get him hooked up on the big daddy," he said as he hoisted the shark up by the shank of the giant hook. The baby predator looked resigned to its fate. Sample tossed it overboard and let out the line for several seconds. When the sinker reached the bottom, he flipped the bail, cranked a few times, and put the rod back down in its original spot. He tied the pole down to the pier with yellow nylon rope.

"There, now we can talk."

I waited, while he stood there with a dumb look on his face. "You texted me, Samp."

"So I did, So I did. So how's it going, Fuzz? How's your mom?"

"She's in jail. How do you think she feels?"

I'd put her there.

We both knew it.

The obligatory awkward silence descended. Even the waves seemed to stop slapping at the pilings. Mercifully, one of the old salts hacked away like a lifetime smoker.

"You still doing the PI gig?"

"You know I am," I said.

"Still doing, domestic stuff? Ya know like catchin' daddy puttin' his thing where he shouldn't?"

"You're not married, Samp. Where are you going with this?"

He stepped closer so he could speak in a lower tone. "There's a girl I want you to follow and take pictures of who she gets with."

"Ok, Samp. Who's the girl?"

"She's just a girl," he said. "She's gettin' herself in trouble."

"Like I said, Samp. Who's the girl?"

He had a look on his face I recognized. It was the same look I saw staring back at me from the mirror, after I'd awakened from one of my dreams. The bad ones. The ones, where I dreamed that my fiancé was still alive.

I said, "Are you in love?"

"No, No, No. Nothing like that. It's just she's a good kid. Smart kid. She's got a good future, if she don't go messin' it up. Ya know how it is."

I tried to formulate what a good future looked like to Billy Smith, but I came up empty. "How are pictures of her going to help that? Is she under age? Are you going to take the pictures to her parents? What's the deal?"

"Nah, she ain't under age. She's pullin' tricks."

I said, "She's a whore?"

"No it ain't like she's walkin' Yaupon Drive. She's just meetin' guys at hotel bars and dressed all up in those rhinestone dresses."

"She wears rhinestones?"

"Yeah, you know them sparkly things like the chicks wore to prom?"

"Sequins?"

"Yeah, sequins. The girls that dress like that at the hotel

bars are pros, Fuzzy. She's a good kid. I don't want her goin' pro."

"So say I take pictures of her doin' the nasty. Say I even catch her transacting. What exactly do you think you're gonna accomplish with my pictures?"

"She says she ain't pullin' tricks."

"You asked her if she was a whore?"

"She ain't no whore, Fuzzy. But yeah, I kinda asked her, you know? Why she had so many dates, and with older guys. I was cool about it though."

He caught me with that one just as I swallowed a mouthful of beer, and I fought the urge to spit it back out. "And how did she react to your slick line of interrogation?"

"Oh, she got what I was askin'. I told ya, she's a smart one. She giggled and patted me on the cheek and said, 'Ah, Billy you ain't got nothin' to worry about I only got eyes for you.' I said, 'Honey, you need to be careful with what you doin' there's bad folks out there.' She said, 'I ain't doin' what you think I'm doing.' And got some nasty look on her face. She kinda been avoidin' me ever since."

I said, "I still don't see what pictures will do for you."

"If I can confront her with the evidence that she's lyin', I think I can get her to listen. And if it's all there in black & white, she'll see what she's doin' ain't smart. I know it."

"I shoot in color and digitally."

"Whatever," he said. "Whaddaya say, Fuzzy? You gonna help a brother out?"

"What's her name?"

"I knew I could count on ya. Her name is Marisol Rodriguez."

"How do you know her?"

"I know her brother. He's over at CAU on a full-ride. He plays that receiver, who also blocks on the line."

"Tight end," I said. "What's his name and is he one of your customers?"

"Jandro Rodriguez. Short for Alejandro. In high school, he went by Alex, but got tired of all the A-Rod shit. So now he goes by Jandro. He buys from me from time to time, but don't hold that against his sister, Fuzz. She ain't ever bought from me. She's just sorta around a lot. I think she likes to hang out at the college, meet his friends you know?"

Sample was an interesting character. He was quick to uphold this girl's honor. A girl who he assumed was a prostitute. But he wanted to be sure I knew she says no to drugs. "How old is she?"

"I dunno. 18 or 19 maybe? She outta school."

"Ok, and how long do you want me to peep on her?"

"I dunno maybe a week. We gotta get her with a john."

"I get $100 a day, plus expenses."

He whistled. "Damn, Fuzzy. That is harsh."

"It's my normal rate," I lied. I didn't tell him I was discounting him by half for the help he'd given me in the past.

"What kinda expenses you talkin'? You gonna charge me for gas or something?"

"You say she works the hotel bars. I'll be spending time in them. I can't sit in the bars at night, drinking nothing but ice water without drawing attention, or worse, being asked to leave. Don't worry. I'll keep my receipts."

"Wow, I need to have your job. On top of the fee, you get your bar tab picked up."

"Look this is probably a fool's errand, anyway. You don't have to hire me at all."

He shoved my shoulder and left his hand there. "Take it easy, Fuzz. I'm just bustin' your balls. But let's make it four days."

"Deal," I said.

He patted my shoulder, and when he removed his hand, I

saw the dark stain of fish blood on my jacket. "Say you don't give a discount for cash. Do you?"

"Sorry Samp. I keep it on the level with Uncle Sam. Cash and check spend the same for me. But cash lets me start right away without waiting on the check to clear."

He looked hurt. "Fuzzy, damn, how long we known each other?"

"I'm kidding, Samp." The smell of the fish blood he'd left on my shoulder crawled down my insides and turned somersaults inside my stomach. He had some rags, but they all looked worse than the slime he had just left on me. "So where do I find this Marisol Rodriguez?"

"She'll probably make her way to the Coral Beach some night this week. But, I can't really say with Turkey Day comin' up."

"You know where she lives?"

"I don't want you goin' where she lives, Fuzzy. She lives at home, and I want no one catchin' on to you."

"Sample, you are hiring a private investigator to spy on someone for you. You're paying me, because I don't get caught doing it. It's kind of my thing."

"All the same, Fuzzy. I don't think it's a good idea."

"Ok, but it might take me more than the four days just to luck out and stumble upon her at a bar. You got a picture of the Happy Hooker?"

"Don't call her that. Nah, I ain't got no picture of her. But just check her out on Facebook, Instagram, Twitter, she's got lots a photos on there."

I wondered if he was stalking her online, but I didn't ask, because he pulled a wad of bills out from his pocket. "How much you need upfront?"

"No retainer, Samp. I know you're good for it. But if you can front me a hundred for the expenses that would help. I'm running a little dry right now."

He held out the bill, not letting go of it when I reached for it. "This girl is beautiful, Fuzzy. I mean like movie star looks. When you see her, don't get no ideas."

"Ideas?"

"Yeah, ideas. You got them weathered, jock, good looks, even with that gray hair. Like that Greek god or something. You know the one they always talk about."

"Adonis?"

"Yeah, Adonis. Don't go pulling no Adonis shit on the girl."

I snatched the hundred from his hand. "I don't think Adonis was 'weathered', but don't worry, Free Sample, I won't pull any Adonis shit."

"Ah, don't start with that Free Sample shit, Fuzzy. That ain't right."

"I'll start tomorrow."

I left him there questioning his manhood.

2

I woke up the next morning to a clap of thunder followed by the drumming of quarter-sized raindrops on my tin roof. Home was a humble abode. Two years ago, my friend and former teammate, Jimmy Alou offered me a renovated maintenance shed at the Murrells Inlet Yacht Club, which he owned. In exchange for free rent, I provided a security presence at the marina at a time when he was experiencing a rash of burglaries at boats moored there. The burglaries stopped right after I moved in, and though I can't say I had anything to do with the sudden downturn of crime, I fell into a low-cost living situation, which suited me just fine.

It wasn't much. Room for a sleeper sofa, a TV, and a small kitchenette with dorm fridge and microwave. I took my showers and trips to the john at the boathouse locker room. But for someone, who didn't entertain much and who wanted to work as little as possible and who played a kid's game for lunch money during the summer, it worked out pretty well.

I found my laptop under a pile of dirty laundry beside the TV, and spent a good fifteen minutes trying out passwords on

Facebook, until one worked and I could search for Marisol Rodriguez.

I wouldn't say she had the Hollywood looks that Sample claimed, but she was a cute girl, that looked like a co-ed preparing for Rush Week on Sorority Row. Her hair changed colors and styles, throughout the pictures. The latest picture had her in blonde, wavy hair to her shoulders, bright red lipstick contrasting just the lightest of eye makeup. She appeared to go to great lengths to hide her Latin ethnicity. But her sad and dark Aztec eyes gave it away. I transferred a recent picture to my phone, but I took the time to commit her features to memory.

One cheek, which dimpled when she smiled. Check.

Light evidence of a crescent-shaped scar on said dimpled cheek. Check

The slightest of gaps between her two front teeth. Check.

When I felt I had her image filed away, I turned to searching for her address. It wasn't easy. If she was eighteen or nineteen years old, as Sample said, she probably still lived at home. Which meant I needed to learn her parents' names first. I headed back to Facebook and scanned her friends list. Nobody looked like Mom or Dad. There were too many Rodriguez's on the Strand to try every address.

I decided on a long shot and called my Uncle.

Cricket, the African-American receptionist at the Ted Collins Law Enforcement Center, answered on the first ring. "Myrtle Beach Police. How may I help you?"

"Hey Cricket, it's Fuzzy Koella. Is Rod around?"

"Hey Fuzzy! I'm not sure. Let's find out."

The background chatter of the police department's lobby fell silent. I flipped through the images I had in my mind of Marisol Rodriguez. I was trying to recall her scar when my Uncle broke the silence. "Gilbreath, Myrtle Beach PD."

"Hey Rod, It's Fuzzy," I said.

"Fuzzy, how's your mom?"

He knew she was in jail, and he knew I put her there, too. He had tightened the cuffs on her wrists when they took her away. "Um, she's okay. Probably the best she could be under the circumstances."

"Yeah, listen. Tell her I'm gonna get out to see her. I just haven't had the time. We're still on this Hammer case."

The case of Maxwell Hammer's murder had hijacked the news for greater than a year now. In fact, the murder occurred the night before I began working the case that ended with my mother accused and eventually convicted of voluntary manslaughter. They had found Hammer, a popular city councilman, in his car in an alley off Yaupon Drive, a section of town with a reputation for its prostitution. His pants were at his ankles, and he was sliced open from midsection to sternum. I didn't care about the Hammer case back then, and I didn't care about it now.

"Will do. Look I need a favor."

"I figured as much, Fuzzy. That's pretty much the only reason you call. Just don't go tracking shit all over the floor this time. Okay?"

Uncle Rod's way with words always left me feeling guilty, or that I somehow wasn't living up to his higher expectations. "Right. So this should be simple. Need to see if y'all have ever pulled in a girl for soliciting by the name of Marisol Rodriguez."

I heard him tapping away at a keyboard. "What do you want with this Rodriguez?"

"You know I can't share too much, Rod." We pretty much go over confidentiality in all of my calls for favors.

"Right. But your track record isn't great, I don't think I need to remind you. Hell, the last of these favors ended up with me visiting you in the hospital."

I said, "This is different. Hell, the only thing I'm looking for is a last known address."

"You said Rodriguez? Marisol?."

"Yeah, you got a record for her." This might be easier than I thought. If she had a sheet for prostitution, I could just get Cricket to scan me a copy of her arrest record. If Sample only wanted to confront her with proof of her tricking, the record would be more convincing than any pictures.

"No record of a Marisol Rodriguez ever brought in for prostitution."

"No? All right, it was a long shot."

"But we have one here for an open container on her 18th birthday." He said.

"Yeah, when was that?"

"Last summer, looks like the officer let her go with a warning. Which means he tested her for intoxication, and she passed. No other records on her. What makes you think she's tricking?"

My stupidity knows no bounds. Based on an assumption of an ignorant drug dealer, I had drawn a cop's attention to some teenager girl. "Yeah, I'm not gonna go there, Rod. Do you have a last known address?"

"It's a shame I ain't a dirty cop. I could retire on all the information I feed you. Eleven hundred, Pridgen Road, Unit G-8. I trust you can find the place."

I recognized the address. It was an apartment complex called the Carlton Arms. It had been there when I was a kid. And it had been there last year on the night when my mother killed Ray Burris.

"Got it, thanks Uncle Rod."

"Don't give me that Uncle shit," he said, and the line went dead.

It occurred to me that Sample may not have been

protecting Marisol Rodriguez by not sharing her address. He may have been protecting me.

THE CARLTON ARMS apartment complex had changed little since my childhood. We called it the Communist Stronghold. It's drab, gray stucco buildings, arranged in a strict grid, peered out over the neighborhood above its oppressive perimeter fence of painted concrete pillars and wrought iron. The spiked *fleur de lis* looked like the bayonets attached to a World War II soldier's weapon. Faux gas lamps flickered amber light from black posts matching the wrought iron. They would continue day and night.

The stronghold appearance failed at the entry. No gate. No guard.

The rain slowed from downpour to steady, and the washed out look of the skies did nothing for the Arms' depressing aesthetic.

I found G-building and parked across one bay of cars from it with a clear view of the building.

In the rear-view mirror, I saw C-building. The building where my mother killed Ray Burris. Because of my experience working that case, I knew how the units worked. Each building had three stories. Four units per floor on the 2nd and 3rd story. Two units on the ground floor. Each of those units included the upgrade of a garage unit, which took the place of the dwelling units. Because it was almost impossible to maneuver in an out of the garages, many of these residents ended up parking in the lot like everyone else using the garage as an enormous, chaotic storage closet. None of that mattered because G-8 would be on the top floor facing me on the right, as I looked at it. A gray Volkswagen Beetle, one of the new models, sat like an obedient puppy in the short driveway in front of garage beneath G-8. There was another Beetle, an original, parked three spaces down. Its color was hard to determine through all the rust. Two Chevys – a Corsica and a Citation. A black Ford Probe. Remember those? A white Ford Ranger with the ghost of a business label bleeding through a cheap paint-over job. Some Hondas, Nissans, and Toyotas. All models from the last decade. The lot wasn't full. Most of the residents were away, making the beds at deserted hotels or bussing tables at empty restaurants.

The lot was strewn with dead leaves and rainwater. A storm drain carved into the concrete curve between building G and H had a mouth of rebar teeth clogged with candy bar wrappers, empty soda bottles, and Styrofoam fast-food cartons. I hated litter. It was low-class. But I realized that the act of littering was not indicative of class. The cost of clean-up was.

I sat there for two hours hoping to get a look at Marisol Rodriguez without knocking on her door. Unit H-2 had a lot of activity. A motley crew of teen-aged to early 20s visitors-- scruffy mop heads, preppy rich kids, well-built jocks, white, black, male, female--drove up, spent less than five minutes, and reappeared with a hand in pocket, protecting their purchase. Competition for Sample? Or maybe part of his operation?

Didn't matter, I wasn't there to further the War on Drugs.

I was just about to give up, and go knock, when I saw the door swing open and a head of blonde hair appeared above the half-wall at the stair landing. Then it disappeared as she descended the stairs.

The rain slowed to a sprinkle.

Marisol Rodriguez reappeared at the bottom of the stairs.

Thick saliva filled the back of my mouth.

She wore a blue knit hoodie opened to show a bright yellow, loose-fitting T-shirt and stretch black Yoga pants, which came to just above her tanned ankles and blinding, white Keds. She pulled the hood up over her blonde hair before scurrying over to the new Beetle.

Beauty came with privileges, I guess. The resident at G-2 let her park in his space. Had to be a man. No woman would lend her space to Marisol Rodriguez.

Another figure appeared outside the door of G-8. A short, Latino with disheveled black hair, bushy eyebrows, and a shadow that had crawled well past five o'clock. He wore a stained white wife-beater. His dark shoulders and arms had gone soft with a layer of fat over the memories of muscle from a lifetime of manual labor. He draped his forearms over the top of the half-wall and stared out at the world. Deep creases burrowed into his forehead.

I had no kids, but if I had a daughter, she'd have the same effect on me.

Inside her car, Marisol fooled with the rear-view mirror.

Thinking she had caught on to me, I slid down in my seat.

But she was touching up her makeup in the mirror.

Even at a distance, I knew she didn't need it.

After doing something with her eyes and applying a touch-up coat of lip gloss, he backed out and pulled away.

The man up the stairs, who I assumed was her father, watched her progress out of the lot.

I waited on him and he obliged by going back into his unit. I took off at a speed that could get me a reckless driving ticket and caught up to her as she turned left onto Thirteenth.

A tickle at the back of my skull got me to check the rear-view. A white sedan like a thousand others. The driver had hair the color of an orange rind. He followed six car lengths behind.

I tracked Marisol from the same distance.

What the hell was going on? Had I seen this car in the lot

at the Carlton Arms? Couldn't have, I would have noted someone else on a stake out.

Marisol tooled her Beetle around like it was a go-kart, weaving through traffic as if it were plastic orange cones on a track.

Keeping up with her whimsies was difficult, especially on the rain-slick streets. Doing it without revealing myself was not. Marisol wasn't a driver who watched the trail she left behind.

I checked on our red-headed stranger and saw he had fallen behind a florist's delivery truck. He kept pulling to the left, straddling the yellow line, to get a peek at us around the truck.

Marisol had two tails.

She signaled to take a right on Kings Highway and came to a rolling stop at a red light.

I pulled beside her in the left-hand turn lane.

Our tail pulled up behind her as she made a right on red, following close behind.

I made a right-hand turn from the wrong lane on red. Three months ago, it would have gotten me a ticket and a call to my insurance company, but Kings Highway was dead, and all I got was a honk and a finger from the floral truck.

We settled into an evenly spaced convoy at about seventy miles per hour.

The miniature golf courses and pancake houses and bargain beachwear shops thinned out, and soon we were picking up speed and out of the main drag of the Beach. She covered that three miles in two minutes and slowed into a turn lane in front of Duck's Gym, a big box gym that was all glass and chrome.

The white sedan continued down the highway.

It was too much of a coincidence. I still say he was tailing us.

Marisol whipped into gym's parking lot and drove diagonally across the field of empty spaces to a spot beside the handicap parking out front. She was out of the car and striding to the glass storefront before I parked a football field away. She pulled the hood over hair against the spitting rain.

I sat there and watched her disappear. I was a Duck's Gym member, and it would do no good for me to follow her inside. The front desk would blow my cover as soon as I walked through the doors.

Minutes later, Marisol came back out with sheets of white paper folded in her hands. The clouds peeled away from the sun, and Marisol's hair captured its glory. The rain stopped, and she left the hood down.

Some charmed life this girl leads. Steps outside with a handful of paper and the rain stops.

She got into her car and sped off. I went inside to investigate because that's what I do.

DUCK'S GYM, was like all the super gyms that had sprouted up around the country at the turn of the century, and have somehow survived despite having to cut their rates by as much as seventy percent to stay competitive. A modern, round reception desk scrolled on the edges with cyan neon piping, served also as a display case for various protein powders, pseudo-healthy protein candy bars, and whatever other unregulated, but legal, performance enhancing substances they hocked. They marked all the prices up at least three hundred percent. Duck's made their sales on the impulses of endorphin fueled gym rats. Behind the desk sat a blonde, tanned, and smiling Terri, attired in spandex workout clothes. Behind her several Duck's Gym t-shirts hung from hooks fastened to a glass block wall.

"Fuzzy!" She leaned forward, arms crossed and elbows resting on the desk, in a way that tested the bounds of her tight, lime green Lycra top.

"Hey, Terri. How's it going?" We had maintained a friendly, flirtatious, competitive relationship over the three years of my membership at Duck's. The competitiveness always escalated around the time of membership renewal, but it never completely vanished throughout the rest of the year.

"A'ight." She had held onto a slight, Cajun accent, an heirloom from her childhood, growing up in the New Orleans suburbs. "Haven't seen you in a while, and when I do you walk-in in street clothes." She tucked a lock of blond hair behind an ear, tilted her head, and cocked one eyebrow. "You're not cheating on me are you?"

In my weaker moments, I imagined what it might be like to peel her out of those workout clothes. The beach was full of Terris, who worked at gyms like this. Because of that, I told myself it wasn't the fantasy she projected that kept me renewing. Right.

I said, "Don't worry, girl. I only have eyes for you. Plus with the albatross you've hung on me that you call a contract, I'm stuck here for at least another six months."

She laughed more than my dig justified. "So, what's up then?"

"The good-looking blonde that just came in..."

She leaned back, frowned. "I recall no one matching that description."

"It's all relative, honey. I said she was good-looking. Not gorgeous like you."

"Oh." She drew the "Oh" out, as if in a great revelation. "Her."

"Right, her," I said. "What did she come in for?"

She scoffed, "Looking for a job."

A job. Sample's case for the girl being a prostitute was

weakening with my involvement. "You don't think she'll get it?"

"Oh, I don't know. It's funny, she was a member here a few years ago. Don't you remember her?"

I didn't, and I guess it showed.

"Yeah, well. She was one of those gym cats. Spent her whole time flirting with guys. Laughing at all the right times. Rubbing up against them just enough to make them aware of her, but innocent enough. Like it was incidental. You know the type?"

I did.

"Yeah, so, she's that type. Now she wants to work here? Like she is some sort of expert. I never once saw her workout, when she was a member. Maybe five minutes on a stair master."

I just nodded my head. I didn't point out that I had never once seen Terri use any of the gym equipment.

"She used the gym like it was a nightclub or something."

"Her money still spent the same though, right?"

"Sure, but it's not the image we want. We don't want to turn away the real gym rats." She squeezed one of my biceps to let me know I was one of the preferred clientele.

This girl was trouble.

"That's all? She just wanted a job?" I asked.

"If I owned this place, I wouldn't give it to her. She'd pick up a check for doing nothing but flirting."

A chuckle escaped me on that one.

But she didn't notice. Her eyes dilated, "Wait a minute, aren't you some kind of detective, too, this time of year?" And before I could answer, "What the dish on this Rodriguez girl? Something juicy?"

She rocked back and forth on her elbows, drawing my attention to her breasts framed between her arms. I failed to keep my eyes on hers. I figured she saw success in my failure. Time to be careful.

"Nothing juicy. Just a concerned dad making sure his girl is looking for work as she says?" As lies go, it was a weak deliver, but I couldn't think straight exposed to her globes of hypnotism.

"He's paying you for that?"

"Hey, I told him that he could do this as easy as I could, but he insisted. Who am I to turn away easy money?"

"True that," she said. It sounded about as out of place as the F-Word in a pastor's mouth.

"But hey tell nobody about this. I can get in big trouble with all the client-investigator privilege stuff. I'm not supposed to share this." Total bullshit. An attorney hadn't hired me. But if the privilege stuff worked on Uncle Rod, it would work on Terri the Blonde, Queen of Duck's.

She made a play of locking her lips and tossing the key over her shoulder.

"Good girl," I said. Now that I'd gotten that out of the way, I pried deeper. "So, you say she flirted a lot. She ever hookup?"

She stared at me slack jawed. "What does that have to do with her lookin' for a job?"

I said, "She is a good-looking girl. Not Terri, out of my league good-looking. But good-looking. I'm just weighing my options in case she works here.

More slack jaw. Then she giggled, and baby punched my shoulder, "You dog! I don't remember for sure. She was big with the high school boys, so I didn't pay too much attention. She came on strong, and they were high school boys. I can't imagine them not taking the bait."

"Bait?"

"Yeah, she focused on the preppy ones. The rich kids. She was looking for ones that could give her the stuff, because her family couldn't. I didn't get the impression, she had much at home. And she was always late on her fees."

A picture developed of Marisol Rodriguez that aligned somewhat with the picture in Billy Smith's head. That picture would be of no value to Sample, other than it led me to believe that I wasn't completely on a fool's errand.

"Was she good at it? The bait, that is."

She scoffed again. As if I were asking Tom Brady if the latest first round quarterback pick was any good. "I guess down there in the Pee Wee league, she managed okay."

"Okay," I said. "Hey, thanks, Terri."

As I turned to walk away, "Hey, Fuzzy. I think we're playing in the same league." She tucked a few more strands of hair behind her ear. Where did all that hair come from? How was it that the girls, like Terri, always had loose hair that needed tucking at the opportune time?

I dragged myself away from her and back outside where I hoped that a cold rain shower would dump on me as I stepped from the curb.

I had no such luck.

3

When I got back to my car, I remembered that I was supposed to visit my mother in Columbia, and that there were only thirty minutes left in visiting hours. I wouldn't make it out of Horry County in that time. So, a phone call would have to do.

Mom was her normal, of late, serpent tongued self. "You aren't gonna make it, huh? Son?" The "son" was spat, as if she needed that title out of her mouth, out of her mind.

"No, sorry, Mom. I'm working on something. I am still planning on being there for the Thanksgiving Dinner though."

"You're working on something, huh?" She paused, and I heard her dragging on a cigarette. "What are you gonna do, exhume your daddy? Maybe try him for slapping me around?"

Turning my mother into the cops, whether she deserved it or not, was hard. Watching her trial, and seeing any hope of her being exonerated slip away, was depressing. But the darkness that I had to endure, every time I visited, every time I called? That darkness was almost too much to stomach. The shadows that now cloaked my mother's soul, appeared in many ways. For example, I had never heard of any instances where my dad had abused my mother, before he had succumbed to cancer. In fact, my mother had always held my dad up as the perfect husband, every time any other man, including her current husband, had let her down.

"No, Mom. I'm working on something for Billy Smith. Do you remember him?"

"Sample? Yeah, I remember that little shit. Is he still dealing?"

"Yeah, I guess, I dunno."

She said, "He tried to trade me some of that shit to get with me one time."

I didn't believe her, and I questioned her mental state. Sometimes I had to remember that as hard as turning her in was for me, it could not have been no Sunday stroll on the beach for her. I needed to get off the phone with her, or I would be in no state to work tonight.

"Okay, Mom. Like I said, I'll see you Thursday."

"Whatever," she said. The line went dead.

I missed the days, after her incarceration, when she wouldn't talk to me at all.

WITH LITTLE ELSE TO DO FOR the next few hours, I found myself at Molly Maguire's, a strip club on the mainland side of the intercostal waterway. The season was over, and it was mid-day on a weekday, so Maguire's was dead. Two middle-aged, pony-tailed men sat at the rail of the main stage, or I should say only stage. A short beauty with black hair wearing a fluorescent green string bikini walked circles around the dingy brass pole with one arm draped around it. The bass line of some vaguely recognizable pop song hammered in my ears.

She completed her rotation around the pole, and reached behind her back to loosen the strings of her top. Her doe eyes settled on me.

I wanted to pull my eyes away from that stare. I'd long ago learned that staring into a stripper's eyes was uncomfortable -- for me and the dancer. But I couldn't help it. Her eyes were like glue.

She flashed a crooked smile like a gambler who had just bluffed you into folding.

I forced myself to break the pull of her stare only to realize that she had removed her top. Her breasts sagged and were a little on the small side but framed in beautiful tan-lines.

She noted my admiration, giggled, and cocked one eyebrow.

I stepped towards the stage, digging in my pocket for some bills.

"Hey stranger." Hands blindfolded me from behind. The voice and the mounds of breast flesh pressing against my back led me to deduce that the hands belonged to another stripper.

"Hi Veronica," I said.

She removed her hands, and turned me to face her. Veronica was a short, raven haired dancer, too. She wore a white mesh, loose fitting top that did little to cover the darkness of her nipples against her pale skin. "How'd you guess?"

"You're my all-time favorite girl," I said. "And I'm not that friendly with other dancers."

"You're sweet," she said. "So, whaddya think?" She looked over at the stage, where the girl was stepping out of her g-string. Like most of the girls, she was shaved bare.

"About what?" I said.

"Onyx. You like her. Don't ya? I saw the way you were looking at her. I had to come out and play defense. Can't lose one of my regulars to the new help."

"She's cute," I said.

She punched me in the shoulder.

I fake grimaced. "Hey watch it."

"Oh my gosh, Fuzzy. Is that your bad shoulder? The one that got shot?"

I laid it on thick, and rubbed my shoulder, but I couldn't keep a straight face.

"You asshole."

"Hey, it was the shoulder. But it's been over a year, and it doesn't hurt very much anymore."

She stepped to a white formica table riddled with cigarette burns, and patted the vinyl seat of one of its chairs. Her smile and ice blue eyes were brilliant in the darkness of the club. "Step into my office."

As I sat, she crawled onto my lap and traced light circles with her fingernails on the back of my neck. "You're becoming a stranger, Fuzzy. How long's it been?"

Veronica was a late 20s stripper, who cycled through all of the Grand Strand clubs, going where she made the best money. This made her a crafty veteran, and also a good reference for my best pool of potential clients. Strippers often needed the type of help I could provide, and they always had a lot of cash to pay for it. Veronica was a good pipeline to that work. She also was the closest thing I've had to a girlfriend since my fiancee's death eight years ago. I rested my hand on her silky thigh. "I don't know. Couple of months, maybe?"

"So where have you been? Have you turned me in for a newer model?" She smiled, as if she were just busting my balls. But the smile didn't reach her eyes.

It was a good question. I wasn't even sure why I hadn't been into any of the clubs. Either to drum up work or to cash in on the benefits of Veronica's friendship. "I've been busy with work," I lied.

She laid her other hand on my chest. Between it and the

job she was working on the nape of my neck, the strumming began in my solar plexus. "So what brought you in today, then?"

My tongue thickened and my throat felt dry. "I, uh..."

She looked down to my lap. "I think someone misses me."

I hadn't realized the effect she was having on me. It had been years since I had so publicly displayed my arousal in a club. You get numb to it after awhile, but I was anything but numb to it now, and the self-awareness would do nothing for hiding it now. I shifted a little to slide her hip a few inches away from swelling loins. I wasn't sure why I had come into Maguire's. Typically, I come in to troll for work and enjoy the scenery. Or come in to see Veronica, and tuck dollars in her G-string and lure her back to my place after her shift.

Or both.

Troll for work and Veronica.

But I had given no thought to either today. After the call with mom, I pointed the car to Maguire's, and here I was. Somehow even with a raging erection, I managed some thinking with the big head. "So, I came in for a reason."

"I can see that," she said, and scooted her hip back against my crotch.

"Very funny." I leaned back and reached into my pocket and cleared her ass from my current situation, again. I brought out my cell phone, and started scrolling through the pictures on my camera roll. When I found the picture from Marisol Rodriguez's Facebook page, I handed her the phone. "Look, I said. "Have you ever seen this girl? Maybe in the clubs?"

She immediately nodded. "Liza."

"Lisa?"

"No, Ly- Za", she corrected.

"That's not this girl's name."

"Really, Fuzzy? Liza was her stage name. I don't know

what her real name is. She worked at Daisy Doe's for a few weeks. She was popular with the south of the border crowd. Unfortunately, that isn't the best paying crowd, and I think she needed to hustle the DOWDs or she wouldn't make it. She never got that chance because of her brother."

"What did her brother do?"

"Nothing, he just came into the club. Liza saw him, and spent the rest of the night on look out from the dressing room. It's actually pretty common. I've never had to deal with it, because my family is all up in Michigan and they're the only people in Michigan that don't vacation in Myrtle Beach every year. But, yeah, girls get a little freaked when family members come in to the club." She shrugged. "I think Liza over reacted. She never came back in after that, and I haven't seen her at any of the other clubs. It's a shame. If she could have learned to not spend so much time at the immigrant tables and learned a little hustle, she could have made good money. And she was young enough to do it for awhile."

"DOWD?"

"Right, DOWDs are the gravy train."

"What is a DOWD?"

"Dirty Old White Dude." She smiled, rested her head on my shoulder. "Like you old bear."

"I'm 31."

"Yep you're old."

"And how old are you?"

She lifted her head. "You don't expect me to answer that question?"

I dropped the age thing. "Hey, do any of the girls, you know...I don't know... Go home with guys?"

She giggled. "I can think of one."

"That's not what I mean. I'm talking about for pay."

She giggled again. "You mean like take-out?"

"Yeah. I'm not sure what's so funny. I mean... not like you or I. Like pulling tricks?"

"Fuzzy, do you remember what I was like the morning after the first time I was with you."

"Yeah, you cried." I did, too. I just stepped outside, and did it while she slept. "But like I said back then, it wasn't like that."

"But it was. I hustled you for a number that night, and I decided if I got there, that I would finally agree to see you outside the club. You were my first and only take out."

I had no words.

She patted me on the chest. "Of course, it's not like that now. And even back then I wanted to see you. I just had a code. No customers. But I proved to myself that everything has a price." She frowned and chewed on the corner of her lower lip. Some of her lip glossed smeared onto one of her incisors.

I had to change the subject. "Ok, but other girls? Do many of them not follow this code?"

"Most of the clubs claim a strict no meeting customers outside the club policy. But they all look the other way, they know a lot of the girls are offering extras both in and outside the club. Hell, have you noticed on busy nights how many of the girls never make it onto the stage?"

"Now that you mention it. I guess you're right, but don't you have a regular rotation?"

"Sure. The point I'm trying to make is a lot of those girls shouldn't even be here. They come in dressing sexy, act like a dancer, and pull tricks in VIP or outside the club, and they never pay the house like the dancers have to. The club looks the other way on this, too."

"Do you think Liza could be playing this game now?" I asked.

Perplexed, she said, "Huh? Oh Liza. No, I don't think so.

I never got the impression she was doing take-out when she worked at Daisy's, and she seemed freaked at the possibility of running into her brother again. I don't think she's stepped foot into a club again since that night.

"How long ago was this that she worked at Daisy Doe's?"

"Three months? Six? The nights blend together now. So why all this interest in the girl?"

"I'm working a case."

Her eyes went wild, and she cupped a hand over her mouth. "Did something happen to her?"

"No, she's fine. I'm just trying to get a handle on her."

"Oh my god, Fuzzy. You're digging up dirt on her for her family? And here I am shoveling for you."

"It's not her family. And look I just came in to see you. I had no thought of asking about the girl when I came in. It just occurred to me to ask about her, when I was trying to keep my mind off other things."

She looked at my lap and said, "Other things are still occurring."

And so they were.

"So I get off early tonight, you up for a visit?"

I said, "I'm working this case tonight."

"All night?"

I became acutely aware of the soft pressure of her hip in my lap. "Not all night," I admitted.

4

———

The Coral Beach Resort was a typical, sprawling, pastel stucco with neon-piping hotel on Ocean Boulevard. I parked a block down from it at the public beach parking, fed quarters into a parking meter, and walked back to the lobby. The streets were empty. Myrtle Beach was a ghost town in November.

Like most of the resorts on Myrtle Beach, the bars were open to walk-in traffic, so I got no resistance from the front desk when I strolled past them to the bar which was next to a fine dining restaurant. I'd been here before, and I knew they had two beach bars outside. One poolside. One oceanfront. But even if they were open, I couldn't imagine Marisol Rodriguez meeting a john outside in the 50 degrees breeze.

A plump brunette in a tight, white T-shirt wiped down the glossy, black bar top. She looked up at me as I took a seat. "My first customer. What'll ya have?"

She had a friendly smile, and the Coral Beach logo on her T-shirt pleasantly bent around the contours of her bust. The top of a lacy, black bra peeked out above the low-cut neck of the shirt. The pale halo of tan lines peeked above the bra. I can't recall what color her eyes were.

I said, "Pretty dead, huh? It's amazing. I was in here on Labor Day weekend, and this place was crawling with tourists and drunks."

"Try coming, Memorial Day weekend." She draped the towel over her shoulder. "So, what'll it be?"

"I see you have an Oatmeal Porter on tap. How is it?"

Her cheeks puckered and her nose wrinkled. "Don't ask me. I can't stomach that shit." She grabbed a shot glass. "I can give you a taste, though."

The beer taps were on the back wall of the bar, and when she turned, I noticed her ample butt cheeks poured out of tight, short black biking shorts. She wore knee-high rainbow-striped socks, and Doc Marten boots. The get-up seemed out-of-season and out-of-place for the restaurant bar. And out of context for her figure. I liked this girl for it, though. Her self-confidence was refreshing.

She put the shot glass in front of me. "Bottoms up."

I threw it back as if it were a shot of whiskey. It had a rich, almost coffee flavor. "We've got a winner."

She poured me a pint. "You don't look like a golfer."

"Not much of one," I said. "Why?"

"Most of the customers this time of the year are here to golf. They come down for a week to golf, and get away from their wives, because all the courses are closed up north."

"Yeah, I know. I'm sort of a native."

"So what in the hell are you doing here? It can't be for the price of the beer!"

I took a pull on the beer, scrolled to Marisol's picture on my phone, and asked her to look.

"Mari?" she said. "What about her?"

"So she comes in here?"

33

She nodded at the entry behind me. "Honey, she just walked in."

Marisol Rodriguez sashayed towards me wearing a sparkling, blue dress with a hem that came a good six inches short of her knees. She carried a matching clutch purse in one hand. A cellphone the size of a small tablet in the other. As good as she looked in her civvies, earlier. She was breathtaking, now. I felt for Sample. This girl's look was like sorcery.

"Hey, Michelle. Any sign of my friend, yet?", Marisol said.

"No, but..."

I gave Michelle a look that could bite her tongue off.

Marisol Rodriguez took up a seat beside me and crossed her legs in a way that was more sensuous than should be legal. "How about a drink, Mister?"

I weighed my options. I could have argued that she didn't look of legal age. Or I could have played not interested. But those weren't options if I wanted to keep my cover. Any red-blooded man would have bought her that drink. So that's what I did.

"Michelle," I said, "bring the lady a drink."

Michelle rolled her eyes. "Mari, you're gonna get me fired one of these days."

I played dumb. "What do you mean?"

She rolled her eyes again, and made Marisol a colorful red, juicy drink complete with plastic umbrella.

Marisol held her glass up for a toast, and I tapped mine to her rim. "To new friends," she said, "while waiting on old ones." She kept her eyes on me as she took a sip from her glass.

"I think we've met before," I said. "But I thought your name was Liza."

Her glass stopped right before her mouth, still looking up

34

at me. But she recovered. It was only a momentary pause. "My name is Marisol," she said.

I grinned and waited for her to notice it. "I must be mistaken. Nice to meet you, Marisol." She had to be the girl who danced at Daisy Doe's. The girl that Veronica remembered. I'm not sure what that had to do with anything. It certainly didn't mean she was a prostitute. Especially when you consider that Veronica remembered her as someone that didn't take dates outside the club.

I saw someone enter the bar over her shoulder. He was mid-height about ten years older than me and he looked like a former athlete that had gone soft in the middle. He had a face with bulldog jowls and a bushy red mustache that would be the envy of any adult film star. His hair was the same rusty color, and glued into place by a full can of hair spray. Broken capillaries on his cheeks mapped out every drink he'd ever consumed. He shocked me by sitting down beside Marisol.

She smiled and turned to face him and offered a cheek.

"Hey, beautiful," he said and pecked the cheek.

"Hey, Daddy," she said.

Daddy noted my stare and wrinkles formed in his brow. "Who's your friend, baby?"

She looked back at me, her chin resting on her shoulder like so many shots you see on the covers of the glamour magazines. "A new friend," she said. "But I don't think I got your name. What's your name, friend?"

"Fuzzy," I said.

"Fuzzy! I love it!" She laughed, as if she'd had three more drinks than the half empty one in her hands.

Michelle cocked a hip onto the beer cooler behind the bar. As much as I admired Michelle, she was easy to forget in Marisol's presence.

"What can I get you, Tommy?"

So Daddy, who I assumed was not Marisol's father, had a

name, and it was Tommy. Not Tom or Thomas. Tommy. An ideal name for the man courting a girl young enough to be his daughter.

"Nothing, Michelle. I just came to pick this one up," he said.

Marisol grinned at what appeared to be an inside joke and swirled the ice and the remains of her cocktail.

"Finish that up, baby. I've got other plans for you". He stood up, patted me on the shoulder and said, "Nice to meet you, Frizzy."

"Fuzzy," I corrected.

"Yeah, whatever." He turned and started out the way he came. "You coming, baby?"

Marisol tossed back her drink and leaned into me. Arched an eyebrow. "Thanks for the drink, Fuzzy." Beneath the smell of a teenager's perfume, I could smell cucumber melon body lotion on her neck. It was the same lotion that Veronica used.

"My pleasure," I said. "Better hurry off, Daddy is waiting."

She shook her head, and sauntered off with an exaggerated, drunken sway. I wondered if it was for effect, or if she had started before she had arrived.

"So, Fuzzy, is it?" Michelle wiped down the bar where Marisol had placed her glass. "I guess it's just me and you, again."

I watched them all the way out of the bar. He marched a straight line like a twenty year vet, she had her head resting on his rigid shoulder. I once had a cat who nuzzled me like that when it was hungry. As soon as it got what it wanted, it returned to ignoring me.

"Don't get too interested, Fuzz. She's a drain on the wallet."

Michelle continued to wipe the bar like she was trying to remove its lacquer. She looked up at me from below her brow.

"Yeah?" I said. "High maintenance?"

"I'd say," Michelle said. "Most pros are."

I made my best dropped jaw shocked look. "You mean like -- ". I left it hanging there without saying the word prostitute. I added a smiling frown and approving nod.

Now it was her turn for the faux shocked look. "You guys," she said. "You want another?"

I was down to the last swallow of beer. I hadn't thought this through, which wasn't unusual. How was I going to catch Marisol in the act?

Michelle stood with a fist on her hip in a mock impatient look.

Ah, what the hell, it was a worth a try. "Say Michelle," I said, "Do you have a way of finding out what room Marisol and Tommy are staying in?"

She swatted me with her damp bar rag. "What are you, some kind of creep?"

"Probably, but not for the reason you think," I chuckled. "Look, I promise my reason is mostly innocent."

"Mostly, huh?" She leaned forward with both elbows on the bar and looked up with wanting dark eyes. In the dim light of the bar, they were so dilated that they looked like glistening pools of black ink. "You don't look so innocent."

The fabric of her T-shirt strained under the added stress she put it under in the current pose.

She noted my attention. "Nah, you're not a creep," she said. "Just a typical guy. Still, I can't just give out guests' room numbers."

"I understand, but hear me out." Now, I had to come up with a good reason. Like I said, I often, don't think these things through. I went with the truth.

I reached into my wallet and handed her the laminated card which served as my private investigator's license.

She looked at it, looked up at me, and said, "No shit?"

I shrugged. "I cannot tell a lie. Well, that's not true. With that thing," I pointed to the license. "I often have to, but in this case. I'm not bullshitting you."

"That still doesn't tell me, why you need Creep-o's room number."

With her lifting the creep tag from me to Daddy, I felt things moving my way. I kept with the truth -- mostly. "Well what do you know about the work private eyes do?"

"I don't know. Are you packing right now?" She said out of the side of her mouth in her best Bogie voice, or was it Cagney? I don't know, but it wasn't very good.

When I didn't immediately answer, she leaned back and took a step away from me. Her t-shirt crawled up at her waist line and exposed a pale roll of belly fat. "Oh my god," she said. "You are. Aren't you?"

I kept a straight face for maybe half a second, but the look on her face made it impossible to keep up the act. I grinned. "Nah, silly. I don't need a piece on a typical peeping job."

She tossed her towel at me, this time. It hit me in the face and landed in my lap. "So you are a creep?"

I looked down at the rag in my lap and back up at her. "You know your tip is going down the drain with this treatment of the customer. I think you need to help me out here to recover."

"Oh, so now you're trying to bribe me?"

"Comes with the territory, baby."

"Oh wow, you are laying it on thick now," she said. "Why don't you just call me a dame?"

"Would it work?"

She leaned forward again, propped one elbow on the bar, and supported her chin on her palm. Her smile erased the image of that roll of fat.

"That's a honey of a T-shirt you got there Michelle."

She noticed my eyes weren't on hers, and stepped back

from the bar again, and chewed on the corner of her lip. She was mulling over my proposition.

She was the kind of girl that needed to be tossed into the deep end. I got up to leave. "How much do I owe you for the beer?"

"Wait a minute," she said. "How much of a tip are we talking?"

Everyone had their price. "Fifty bones?"

"I could get their room number, if I played it off with the front desk, and said they asked me to have some drinks brought up." She gnawed on her lip some more.

"Look Michelle, I understand if you can't do it, but I can't wait here forever. At this rate, they'll be checked out by the time I get in position."

"No I can do it," she assured. "But look you have to come by sometime when this is all over and tell me all about it. It's not everyday I get a PI for a customer."

"I can't tell you everything, but I'll stretch what I can tell for you." Sometimes you had to make them feel special. Who am I kidding? You always had to make them feel special.

She held her hand out to shake on it. "Deal."

I took her hand and looked her deep in the eyes. "One other condition. I get your digits."

She pulled a pen out of some pocket I didn't know existed in her shorts and leaned so far forward that some of her poured out of the top of her shirt. Twin brown crescents of her areola peered out from the edge of her bra. She turned my hand up, and wrote her number on the palm, including a little heart insignia at the end.

I felt like I was in middle school again. Who doesn't want to feel that at 31 years of age?

"You have to use it, now," she said.

"Yeah, Yeah, Yeah," I said. "Now run along and get my information."

She wrote the number 315, under her phone number and winked at me.

Shock must have appeared on my face.

"He asks for the same room every time, and he has an arrangement that I bring up some wine after about an hour."

"Michelle you are a girl of mystery and intrigue."

I pumped Michelle for some information on the lay of the land on the third floor, and even engaged her in a simple strategy to get some more face time with Marisol or Daddy, or both, when Michelle made her delivery. It wouldn't get me the money shot, but I wasn't sure I'd ever manage that. Sample might just have to connect some dots. If I couldn't get him photos of her doing the nasty and taking money for it, he'd have to make do with images of her sharing a hotel room with a man more than twice her age.

After about a half hour of flirting with Michelle and nursing a second beer, she flipped a switch and shut down the lights behind the bar.

"Wait a minute," I said. "Who watches the bar?"

She waved that off. "It's off season, and we're under-staffed. As long as I have no customers I'm okay."

We took the stairs. When we reached the landing on the third floor, she turned to me. "Okay, their room is three doors down on the left. I will do my best to get you a view of them."

I pulled out the small Canon camera that I'd used for 3 years. There was newer, better technology, but it would mean learning how to use it, and it beat using the camera on my phone.

Michelle strutted off. A little ass sway in her step for my appreciation.

I watched her at the door through a thin glass vision panel in the door. It had wire criss-crossed inside it because it was a fire-rated door. I held my camera to the glass, and aimed it so

I would not obstruct the shot, and focused on Michelle, who had now stopped in front of the door to room 315.

She knocked on the door and stepped back from it. She made a play of looking down the hall to something she had heard down there. The door opened, and she continued to look down the hall. She played it well. Daddy stepped a few feet out of the door in a white terry robe. His face was flushed from the indoor activities and matched his rust colored helmet of hair, still plastered in place. Smiling, he said something to Michelle and reached for the bottle of wine she held at her waist.

I clicked off three shots of him and then focused on the doorway hoping to catch Marisol. No luck.

Michelle kept up the act as we had planned it. She gestured with her hands and had an apologetic look on her face. Daddy shook his head and smiled. Michelle held up one finger to let him know she'd back in one minute with his check and then hurried back in my direction. As he watched her head in my direction, I stepped away from my looking glass.

She reached me.

"Good job," I said. "Did you see Marisol at all?"

"Nope, it's like I told you before. She never comes to the door."

"Okay, well, let's try again."

We waited about ten minutes before I got back in position and she returned to their door, and produced the check. It was just as she predicted. Tommy came to the door, and signed the check. I took two more shots and even risked a full frontal face shot as he watched Michelle's ass as she strode in my direction. It wasn't much of a risk. His eyes were not up looking at me.

With that done, I sent Michelle back to her real job. I eased a ball-point pen between the door and the jamb, so I could hear anything going on down the floor. I sat with my back to the wall and waited.

It seemed like an eternity, and the floor remained dead silent for that time, but only ninety minutes had expired before I heard the door open. Then I heard her voice.

"Yeah, Daddy, maybe after the game?" She said. "You know Christmas is coming up?"

I swung into position and clicked off several shots.

She was standing with one foot splayed in front of the other, in a fashion model's pose. Even from where I stood I could tell her smile was fake.

"Come here," I heard him say from beyond the door.

She shook her head and stood in the center of the hall with her hands on her hips and her chin raised. It was to my good fortune, as he emerged from the room, wearing nothing but a towel around his waist. His blubbery hairless torso was bright red and damp. He reached for her waist, and they play wrestled in the corridor like lovers sometimes do. He made a play for more kissing and hugging. She wriggled free of his advances.

I kept working the camera.

As the action died down, I caught him sliding a small wad of folded bills into her tiny hand. She made a production of tucking them into the crease between her breasts.

I took that photo too.

Then, the flirtatious play immediately stopped. Marisol's head snapped to look at the other stairwell on the opposite side of the floor. Its door thudded shut from about half a foot open. Marisol's eyes went wild, and she ran the fingers of both hands into her blonde locks, and held them there.

She must have seen someone standing in that doorway. She stood on her toes and pecked Daddy's cheek, then turned and walked towards me.

I hauled it down the stairs, leaving the pen I had propping

the door in place. If she saw it, she would suspect something, but removing it would mean the door slamming shut.

I made it down to the second floor landing just as I heard her open the door above me and slid into the hallway on the second floor. At six-five with a full head of prematurely gray hair, I'm easily recognizable. So I stepped into an elevator lobby outside of view from the hallway. I waited there for a five minutes, acting like I was waiting on a car. No car and no one came. When I figured Marisol had either made it to the bar or left the building, I resurfaced in the hall, and walked back to the other end. I climbed the stairs to the third floor and noted the smell of tobacco. It was faint enough that whoever had been in the stairwell had not been smoking. They probably carried the smell around in their clothes. Heavy smoker. Maybe not even my guy. Or girl.

I stood close to the door and peered through the glass in the door. Their room was a much greater distance from my spot. I imagined our peeper leaning into the glass to get a closer look, as my forehead touched the glass, the latch on the door released and it creaked open. That's probably what happened, and how our friend's cover was blown.

Did our friend also enjoy fishing for sharks? I knew Sample smoked, but did he do it heavily enough to leave this odorous trail?

I HAD no recollection of the twenty-minute drive, as I spent all of it pondering what I had just witnessed, and the further questions it posed. What was the nature of Daddy and Marisol's relationship? Was it purely transactional? They would have differing views. And Marisol's opinion was the one that mattered.

I had seen Daddy someplace before. I couldn't place it,

but I felt he was some sort of public figure. I spent half of the drive trying to recall where I had seen his puffy face before tonight. When I had used up all of my excess frustration, and was through figuratively pulling my hair out, I moved on to other perplexities.

Like who was my counterpart on the other side of the hall? Outside her beauty why had Marisol Rodriguez attracted so much attention? Was she being stalked by someone besides me and my client? I had convinced myself that Sample would never have done this. He didn't smoke heavily, so it wasn't his smell in that stairwell, and why would he risk this when he had me peeping on her? Unless his infatuation had run straight to a mental illness. I didn't think so. Maybe Daddy had a jealous wife at home, who had hired some of my competition to do what I was doing? That was the most likely conclusion, which meant I could not accept it, and I had to keep picking at the scab.

I had just determined to leave it all alone, and deliver my pictures to Sample and pick up my fee, when I pulled into the marina. It was dead still. The yachts and cabin cruisers were motionless on the flat dead seas, and lights illuminated their cabins.

I pulled around the boathouse to my home.

A black, convertible Miata sat in my parking space. In the driver's seat, black hair teased high above the seat back.

I pulled beside the car. My fingers curled around the number Michelle had written on my palm.

She turned to face me. Her pale skin flawless in the dark of the night. Her ice-blue eyes luminescent in the moonlight.

My lady awaited. Veronica.

5

The sex had been selfish and hungry. When I awoke in the morning, the impression left by her on the bed was cool to the touch. I couldn't recall a word spoken between us.

Now, I sat across from my step-father, Paul Pope, and my mother at a molded plastic picnic table inside a visitor's hall at the Horry County Women's Detention Center.

My step-father was a smiling man of salt and pepper hair and blues eyes, which sparkled in contrast to his perpetual sunburnt face. His only shortcoming in both mine and my mother's eyes was that he was not my father.

That my mother was a beautiful woman was undeniable. She still had the beautiful, if disheveled, blonde hair of her youth. Her eyes were a deep blue, like the ocean seen from a plane at 30,000 feet. They squinted when she smiled, and men would fall over themselves for her attention. However, over the last year there had not been a lot of squinting and smiling. Some luster had eroded away from my mother's good looks with the darkness that had taken residency in her soul. In the current environment she still stood out like a rose in a bed of weeds, but I worried my mother, of the squinting and smiling eyes, was gone for good.

She traced circles with her yellow, nicotine stained thumbnail on her palm. She watched these circles as a way to keep from looking at me.

The visitor's hall was in the disrepair you would expect. Roof leak stains dotted the ceiling tiles. The vinyl floor was scarred from years of furniture moves, and the walls were coated with the brownish tar put there years ago when they permitted smoking indoors.

Half the people in the room were dressed like my mother in dark orange jumpsuits with HCDC stenciled on the back. The rest of us were family and friends here to visit their loved ones for Thanksgiving dinner.

The leftovers from dinner sat before us on paper plates. They all seemed untouched as if all we did was just move the food around on the plate. In my case that was true. It had tasted like a frozen dinner that had sat in the back of the freezer for over a year. My mom appeared to have lost about ten pounds over the last year, and I could see why if this was what they served on Thanksgiving day.

Paul broke my thoughts on dinner by asking, "Fuzz, what are you working on these days?"

I didn't like talking about my cases. Especially not with family, but I knew he was just trying to break the ice forming in the space between my mother and me.

"Simple stuff, Paul. Mostly domestic stuff."

Paul continued to smile and his head bobbed like one of those collector figures they had out at the ballgames.

"Do you mean you have moved on to tearing other families apart besides your own?" Mom said.

Now she looked at me and held my eyes. She squinted, and she smiled, but they weren't the eyes of my mother, and it wasn't her smile. They were those of a serpent.

It was my turn to break eye contact. I looked over her shoulder to a TV mounted on wall brackets in the corner of the room. An enormous woman with jet black hair, and prison art on her arms, and coarse black hair like an animal's on her neck was pointing a remote at the TV and clicking through channels. She made it through what must have been fifty channels before she gave up, and dropped the remote to the floor, and returned to a table and sat down across from an enormous man with a bushy beard. Either a brother or spouse or boyfriend.

My mom said something, but her voice was just some sound in the deep recess of my mind. I could not make out her words because I had focused on the TV. It had settled on a local news program that was reporting from the football practice fields at Coastal Atlantic University. A young attractive female reporter, who looked as if she could be a co-ed at the school, interviewed a coach. It was a familiar face from the night before.

I stood and trance walked across the room. At my back, I heard my mother's voice rise above the chatter. "Fuzzy, Fuzzy."

I stopped in front of the television. Subtitles scrolled at the bottom of the screen. Daddy, who happened to be Thomas Cain, Head Coach of the Coastal Atlantic Manatees football team, explained the importance of this Saturday's game against the Louisiana-Lafayette Ragin' Cajuns. In their first season in college football's premiere division, the Manatees were one win, their last game of the season, away from qualifying for a postseason bowl game.

My shoulders bunched up and I could feel the stiffening of cartilage in my jaw and the throbbing of a vein in my temple. A picture formed of the task I was hired to perform for Sample. All the people involved made me feel sick. It wasn't the normal disgust I felt when I watched my subjects resort to the animalistic base of our nature.

It was worse.

I thought of Sample's blackmail scheme. Did it involve Marisol? Was she acting like the black widow? And Tommy Cain was no angel. Snared in her web or not. A man in his position, preying on a near-child?

Sick.

I turned and strode past my mother and Paul. "Happy Thanksgiving, Mom. I have to run." I didn't stop to kiss her on the cheek or hug her or shake Paul's hand. I kept walking past them.

"Fuzzy, Fuzzy," again at my back.

I took a deep breath and carried on.

Paul caught up with me as I stopped at the desk to turn in my visitor's badge.

"So, that's how it's gonna be, Fuzzy?"

"I have work to do, Paul."

"Just like that?" he said. "On Thanksgiving Day?"

"Yeah, sometimes my work doesn't take a holiday," I said.

"Don't do this, Fuzzy. I know she's being tough on you right now. But you only get one mother."

Thanks for reminding me, genius.

He put his hand on my shoulder. "C'mon, Fuzzy. Let's go back in there and be there for your mom."

I resisted the temptation to swat his hand away, because, as usual, Paul's heart was in the right place. Of course, he hadn't been the focus of my mother's scorn for the last year. If she had heaped on that bile on him, would he would be so adamant about us being there for my mom?

I left him standing there without a word.

The parking lot pavement was webbed with cracks and had faded to near white and reflected the heat from the afternoon sun. Despite the heat which had risen into the low 80s, I stood beside my car, and searched for a number on my phone, and made a call.

"2nd Avenue Pier and Restaurant," a familiar voice answered.

"So, you are open today?"

"Unfortunately, yes. The Pier is open today. The restaurant is closed."

I recognized the voice. It was the clerk from the other night. Mr. Out by Eleven.

"Cool," I said. "You open till eleven?"

"Nine tonight," he said. "We have families to go home to, too. Ya know?"

"Great," I said.

"No exceptions," he said. "I have to kick..."

"I know you have to kick me out by nine."

He started to lecture me.

I cut the connection.

I'd give the pier a shot at sundown. Sample wouldn't be out there in the daytime, but the Thanksgiving holiday wouldn't keep him from hunting sharks at night. I also figured that the pier had become a good source of the potheads that were the lifeline for his business.

MYRTLE BEACH WAS EVEN DEADER than usual on Thanksgiving Day. Most of the businesses were closed. Even those who kept the shutters open during the off-season recognized a losing proposition. There were two exceptions.

Strip clubs and Fishing piers.

I had pulled through the full parking lot of Molly Maguire's, and drove around back and saw Veronica's Miata.

It gave me a sour stomach. She showed up late last night and got used by me, only to get up and go to work chasing dollar from old guys, who were no better than me. I chose not to stop in to see her and continued back onto Highway 501 towards the beach.

I pulled into the last open spot at the 2nd Avenue Pier. Fishing and strippers were the only businesses alive on Thanksgiving in the Strand.

I dropped quarters into the meter before I saw the sign reading "Free Parking on weekends and Holidays - Sept - April". It was one of those days.

I stepped into the bait shop with the sounds of door chimes tinkling in my ears. A hag of a woman wearing a faded pink ball cap and a mostly toothless grin stood at the counter before the Pier Nazi. He lorded over the place, perched on his stool, smiling and chatting with his friend until he looked up to see me enter. He looked at his watch.

"Only open till nine, tonight pal. Probably not worth the rod rental."

The hag turned to me and lost interest in the pier Nazi. I kind of understood what Veronica went through every day of work, the way this woman was checking me out. The Nazi didn't care for it one bit. "Um, so what'll it be?"

"Just a walker's pass, no rod or bait." I said.

"Geez, mister. Don't you have anything better to do on a day like today?"

He was trying to talk me down a bit due to the attention his girlfriend was giving me. I let him have it.

"I like the Ocean," I said. "Besides who can stand spending the whole day cooped up in the living room with family?

The lady laughed a little more than that deserved. The fat guy handed me the ticket stub. "Remember..."

"Out by nine, I get it," I said.

He looked hurt as if I had stolen his thunder. I left him to his lady friend.

Fisherman lined the pier, and it was dusk, so it was easy to navigate my way to the end.

There, I found Sample.

He stood shouting encouragement to a pimpled, shirtless teen, with Sample's build.

"Keep that rod tip up, Davie. This bad boy will take you and the rod in," he said.

Davie was on his knees trying to leverage his boat rod using the wood railing as a fulcrum.

"Sample," I said. "You got a minute?"

He continued watching Davie fight the fish. "Hey Fuzzy," he said. "What's up?" And then, "Reel! You little mother-fucker! The bastard is tirin', but you can't give him a chance to catch his second wind."

"Sample? We need to talk."

"So talk, Fuzzy. Jesus, it ain't like I got an office out here."

"It's about the case you have me working," I said.

Davey couldn't get the reel to budge. I wondered how long he'd been fighting the fish. His rod was bent over, nearly in two, small squeals of the drag came in spurts as the kid held on for dear life.

"I know why you hired me now," I said.

He looked over his shoulder at me, with a meth users eyes. "What are you talking' about, Fuzzy? I told you why I was hiring you."

I jammed my hands into the pockets of my jeans. "You're going to blackmail him aren't you?"

Davey caught his second wind and cranked at his reel, completing one revolution every two or three seconds. Sample looked at me sideways.

"I'll ask again," he said. "What the fuck are you talking about?"

"I got the pictures you were looking for Sample," I said.

"Good. Let's have a look," he said. "But after Davey pulls Jaws in."

"I don't have them with me," I said. "And I don't have the time to wait while you two fish."

He inhaled. Held his breath and exhaled his shoulders dropping in recognition. "Fuzzy, could you please spit the food out of your mouth? I can't make out any of the shit you are talking."

Sample either was a much better actor than I would ever have given him credit for or he didn't know what I was suggesting.

I tried again. "The guy she is getting with is someone with a lot to lose. You knew, right?"

"Old dude with Santa Claus cheeks and a helmet head?"

So, he knew.

"Yep."

"Who the fuck is he? That I'd want to blackmail?"

Or he didn't.

"Look, I gotta run, Sample. Good luck with the fish."

The kid was screaming now. "Billy, Billy! I'ma need the gaff!"

Sample leaned over the rail. "Oh, shit. That's a big boy!"

I stepped to the rail. A six foot black-tip shark with a fat, pregnant belly floated on the surface of the ocean. Davey's line was taut and ran from the fish's mouth.

I looked to Sample. His eyes were still dazed from whatever he was on, but something darker lived there.

I patted him on the back. "Take it easy, Sample. I'm out of here."

He ignored me and continued to stare at the impotent shark. Beside him Davey kept asking for the gaff.

I stepped away from the rail and turned to walk away.

"When are you bringing those pictures by?" he said.

"I don't know, Samp. I have a few visits to make before I do that."

"That's not what I paid you to do."

"I know," I said as I walked off.

I wasn't sure what was wrong with Sample. That's a question I could ponder the rest of my life without an answer. But tonight? He seemed more out of focus. He was heavily medicated, sure, but my news seemed to pull him in and out of his stoned state. It concerned me. Halfway down the pier, I turned to look back at him.

The white belly of the shark shined fuzzy with moonlight, and traces of blood streamed down its sides. It lie there lifeless or nearly so, but Sample, bent over at the waist, held an old, scarred wooden baseball bat, the size we would have used in little league. He rose, the bat swinging back high over his head, and chopped the bat down upon the shark's head. He repeated this a number times, leaving his feet as he drew the bat back to give him more momentum on the downswing. Each time the bat smacked the motionless fish, its tail lifted a foot off the pier at impact. The fisherman lining the pier watched in stunned silence as Sample tortured the defenseless predator.

I hurried down the pier and grabbed Sample's forearm before he began another attack.

Sample's eyes were streaming tears.

I removed the bat from his hand. It was a small bat, maybe 28 ounces. I felt nausea growing in my esophagus, and looked away to the shoreline, and settled on the yellow light from a tiki torch lighting the pathway to one of the hotel bars. It was a trick I had learned on fishing boats to fight off sea sickness. It seemed to be working on this too.

When I came out of my nausea spell, I noticed I had draped my arm over Sample's shoulders, and he had turned into my chest and was muttering something.

I leaned back, so I could hear what he said.

"God, Fuzzy. I didn't want it to be true."

I wasn't much of a bro-hug guy, and I was becoming increasingly aware I was amid a pier full of fishermen with my arm draped around a shirtless man. I patted Sample on the shoulder. I didn't know what to say. So I said nothing.

The second time I gave him the reassuring pat on the shoulder. Sample got the message and swiped his tears away with the back of his hand.

"Just get me those files, Fuzzy."

I left him there without answering. I felt the dead shark's hanging eye watch me as I walked away from him.

6

I couldn't get the image of Sample torturing the shark out of my mind. His anger made me wonder if Marisol was in danger? It seemed I had two options: Bring Sample the photos and wipe my hands of it or address the possibility he was trying to blackmail someone who had a great deal to lose with the evidence I possessed.

I had none of it figured out by the time I returned to the darkened parking lot of Molly Maguire's.

The lot was still full, and I pulled in between a navy '57 Chevy and a cherry red '58 Corvette. Both convertibles. Both with tops down. The Chevy had a small posse of teenagers sitting on the hood and leaning against fenders. They were the kind of fake gangbangers that had infected the Strand over the last few years.

I got out of the car and headed for the club without making eye contact.

From behind me I heard, "Yo, chief"

A short, alabaster-skinned kid, with hair only a shade darker, held his chin up in defiance. "Do you need someone to look after your car?"

I knew the scheme, and most of the time I would have pulled my piece and put the fear of God into this kid and his punk friends, and explained that no, I didn't need him to look after my car. But the scene with Sample had me feeling less than hard-boiled. So I reached into my wallet and handed him a five-dollar bill.

The kid looked at it, and scoffed. "Five bucks, ain't gonna do it chief. I'ma need twenty to do the job right."

Fingernails dug into the skin on the palms of my hands. "It's all I got, Casper," I said.

"What the fuck is this Casper shit?" He stepped forward, and two his buddies slid off the car.

I turned and walked away under a shower of profanities. I made a show of untucking my shirt, so they could see the Glock 19 tucked in the waistband of my jeans. It slowed the stream of f-bombs and other obscenities.

They didn't pat me down at the doors to Maguire's, because I was a regular and Paddy Meibaum who worked the door knew I was packing, but also knew I was unlikely to use it, unless I had good reason.

Inside, Maguire's was crawling with a motley crew of college kids, sunburned construction workers, and middle-age divorcees dressed like they just came off a cruise boat.

Then there were the girls. Enough of them, so it looked like a weekend night. They walked in slow laps around the floor, weaving in between tables, hoping to catch the eye of some eager guy, in which case they would lean down and whisper into his ear, "Do you wanna dance?" Most of the time the answer would be no, but dancers were persistent. And they would adjust their hustle as necessary. Sometimes that meant investing time in sitting with the customer, and engaging in inane discussion with him, pretending to be interested in his tales of prowess in the office or on the golf links. This was the approach that worked on me, but I had no intention of sitting and becoming the prey. It was a good thing, too, because I saw no empty tables.

And Veronica was on stage.

She had removed no clothing yet, but she had some enormous black guy's bald head buried in her breasts. She bounced them back and forth off his face to the rhythm of some hip-hop tune blaring from the house system. When she stood back from him, the dude was smiling as if he just learned to ride a bike for the first time. She pulled back the garter on her thigh, and he snatched a couple ones from a folded wad of bills in his hand and slid them up her leg. She gave a little, "Oh." When his hand grazed her thigh. She had told me in the past it was her subtle way of letting the customer know he was treading shaky ground. I'd been guilty of it a time or two in the past. She snapped the garter over the bill, and stripper strutted back to center stage.

She walked circles around the pole, one hand lightly gripping it. The black guy stood dumbfounded in his place watching, as her other hand reached behind her back, and worked her black bra loose. Strippers were talented and resourceful girls.

I decided to get a closer look, before the dude dropped too many dollars on her, and I lost Veronica's attention. I walked up beside the guy.

"What's up?" I said.

He bobbed his head and rolled his shoulder to the rhythm of the music.

"She's something else, huh?" I said.

He shook his head with a wide smile on my face. "Man, you have no idea."

I wasn't sure what he meant by that, but if it had something to do with a dance or VIP room he had gotten from her, I didn't want to hear about it. So I pulled out two ones and turned my attention to my girl on stage.

She was topless, now, and I could see light blue traces of veins translucent in the pale skin of her breasts. Her eyes settled on me, but she played it off, not even cracking the slightest of smiles and looking over my head to the bar, she hip swayed my way. All business.

She crouched down in front of me, so she was eye level with me, and draped both of her forearms over my shoulders.

I reached my hand over to the side of her leg and slid my two ones beneath her garter. I left my hand resting on her thigh. She didn't give me an "oh."

She leaned closer, her breasts pressing against my sternum, and nuzzled her cheek against my collar bone. Tilted her head up, hair brushing my chest. Light breath against the side of my neck. Her erotic voice whispered in my ear. "Your money isn't any good here."

She nipped the lobe of my ear. Giggled. Stood up and sidled over to her other customer.

I stood there, dumbfounded, like he had been moments ago. She still had that effect on me. The other girls didn't anymore.

When she was done with Big Daddy, she strutted around the main stage making eye contact with every horny eye in the room. Two college buddies stopped her on the other side of the stage. It was a short pit stop as one would expect. She swatted them each in the face twice with her boobs, squealed "Oh!" when they groped her, and earned a dollar off each of them. She pivoted towards me and rolled her eyes while they exchanged high-fives and walked back to their tables.

Now, she strode toward me, her gait that of a runway model. When she reached me, she hopped into the air and landed in a split. Then another leap, landing in the crouch position before me. I'd like to see Johnny Bench pull that off in five inch, platform heals.

Her head cocked, one eyebrow raised. "So what brings you in, Fuzz?"

The DJ informed us in a deep movie trailer voice that this was Raven's last song, and that all the gentlemen should make their way to the stage to tip her and ask about a private dance. Next on stage would be, "Cornbread."

"I hoped to make up for last night," I said.

"You're sweet, but whatever do you mean?"

It sounded like something from Gone With the Wind. She was sucking the wind out of my chest again. "Ah, I just don't think I was there for you last night," I said.

She pulled me close to her by my shirt collar. "Why don't we get out of here?"

"Really?" I said. "You can do that."

Crooked grin now. "What are they going to do fire me? I'd be back in six months after making the rounds at all the other clubs. Nobody owns me, Fuzzy."

"Come on Gents, let's get Raven out of those bottoms," came over the house system.

"Should I tip you to get you 'out of those bottoms', hmm?"

She wagged a finger at me, like a scolding teacher. "You wait and you can get them off me for free later."

What do you say to that? Nothing, but "yes, ma'am?", right? I stood there like an obedient puppy waiting for my treat.

Customers now lined the stage with desperation in their eyes and money in their fists. I stood back from the stage and left her to her work.

"Lucky man," I heard from my side.

It was Big Daddy, who had a grin on his face like a kid who'd just been told a salacious secret about one of the mothers in the neighborhood.

Veronica made her way around the stage collecting a pile of cash that would be the envy of any capitalistic entrepreneur. She never made it out of her bottoms. By the time Cornbread had taken the stage, Veronica was at my side, kissing me on the cheek, and running off to backstage. Over her shoulder she shouted, "Just give me a minute to change."

I decided that the troubles of Sample, Coach Cain, and Marisol could wait for the night.

THE LOVEMAKING WAS an act of mutual giving this time. We built up a rhythm, almost a cadence, right up to the time both of us reached release. The male beast, by its very nature, is one which seeks conquest and cares only of self-gratification. It is easy to forget, as I had, that in tending to the female's need, in return his own pleasure would be returned twofold. And a repeat performance was more likely.

Veronica pulled herself up on her elbows at my side and demurely reached behind and yanked my flannel blanket up over her shoulder so her breasts were not exposed.

"That was nice," she said.

I looked deep into those ice-blue eyes and nodded.

Somewhere behind those eyes, Veronica was turning something over in her mind. She struggled with it.

"What?" I said.

"Nothing," she said. Then told me, "Fuzzy, how come we never talk?"

Oh brother, I was in trouble, now. I played stupid. "What are we doing right, now?"

She dropped her bony chin to the fleshy mass beneath my collar bone. It dug into a pressure point.

I fought the urge to grimace.

She looked up underneath her brow, a frown on her face. "You know what I mean?"

I felt a finger nail tracing a line from my sternum to navel to beyond. And I couldn't help myself. I was ready for action again. I found myself resisting urges again. "What do you want to talk about?"

Her hand found me. Her eyes widened. She had me in a vulnerable position. "We can start with why we don't talk. It's like sometimes I look at you and you're not even there. Your mind is elsewhere. Is it work? Is there another woman?"

How do you tell someone you're in love with a dead woman? "It's complicated," I said.

She removed her hand, traced it up my chest, placed it flat upon my sternum, and rested the bony chin there. I'm sure it left an imprint on my pectoral muscle. "I'm sure it is, sweety. Let's simplify it."

I looked down at the tent I was pitching beneath the covers and frowned.

"Un huh, mister. You're not getting out of this," she said. "Is it the situation with your mom?"

I could have gone with that, and embellished it with some half-truths and bought myself a few more weeks of dodging the truth, but that would mean a lot of talking about the situation with my mom. Veronica would no doubt try to fix that situation with her special kind of psychology. It would involve a lot of sex, so that would be fun, but somehow I'd feel like I would have to make it up to her.

"It's not Mom," I said. "Actually, I'm sure there is some of that." I paused. "Same with work."

When I didn't continue, she removed her hand, sat up in bed, and turned away from me. Her shoulders trembled as if she were crying. The blanket slid from her back. She was beautiful there, all woman curves and vulnerable. "That leaves another woman."

"Veronica, have I ever told you I was engaged once?"

She shook her head. She twisted her torso towards me.

I resisted the temptation to take a peek at all the goodies and kept my gaze on her watery eyes.

"What happened?" She said.

"She died."

Veronica gasped and covered her mouth with the tips of her fingers. "Oh my god, Fuzzy. How long ago was this?"

I couldn't keep looking at her. I turned and looked at the small half-moon window in my door. The sky was turning gray with the rising dawn. "Eight years," I said.

I felt the bed shift with her movement. A small spider crawled down one of the mullions, which radiated from the center of the window. "She was killed," I added.

I heard her gasp again. Was I hitting it with her bluntly, using the truth as a weapon I could wield to keep the upper hand? If I laid the foundation now, could I rely on it every time she asked a tough question? Was any of this fair to either her or I? I wished I had just kept my mind on the three stooges -- Marisol, Coach, and Sample.

"Fuzzy?" she said. "You're doing it again."

I turned to face her. "What's that?"

"I was talking to you, but you were off on another planet."

"I'm sorry. What was it?"

"I asked if you were okay?"

It had been a long time since someone had asked me that question. I mean, I get a lot of "How's it going" or "How's it hanging, Fuzz?", but none of that had the sincerity of Veronica's question.

"No," I said.

"Talk to me, honey. I'm not going to bite."

"I could never love you," I said. "Because I am still in love with Angel."

He lips parted and formed an "Oh". Her cheeks sucked in, the words taken out her mouth. She got up, with the blanket clutched to her body with one hand, and hurried about gathering her clothes in the other. I had never seen her so upset. Not even during our knockdown, drag out fights about how she made a living.

"Veronica..."

"Her name was Angel?". She stopped gathering woman things and looked at me. "Angel?" she shouted. "How fucking convenient?"

Sadness replaced the discomfort. It was over.

"I'm happy I could service you here in the real world, but you can have your fucking Angel. I'm out!"

And she was. She walked straight out the door wearing only my plaid, black and red blanket and a pile of her clothes in the crook of her arm. She left the door open. Her car started, and she was gone.

Later, I found her panties lying limply on the pavement beside the tire of my car.

7

Jimmy Alou was the best friend I had ever known. There was seldom a week that went by without us seeing each other at least once since both of us tried out as Freshman for the Myrtle Beach High baseball team some 16 years ago.

We had a standing date for Friday breakfast at one of the pancake houses he owned on Kings Highway just west of the Family Kingdom amusement park.

Lately, it seemed one of us missed, and the other would eat breakfast silently alone at the counter. So, I was skeptical about seeing Jimmy. But like any good friend, he had that sixth sense that allowed him to know when his friend needed him. It was with great relief when I saw him stroll in through the front door trailing sunlight and smiling like a politician.

I stood to greet him.

Jimmy was a short, broad-shouldered middle infielder. He was of mixed Mexican/Asian descent. When he smiled, one dimple formed on one of his cheeks, and while I've never taken the time to confirm this, I'm pretty sure the dimpled cheek changed from time to time. He was charismatic as hell, but also, mostly, sincere.

He took my hand, patted me on the shoulder, and said, "Fuzzy, how's it hanging?" And followed with, "How's Henna K.?"

"She's not Henna K., anymore," I corrected. "She's Henna P."

He tapped a fist against my chin like a fake punch. "C'mon, Fuzz. She'll always be Henna K. to me?"

Henna was Mom. "Yeah, me too. I guess."

"And how is she making it out there? Have you seen her?"

She's consumed with hate. For life, for her current situation, but mostly for me. "She's taking it pretty rough, Jimmy. And she doesn't talk much to me."

He socked me in the chin again. "Ah, give her a little time, Fuzz. She'll come around."

I wasn't so sure, but I changed the subject and asked about his wife, Candy, and the kids -- two girls Macy and Grace, who they called Gracy, both of whom were a perfect mix their parents' good looks and would give their father a heart attack when they reach adolescence in a few years.

"They're fine," he said. It was his turn to change the subject. "You still balling that stripper?"

He had a way with words. "Come on, Jimmy?"

"What?" he said. He slowed it down, "Are - you - or - are - you - not - sleeping - with - that - stripper?"

"It's complicated."

"Then simplify it, and just answer the fucking question." He smiled, and crawled onto one of the backless, spinner stools at the counter.

I joined him. "We got into a fight last night. We may be on the outs."

"So you fucked her?"

"Jimmy, stop it."

A squat waitress, probably about our age, but who looked ten years older, waddled over before us. She had an eighth of an inch of makeup caked on her face, and oily brown hair wrapped high on her head like a beehive. It was a look that didn't help her keep a youthful appearance. Who was I to judge? I'd had a full head of gray hair, since I'd turn legal. "What'll ya have?"

"Coffee, black. And brew us a fresh pot, Brenda. Make it extra strong, not like that watery shit we usually serve."

She looked to me. Pen poised above her checkbook.

"I'll have the same."

"Alrighty, Mr. Alou and friend. I'll get that going."

When she was out of earshot, Jimmy said, "She's probably single, if things don't work out with the stripper."

I said nothing because I figured it was the only way to get him off my case.

"Hey Jimmy, guess who I am working a case for?"

Brenda graced us with her presence again. "Ok coffee is brewing. How about breakfast?"

We ordered. Again, both the same thing. Two eggs, over medium, and a side of sausage.

When she left us again, Jimmy asked, "Who?"

"Billy Smith. You remember him?"

"Sample? Are you kidding? I heard the little shit is selling drugs now. I guess the Amway stuff didn't take off like he'd hoped."

When Sample dropped out of college, he got connected into one of those pyramid marketing programs, like Amway. He would try to sell us and all of his friends and acquaintances on it, hoping to make his fortune by exploiting his friends. He was doing the same thing now I suppose, but it somehow seemed more honorable.

"That's him," I said. "And yeah, he mostly sells weed."

"Be careful with dealers, Fuzzy. Shit can go south quick."

"Funny you should say that," I said. Ever since I started working cases, I've used our Friday breakfast as a sounding board. Jimmy, to go along with his charisma, was a bright and practical guy. "It's a simple peep job with a twist."

He shook his head. "There's always a twist in the shit you work, Fuzzy. Hell, I don't have to remind you the last time you brought me one of these cases with a twist."

He was referring to the murder of Ray Burris by my mother.

"Sample wanted me to take a picture of a prostitute pulling a trick."

"Get the fuck outta here!" He bent over at the waist and laughed so hard I thought I might need to perform CPR.

Brenda returned with two mugs of coffee and a steaming black carafe on a tray. She put the mugs down in front of each of us, and the carafe between us.

Jimmy was still at it.

She looked to me. "What's so funny?"

"My life," I said, and took a sip of coffee. It was somehow both watered down and bitter.

Jimmy got control of himself enough to ask, "He wants proof that a hooker is fucking someone?"

Brenda frowned and walked back to the kitchen.

"I told you there was a twist. And that's not it."

"It gets better?" he said. "Wait, a minute. How much is he paying you for this?"

"Half my normal rate," I said. "I should have gone full rate."

He paused with his mug right before his mouth. "What's the twist?"

"It's not as simple as Sample made it out to be."

"No shit, Sherlock."

We both drank coffee. He waited on me.

I tried to decide how much to share. I went with the full

Monty. "The girl is getting it on with a pretty recognizable face. I think Sample is working an angle."

"Who's the john?"

"That new football coach at CAU, Cain." Despite all my talk about confidentiality with my Uncle Rod and others I never felt the need to explain this to Jimmy. I knew anything I shared with him stayed with him.

He whistled. "So, Sample is trying to move on up, like George Jefferson?"

I nodded and drank more sewer water. It must have shown in my face, because he said, "Yeah, I know it's terrible."

I put the mug down and resolved not to drink anymore. It was only giving me something to do while I worked shit out in my head.

"The problem is that I confronted Sample with it last night, and he's either a great actor or he had no clue what the fuck I was talking about."

"Did you give him his proof?"

"Not yet."

Jimmy reached for his mug, thought better, and started drumming his fingers on the counter instead. "Don't get too deep into this, Fuzzy. Sample's a joke, but he's a dealer, and dealers pretty much all hang with low-life fucks that'll rub you out for a dime bag."

"I was thinking about visiting the coach," I said. "Let him know what's going on. Give him a warning."

Jimmy looked to the ceiling. I knew he was avoiding my eyes, so I couldn't see his disappointment. Fact is, what he was doing, pretty much everyone does with me. I never live up to anyone's expectations. Hell, even Veronica gave me this treatment last night while she was gathering her things. He broke the silence, "Fuzzy, just give Sample his pictures, and get out of this shit."

Although I always shared my cases with Jimmy, and I thought he was intelligent and measured in his advice, we seldom saw eye to eye. And I never took his advice.

"And about that stripper," he said. "Forget about her, there are other titty dancers in the sea. Throw your line back out there. I'm sure you'll get another bite."

Like I said, he was a practical guy, and we never agreed on anything.

8

A fter breakfast with Jimmy, I stopped by another friend's place, Amanda Diamond. Amanda, was a Swiss army knife of skill sets. She always did better by me when I visited her in person than if I emailed her. So, I dropped a thumb drive off with her to make hard copies of my pictures, and spent the afternoon watching an LSU-Arkansas football game on TV at home.

It wasn't much of a game as LSU jumped out to an early 17-0 lead facilitated by two turnovers by the Hogs on their first two possessions. I only paid it half my attention as I considered Jimmy's advice regarding Sample once again. There was a lot of common sense in it. Primarily, the economics. If I gave Sample the photos, I would get paid for my troubles. If I held out just a little longer, I most likely would not, and I may bring the kind of attention that Jimmy had warned me about.

By halftime, I was halfway to convincing myself of wiping my hands clean of this mess, and picking up a check, but Amanda called and I picked up the pictures.

Then, I made it to the parking lot of the CAU practice field right before sundown.

Sports cars and sedans littered the lot. The sedans had gold rims and other effects. A few 15-year-old rust buckets stood out like cavities. The walk-ons' cars, I thought, and backed my pickup beside one of them.

Things were wrapping up on the field. Different squads huddled up with their coordinators to get the pep talk for tomorrow's big game. A large huddle followed with what I assumed was Cain's final speech to the troops before the contest. Hands flew in the air with helmets held high, and the players shouted something I couldn't make out, but no doubt was some variation of "Go Team!" or, more likely, "Kick That Ass". They broke and jogged to the field house with coaches in deep discussion trailing behind them.

During my afternoon of football watching, I had done a property tax search on Thomas Cain in the Horry County online database. Seems Coach Cain paid taxes on three different vehicles - a 2015 Ford F-150, a 2017 Toyota Prius, and the most recent purchase, a 2015 Volkswagen Beetle. An F-150 was parked before a sign that read "Reserved for Head Coach, Thomas Cain". My mad detective skills led me to deduce that this was Coach Cain's truck.

I thumbed through the developed photos while I waited. Fifteen minutes later, a small crew of foul-mouthed kids emptied out the locker room. About 30 minutes later, the last group of stragglers entered the lot just as the sun dropped beneath the bleachers. There were five. All tall, lanky, and black. Except for one. He was a 6'-4" Latino. He went about 220 pounds. There was nothing lanky about this one. The others were receivers, and he had the hands of one, too, but he was built to protect the passer and open lanes for the backs. His Aztec eyes looked familiar.

Jandro Rodriguez.

As they strolled by my truck, I stuck my head out the window, and smiled. "Say fellas, you wouldn't happen to know if Coach Cain was still around? Would ya?"

Jandro's face remained flat. He jabbed a thumb towards the locker rooms. "He in his office and gonna be there a while." He continued walking by without so much as slowing his stride. "He ain't seeing no press either," he added over his shoulder.

The boys drove off.

A light procession of the coaching staff emerged from the field house. First it was the graduate assistants, and I had been wrong about the rust buckets belonging to walk-ons. Then, more senior level coaches, and finally the coordinators, who drove cars the caliber of the kids.

At last, we were down to coach's truck, myself, and a plain, white sedan that was backed in, like me. It was the first I had noticed it. There was a dark shape in the driver's side, but it was unidentifiable like the car in the pale light of the parking lot.

A door scraping open pierced the silence of the early night. Coach emerged wearing a shiny teal polo shirt, khaki shorts, booty socks, and running shoes. He had a cell phone ground into his ear. In the other hand, he carried a stack of envelopes like the one sitting beside me on the bench of my truck.

I took a deep breath and grabbed my package of pictures. I was looking forward to this like root canal work. I stepped out my truck.

Some movement from that sedan, as if the driver planned to get out, too, until he saw my action.

I stared it down for a couple of steps. I may have imagined it, but it looked like the figure slid down half a foot in the driver's seat.

Fuck it, I turned my attention to Coach.

He stood, fumbling in his pocket for keys, beside the truck. He glanced at me.

"Say, Coach, you have a minute?" I picked up my pace into a light trot. "I need a word with you it's important."

He didn't appear to recognize me as he went back to fishing for his keys. When he removed them, he inserted the key into the door.

I was short yardage away when he swung the door open. "It's about Marisol," I said.

The acknowledgment slid onto his face before he turned to face me.

"Frizzy?" he said.

Can you believe this guy? "It's Fuzzy," I said. "I know you have a big day tomorrow, but I think you need to see these." I waved the envelope at him.

"Oh, for Christsakes, not another one of you!" Even in the dim light, I could see his face brighten. "Seriously, why don't you folks spend your time in Columbia or Clemson? You are so transparent in your lack of nuts to go after the big boys. "No," he said. "It's always the Louisiana-Lafayettes or the Coastal Atlantics."

I had no clue what he was talking about. It must have shown on my face because he changed tact.

"What is it you got there?"

"We may want to go some place a little more private," I said, and cocked my head like an accusatory finger at my friend in the sedan.

Coach dropped his shoulders in resignation. "Okay, back to my office it is," he said. "But this had better be good."

It wasn't. So I didn't answer him.

I followed him through a lobby lined with trophy cases and walls all done up in teal and gold. A manatee cresting the surface of the ocean, CAU's mascot, looked down on us from the archway we passed under. We went through a set of double doors, coach holding one leaf open for me with the toe of his foot, as we entered a weight room. It was like nothing you'd see at the finest pay per month gyms. There was no bubbly blond working a counter here, but that was all that was missing.

Maybe, she was off like everyone else?

We weaved through free weight stations and emptied into a locker room through another door propped open by coach. The carpet was plush, cut-pile and teal. The shiny, cherry-lacquered lockers each housed a crisp teal jersey with a solid, gold, Notre Dame-type helmet on shelves at the top. Bright, white spikes lined the bottom of each locker. At least two pair per locker. This was a different field house than the one they had when I was here eight years ago on a baseball scholar-ship. The program had a lot more money to spend than they had in my time.

Cain opened another door. This time he stepped through without holding it open for me. Fortunately, it was not self-closing or it would have smacked me in the face. To Coach's credit, his office was pretty spartan compared to the rest of the accommodations. It was spacy as you might expect. Enough for an executive sized desk and a four seater square table for meetings with his staff to review game strategy. Both were humble pieces of furniture settings, like you'd see from IKEA. Staid, gray level-loop carpet, the kind which held up well to heavy traffic. In comparison, the carpet in the locker room would need to be replaced annually to keep up with the damage it would take from a year of muddy football player traffic.

Coach sat behind his desk and indicated the plastic-molded chair in front of it.

I took a seat and laid my envelope out in front of me. "No computer?" I said.

"It's a distraction, even for someone as old school as me

the internet's pull is too hard. This keeps me focused."
Everyone has their impressive qualities, I guess. I wasn't sure
how to approach my subject, so I went with a blunt, knock
over the head approach. I removed the 8 x 10s, and fanned
them out on his desk, so he had a high level view of the
complete collection. I had spent little time reviewing my
work, because I knew what was there, but staring at them
now I virtually patted myself on the back. The color was
bright, the shots were all sharp, and the individuals in them
were identifiable. It may have been the best half dozen of
pictures I'd ever taken on a gig like this.

"What the fuck?" he said. "Where do you all draw
the line?"

Even through his fleshy jowls, I could see the cartilage
bunching on his jawline. I didn't know who he thought "all"
of us were, but I figured the best way to learn was to let him
tell me. I kept his stare and waited.

He stabbed a finger at one of photos, the one showing
Marisol tucking his sheath of bills in her cleavage, he looking
on dumbly. "What in the hell does this have to do with the
program?" He said. "This is my personal life. What line will
you fuckers not cross?"

His other hand rested on the desktop. I noted neither
hand had a ring on it. Something he probably regretted
because it meant no conference championships, but for me it
meant no wife. It probably explained his irritation, and lack
of fear faced with the evidence in front of him. I decided to
come clean. "Tommy, I don't know who you think I am or
who you think I work for, but I'm here trying to do you
a favor."

He tapped his finger on the picture. "Great, next time
don't do me any favors."

"Someone hired me to take those. At the time, I figured it
was an odd variation of the standard peeper job. Now I think

someone, probably my client, may be looking to blackmail you."

"But not you? Right? You come out of this squeaky clean."

He stood up, so he could talk down to me. "Look here you asshole. You can take those pictures, roll them up real tight, and shove them where the sun don't shine." He motioned with a hand as if he was doing a karate chop. Each word delivered a more violent chop. "You, or your client, won't get one penny from me. Why? Because I did nothing wrong." He stopped chopping to point at the pile of glossies on his desk. "That's two consenting adults."

"Some cash is changing hands. Someone might call that prostitution."

He hurried around the desk, grabbed my arm, and tugged me to my feet. "Get out of here you fuckin' lurch. Get out."

I straightened my t-shirt, as if I had been wearing a coat and tie. Calmly, I gathered the pictures back into the envelope.

Coach's face was as red as a boiled lobster. "Get the fuck out!"

When I stepped out the door, I heard him tapping numbers on an old landline phone.

I made my way through the palatial locker room and stopped in the lobby to scan the trophy cases. It didn't take me long to find it as it was the only baseball trophy. It seemed to stand like an awkward kid at the high school dance. 2009 Southern Conference Champions - Baseball, it read. I had helped them win it. I felt the breeze of nostalgia come over me, and couldn't help but smile. Jimmy caught the pop-up to end it all, while I watched from the dugout with a bag of ice and a towel wrapped around my left elbow. I had carried a shutout into the ninth and had begged coach to let me finish what I started. But I had put the first two on and, as is usually the case, he made the right choice. He brought in our 6'-6", hard throwing righty, Shawn Jackson. We called him "Action". He was black as midnight and did not have the stereotypical closer personality. In fact, opposing batters complained that they couldn't take him serious because he always smiled at them. Even during his delivery. At any rate, Action didn't secure the shutout, but he did close out the 3-1 win, and we celebrated like kids in Williamsport.

Afterwards, I remember making love to Angel in a peddle boat on the bank of the pond in the center of campus. It was uncomfortable as hell for both of us, but something in her eyes that night led me to ask her to marry me. I didn't even have a ring. Couldn't even remember thinking about getting married to her or anyone? But, it seemed the entire world changed that night. I could see my future in the game, in life, and I wanted Angel Serevina as part of it. She said, "Yes." And we completed the doubleheader in her dorm room, while her roommate pretended to sleep. But I was wrong, the universe hadn't changed that night. That came six months later, almost to the day, when she was taken from me by a hit-and-run driver. A witness, that same roommate, said the driver was swerving, like an obvious drunk, but sobered up after clipping Angela on the sidewalk. He sped off in a straight line. Nobody got a license plate, and nobody ever got the driver.

Two beefy campus cops interrupted my nostalgia. They surprised me when they settled at either side of me.

"Identification, please?" Said the cop on my right. They looked like brothers, possibly twins. Both blonde with short, cropped military haircuts, both with smiling, blue eyes, though neither of them smiled, set in pie shape faces. They were both a head shorter than me and built like linebackers gone soft in approaching middle age. They didn't look like the type to beat me over the head with their clubs, but they were stout enough to do it if they had to.

I decided on the sheepish, innocent approach. I handed the officer on the right my P.I. license. His nameplate said, Officer Studbeck.

His pale eyebrows rose. "Oh oh, look what we got here, Beau. A private investigator." He delivered it slowly, drawing out every syllable of investigator. It was a common corn-bread-fed, redneck tactic to mock being impressed.

I let it pass, but I had to push down a need to defend myself. "That's me," I said. "I've moved on from my previous lot in life. Say is Sergeant Holcomb still running things around here?"

Beau laid he hands on me then and turned me to face him.

Again I had to fight an urge building like a turning fork sounding deep in my skull.

"How d'ya know the Sergeant?"

I nodded to the both of them in succession. "I used to wear the uniform, too," I said.

"Yeah?" said Beau. "Well you ain't now, and we got a call to take your ass outta here. So you're coming with us, pal."

I yanked my arm out of his reach before he could grab me and stepped towards the door. I turned my attention to Studbeck. "No kidding," I said. Flashed a dumb smile as if I didn't know the shit I was getting myself into. "Mounted patrol, my last year of school, and then for two years later. Then, I went back to playing ball, and being a bum."

Studbeck seemed to forget he should be roughnecking me off campus and said, "Yeah, what did you play? You say you played ball?"

Beau put the grip on my left elbow, the one where they jab their fingers and thumb on either side of the arm into the hollow above the bony, ball of the joint. It was immobilizing, and an easy way to subdue someone without causing a scene or the image of a cop in a brutal act.

I twisted my arm free. "Watch the arm, Beau." I went back to ignoring him, and said to Studbeck, "Baseball, and I'm still playing summers."

We had reached the doors. "Yeah, what, like a Men's League?"

"I play for the Sun Sox."

"That's Independent League, huh?"

The other one tried to put his hands on me again. I felt it, even before, his fingers grasped my elbow.

I stepped through the doors.

The white sedan was missing. The parking lot empty accept for my mid-90's Ranger, Coach's truck, and a golf cart.

I laughed. "Is that how they afford this field house like the Taj Mahal?" I said, "Y'all partner up in a golf cart?"

"Shut the fuck up," the other one said. "You're coming with us."

The two of them looked each other over as if they hadn't realized they were going for a good cop - bad cop scheme.

I walked towards my car. Past their golf cart.

They followed.

It was easy to be so steadfast when you realized there was no way they would transfer me to Campus Station on the back of a golf cart. I knew that from firsthand knowledge, having patrolled three years on the back of a horse. Yes, calling in and waiting for a cruiser was a possibility, but you only saved that hassle for nasty situations. The time I had used it was a domestic situation - a drunken fuck beat up his girlfriend. I had called for the back-up, as much to insure I wouldn't kick the dude's ass, as I needed the help.

The brothers Piggy followed me to my car, and watched with stunned looks on their faces, as I climbed into the cab. Studbeck tapped his flash light on my window.

I rolled it down.

He handed me the license back. "Can't come back on campus, Mr. Koella."

I pulled away. "Un huh," I said. I would have sprayed them with loose stone, but the pavement was too new, too high quality, to have any.

In the rearview, the two of them were shouting at each other, as if they'd just let a hardened criminal get away.

I drove on.

9

There's something about trying to do the right thing, that always goes wrong. Even worse, when the right thing involves trying to help someone out, who maybe doesn't deserve the help, they seldom, if ever, appreciate it. If I'd just taken Jimmy's advice, I'd be free of all this, and I'd be two hundred bucks richer. Plus, there would be the honor of doing the work Sample paid me to do.

I was relieved that I had not been taken to see Sergeant Holcomb because without fail that always meant spending at least some time behind bars. This case was not worth even an hour's wait in the slammer waiting on Holcomb to get his kicks.

The problem was Sample. It wasn't like he was a great friend, but he was something more than your typical shark fishing, drug dealing client. We had a past. Of late, that past involved him doing me some favors. I owed him something for that, and for the hundred bucks I was carrying of his.

Well, it was less than $50 now, but who's counting.

I had no concern that Sample would resort to the kind of danger that Jimmy warned me about, the typical dealer shit. I just didn't know what to do. Usually that meant getting Jimmy's view. And then doing the exact opposite.

I drove east over the inter-coastal waterway bridge, past the Waccamaw furniture shops lining the highway. I had no recollection of leaving Conway, and it concerned me that I was so deep in thought. Almost as if the car was driving itself and my feet and hands operated the task outside any input from my brain while it processed my current dilemma.

I pulled off the highway, onto a frontage road, and into the parking lot of one of those big box Waccamaw furniture shops. It was dead.

I tried Jimmy.

No answer.

Veronica was as good an option for sage advice, and a strip club visit would be cathartic right about now, but the image of her hauling it out of my place naked with a pile of clothes in her arms scared me off of that idea.

Fuck it, if Coach didn't want my help. Maybe Marisol Rodriguez would.

MUCH LIKE THE drive that got me back to the Beach, I remembered little of my trip to the Carlton Arms. I just found myself backed in between Marisol's Beetle, and a beat up Chevy mini truck, its bed littered with construction debris. It was only 9 p.m., so I didn't consider it too late to go knocking on her door. I should have.

Upstairs I knocked on the door to G-8 and waited. Salsa meringue filtered through the walls and doors. I almost gave up, when the music stopped. The chain rattled behind the door and the bolt of the lock slid open. The door opened maybe half a foot.

I wondered what the purpose of removing the chain was if you would open the door like this.

The face that peered out at me belonged to the little Latino that I had seen the other day. I assumed it was Mr. Rodriguez, Marisol's father. "Who you?", he said in a thick accent.

"I'm here to see Marisol, Mr. Rodriguez."

"Why?"

"It's personal."

"Marisol just a girl. Why do you need to see her?"

The over protective dad wasn't something I had to encounter often in my job. I would need to wade cautiously in these waters, or wait to catch Marisol away from home. I wasn't sure what was behind my urgency, but waiting didn't seem a viable option.

"Mr. Rodriguez, I assure you I mean Marisol no harm, but I need to talk to her. I'm concerned about others' intentions."

A scowl took up residency on his face. "Who others?"

Marisol's voice calling from within saved me, "Who is it Papi?"

He turned to call over his shoulder, but the door swung open a little further, and a bubbly Marisol appeared at his shoulder. Her smile quickly went flat when she recognized me.

"Oh, you," she said.

"Who is he, Marisol? He say others do you harm. I call police."

He moved to walk away, but Marisol stopped him with a reassuring pat on his chest. "It's okay, Papi. I know Frizzy, here. He's helping me out with finding a good job."

Papi considered that for a moment. He looked suspicious, but his love for his daughter blinded his better sense. She winked at me.

"I only need to talk to her for a minute, Mr. Rodriguez. I

assure you that I mean her no harm. In fact, I may have some good prospects for your daughter." I waved my manila envelope at him.

He stepped back from the door. She stepped through the door and closed it behind her.

She wore no make-up, and her face looked like the kind that would get away from her soon if she kept wearing as much of it as she normally did. She crossed her arms across her chest and shivered, despite wearing a navy sweatshirt inscribed with "Myrtle Beach." It was a shirt you picked up in one of the tourist trap shops for $5 bucks. She also had on loose fitting, heather gray sweat pants. She was barefoot. Her nails painted a dark, almost burgundy, red.

"It's Fuzzy," I said.

With the door shutting, so went her smile. "Yeah, whatever. Are you going to tell me what this is all about or are you just gonna stand there checking me out?"

She had a way with words, and she could turn the charm off and on at will. I wasn't so sure I wanted to help Marisol Rodriguez. Though, she needed it. I cleared my throat. "Yeah so you want to do this here?"

"You want my Papi looking over your shoulder?"

"Right," I said. "Um, so what I have here is the result of a job I was hired to do."

She hurried me along with a roll along gesture of the hand.

"How much are you offering?" she said.

That gave me pause. "I don't understand."

"The last guy like you came at me with an offer," she said. "You're gonna have to beat his offer, if you want my help."

"Look, Marisol, I don't think I'm the kind of guy you think I am," I said. She thought I was a john.

"You're an investigator. Aren't you?"

Wrong again, Fuzzy. Score one for Marisol. I cleared my

throat. My weight shifting from one foot to another. I must have looked like a frightened teenager trying to work up the nerve to ask her out.

She flicked the envelope with her middle finger. "What do you have in there? That's what you're here about, right?"

I slid the 8 x 10s out and handed them to her. "I was hired to take those."

The corners of her mouth creeped up. "Who hired you?"

"Billy Smith."

A look of surprise on her face, followed by a widening grin. "Billy?" she said. "What's he got to do with all of this?"

Still stunned that I had offered my client's name so easily, and confused by what "all of this" was, my voice seemed to come from some subconscious space, "I think he's trying to blackmail coach."

"Yeah, but how does he know?"

I pointed to the pictures.

"I don't get it. What does this prove?"

I came out of the fog she had cloaked my mind with. My defense was building. "There's a shot in there where money is changing hands," I said.

"I'm not sure if that proves anything you people can use."

"I agree, but Sample is a low-life. He'll think he's got more than he does with these. Even if his original plan wasn't blackmail, with these in hand, he'll eventually get around to it. It's the way guys like him think."

"Wait a minute who's Sample?"

"Billy. Sorry it's a nickname, we've had for him since college."

"Billy has friends?" she said. She didn't wait for an answer. "Has he been talking to Michaels?"

"Who's Michaels?" I said.

"Forget it. So why are you here?"

It was a good question. I wasn't even sure any longer. "I

shared these with Coach, and he didn't seem to care. He just had me escorted from his office."

She giggled at that.

"I was just asked to take some pictures, when I realized what I had. I guess I got a conscience and didn't want you and he to get hurt. But nobody seems to give a shit, so I guess I'll just hand these over to Sample, and collect my pay. Sorry to have bothered you."

She smiled at me the way a teenaged girl would when the boy got up the nerve, stammered and asked her to the Homecoming dance.

I was sick of her. Everything was some inside joke. I started to leave, but she stopped me, as she had stopped her father earlier, with a light hand to my chest. She kept it there. "Wait, don't go away angry."

I couldn't believe this girl. She was so sure of her appeal, and the annoying thing was she had every right to be. "I'm not angry."

It came out like a hiss, and she stepped back in fear.

"I'm just confused and tired of the games and the trying to do the right thing shit."

"So, why are you concerned?" She said. The anger, which I denied, still showed on my face, because she added, "You say you are trying to help. To do the right thing. What would you have me do now?"

"I don't know, Marisol. I don't know."

I walked down the stairs shaking my head. Halfway down, a bulking shape appeared at the bottom of the stairs. As he stepped on the first step, he appeared under light.

Jandro Rodriguez.

He recognized me at about the same. "What the fuck are you doing here, Chief?"

I was tired of getting called that, too. What did these kids think? All of us non-millennials were Native Americans?

"I came to see your sister, Jandro."

He climbed the stairs, taking two steps at a time. Stopped one below me. On level ground, we would look eye to eye, but from this position he had to look up at me, his Chief. He held his chin up in cocky assurance and puffed out his pecs like some fucking bodybuilding contestant. I was so done with the Rodriguez's. "How you know my name, Chief.?"

"I'm a 'Tees fan, at least I was. You keep calling me 'Chief' and I'll re-think that. I'll let Marisol tell you what I came here for. I'm not at liberty to say."

He held his hands at his waist, and cocked his head to the side, like some hip-hop pose you might see on the cover of a magazine. "Liberty? Liberty? What the fuck, Chief!" He paused for effect. "This ain't the Declaration of Independence."

I shoved my way past him, almost knocking him over. Made my way down the stairs and back out into the night.

"I'ma kick your ass next time you try that," he called down. "And stay away from my sister."

Two cars down from where I had parked my car sat a familiar, non-descript white sedan. I made it for a Nissan, not sure on the model. I'm not a car nut.

In the passenger side of my truck, an Alfred E. Neuman look-a-like with red hair, big ears, and stupid looking face, smiled out at me.

I reached to my back, but my piece wasn't there. I had put it in the glove box, before I went to talk to Coach, which in retrospect, was probably a good thing. Now, however, it left me feeling naked.

I crawled in beside Alfred. "I hope you have a good reason for breaking into my car?"

He continued with the goofy look on his face. His cheeks were peppered with freckles and black heads. His hair was plastered to his head with some industrial strength hair spray. Used in such quantity, that I could smell it in the close confines of the cab, and feel it in the pressure building in my sinuses. "You left the door unlocked. Mr. Koella. This isn't the best of neighborhoods. You know?"

He held a crumpled card in his hand, my vehicle registration. The glove box was open. The light bulb had burned out, and I had never replaced it, but even in the darkness I could see he had removed my Glock.

I snatched him by the throat and pinned him back against the headrest.

"I don't know, who the fuck you are, and I don't give a shit about the neighborhood, but if you don't hand over my piece, right now. I swear to god I will squeeze the last breath out of you."

And I did just that.

The goofy look disappeared as his eyes dilated. He squirmed in discomfort and panic.

I increased the pressure of my grip.

Rapidly, he shook his head. He reached behind his back.

I loosened my grip. "Easy Alfred," I said. "Just tell me where it is."

"Under my right hip," he rasped.

I squeezed a little harder and reached across him with my other arm. I could feel the cold steel of my rod. I tugged him closer to me by the throat, removed my gun, and jabbed it into his side.

"Ok," I said. "What the fuck are you doing in my car?"

He looked at me bug-eyed, and I realized I was still choking the life out of him.

I let him go.

Instinctively, a hand went to his throat, and he rubbed it, as if trying to remove a stain my fingers had left there. "Jesus, you could have killed me."

I jabbed my gun deeper into a hollow between his ribs and waited.

He grimaced. "Like I said, you left it open. I just waited here because I figured it was time we talked."

"What do we have to talk about? I've never seen you before in my life. I think I'd remember."

"But you have, I was at the Coral Beach, just like you the other night."

The other guy. In the other stairwell. I just now noticed the stench of stale tobacco smoke emanating from his clothes. It's funny how adrenaline will do that to you. There's not much I hate more than the smell of cigarette smoke.

"Who are you?" I asked.

He handed me my vehicle registration. "I will reach for my wallet," he said. "I'm not carrying."

I believed him but my judgement had been lacking lately. I stabbed my piece in his side, again, just to remind him of the score.

He withdrew a wallet from his back pocket. It looked like alligator skin. He wore boots that looked like they came from the same reptile. He also wore a black suit, with a white shirt, and a bolo tie. It was a get up like you'd see on a priest in a bad spaghetti-western. He fished out a card from the billfold and handed it to me. I had one, too. I had shared mine with Studbeck earlier in the night. He was a private dick. His name was Shane Michaels.

So, I had a name, an occupation, and the fact that Marisol knew him. He was probably the other guy that came offering her something.

"What's your angle, Michaels?"

He smiled the way a chronic back pain sufferer did when offered a moment of relief. "Only if you're sharing yours," he said.

I reminded him of his current station in life by grinding

89

my rod into his side some more. Surprisingly, it hadn't broken skin, yet. "You first, Michaels."

He shrugged. Patted down a shirt pocket. "Mind if I smoke?"

"Hell yeah I mind if you smoke. I'm gonna have to fumigate my ride already to get the dirty ashtray smell you brought into it. Stop stalling. Start storytelling."

"I'm investigating Coach Tom Cain for my client."

"Who's your client? His wife?"

His eyebrows pinched and deep thought lines burrowed in his forehead. Somehow a dumbfounded look, showed on his silly face. "He ain't married. Is he?"

"I have no fucking idea. I'm not investigating Coach."

"How come you visited him at the school tonight?"

Jab to the side.

He grimaced.

"Your story," I reminded him. "Who's your client then?"

"I'm not at liberty to say."

I thought of Jandro Rodriguez and chuckled. "This isn't the Declaration of Independence, Michaels. Start sharing or things will start to get interesting right about now."

"Ok, so it's not just Cain. He's just the figurehead. It's the whole program. Mostly recruiting violations."

"You're working for the NCAA?"

He swallowed his tongue, but the way he averted my eyes answered in the affirmative.

"What does this have to do with Marisol?"

"Nothing. She's just collateral damage to what's going on over there."

He still couldn't look me in the eye.

"Fuck you, Michaels. She just now told me you approached her with an offer."

Now he turned and looked out the passenger window. When he spoke it was like he was talking to someone in the car parked beside me. "Ok, so I tried to buy her into an entrapment scheme with Coach, but she wasn't selling. I think the dumb kid is in love with the jerk."

The way he said it reminded me of Sample. I wondered if this jerk was in love with Marisol, too. "So, what's Coach into that Marisol could help you with?"

"You name it, they are into it. You saw the cars those kids are driving?"

I nodded.

Waited.

He turned back to face me. "Yeah, I know. So what? Right? They all do it?"

"Yup."

"Their rise to prominence has caught some eyes."

"Oh, I'm sure. Columbia and Clemson don't need another school opening shop in the same market they are working."

He shook his head. "Clemson and USC have nothing to do with this."

He was full of shit or ignorant.

"Ok, so they have some kids driving around in brand new cars. What else?" I said.

"Falsifying grades at the high school level and when they get here. Helping momma out with the rent. Cash in the mail box. You name it. Prostitution."

That caught my attention. "Prostitution?"

"Yeah, there's some evidence that Coastal's recruiting trips may have gone beyond treating the kids to night at one of the local strip clubs. It's actually kinda sick. Most schools engage the help of some of the co-eds. Pretty girls they can use to tour the kids of the campus. Flirt with them. It's always a dicey situation. I'd never want my daughter involved in something like this. These kids," he shook his head. "They come from a different environment than a lot of these co-eds. They see a pretty girl being nice to them. They receive the wrong signal. I think that's where a lot of this increase in reported sexual assault on campus comes from."

"How does that equal prostitution?"

"Right. Well let's just say, there is some evidence that the CAU staff may be paying so those signals are just what the kids are expecting."

"Cain's hiring hookers to pretend they are co-ed recruiting girls?"

"It's sicker than that."

I knew where he was headed before he continued. I felt my grip tighten on the pistol and throbbing vessel pounding at the sides of my head.

"Hey watch it," Michaels said.

I had driven the nozzle of my pistol a full 1/4" into his side. "He's tricking college kids?"

Michaels nodded.

I removed my gun from his side. Rested it on my thigh. My other hand went to my forehead. Thumb and forefinger trying to rub the tension out of my temples.

"And Marisol?"

"That's the angle we were pursuing with her. Set her up as a potential Manatee Girl."

"But she's not a student?"

"We could have handled that," he assured. "It isn't hard to get into CAU. She had the grades, we could have picked up a semester of tuition."

"How nice of you," I said. "Turn her into a prostitute, but that's okay, you'll get her an education for a semester. Then, drop her like the cheap whore you turned her into."

Michaels shrugged. "I don't make the rules," he said. "If it's any consolation, when she turned me down it relieved me."

It wasn't. Partly because, somehow the girl ended up tangled in this mess, anyway. And partly because, Shane

Michaels appeared to be another dirty, old man who had fallen under the spell of this girl just out of high school.

"And yet, she ended up with Cain, anyway. How did that happen?"

"Beats me," Michaels said. "She ended up as one of those recruiting girls, anyway." He seemed exasperated by this revelation.

"But she's not a student."

"I know," he said. He sighed, then continued. "Not long after my offer, she started entertaining recruits."

"Full service?" I said. I tried to imagine Jandro Rodriguez finding out some of his future teammates were bedding down his little sister. It wasn't a pretty picture.

"That's the thing. I have good evidence that some of these other girls are working the sheets, but I haven't ever been able to pin that action on Marisol. She gets all dolled-up, flirts like crazy, and then leaves the kid with the blue balls. Best I can figure."

"But then there's Coach, when did that start up?"

"Right about the same time," he acknowledged.

"But what does that have to do with NCAA violations?"

"Um," he squirmed in his seat. "It, um, paints a larger picture of Coach. His character, and um, she is a girl you know. Hell, she's the sister of one of his players."

He was on the defensive now. "They're consenting adults, Michaels."

"You saw money exchanging hands?"

"Maybe, but what does have to do with your investigation?"

"That could be school funds," he said.

"Or it could not. Maybe it was personal funds. I don't see how Marisol Rodriguez figures in your investigation at all." I reached over and gave him a reminder of who was holding the gun. "Now get out of here."

93

"Wait a minute," he said. "Are you gonna tell me what you're looking at her for."

I told him what Sample hired me to do. I left out the part where he thought she was tricking, and just played it off that Sample was a jealous admirer. There was probably some truth in that, anyway. I also left out the part, 15 minutes ago, when Marisol tried to get a better offer from me. What Michaels explained seemed true enough, but I couldn't be one hundred percent sure that Marisol wasn't on his payroll. I pushed him out of my cab, having told him half as much as he'd shared with me. His smell would be with me a lot longer.

10

I spent two beers' worth of time on a barstool at a dive bar called Flattop's. It sat on the end of a strip center, like a pimple on the end of your nose, on King's Highway, close to Broadway at the Beach. It was my mother's favorite watering hole. I seldom visited it and had not been there since my mother's trial. They had 4 bartenders named Carol, 3 women and one man. I got the man today. He served me with as little said as possible. An outsider wouldn't realize that we had known each other for 15 years. He did not even call me by name, let alone ask how I was doing. It was just, "What can I get you?" and then "that'll be two bucks."

I guess I shouldn't have expected much more - unless more was being tossed out the backdoor on my ass, I guess I could have expected that. My mom was like a team mascot at Flattop's. I was the piece of shit son that took her away from them. Yeah, I guess I should feel lucky he didn't toss me out on my ass.

No one else spoke to me either.

When I realized how depressing all this was making me, I sought more pleasant company. Michelle's number had washed off my hand before I had written it down the other night, but I figured I'd try her at the Coral Beach.

———

THE BAR at the Coral Beach was more active than the last time I was there. Three middle-aged men sat in a line at the bar in colorful shirts and plaid shorts. Two Titleist hats, one Callaway. All with ball markers clipped to their bills. Another group of four similarly attired, sat at a table. It was close to midnight, yet, they all looked like they had just finished their round and they were enjoying a different type of round at the 19th hole.

Michelle was behind the bar. She wore a less revealing, less tight Coral Reach T-shirt. It was untucked and draped long over the ass of her black yoga pants. She leaned over in front of the men, an elbow propped on the bar, laughing at their jokes at the proper times. She watched me from the corner of the eye as I walked pass all of them and took a spot at the end of the bar.

I settled in there for a moment and waited.

The three guys guffawed at some unheard joke. Michelle shook her head and smiled and used the moment to break free of them.

She walked to me with what I thought was just a little extra hip sway. The other night I liked her because she dress like a confident woman 10 sizes less than her. She wasn't dressed like that tonight, but the confidence was there. So was the smile. She had a pretty smile.

"You didn't call," she said.

"My dog ate your number," I said.

Her lips turned down in a mock frown. "I wrote it on your hand."

"I know. It hurt. That little fucker."

That got a giggle out of her, and the smile again. I'm biased, but I think it was more authentic than the one she shared with the golfers.

"Your favorite couple just went up about 15 minutes ago," she said.

I tried to hide the surprise from my face, and I guess I failed.

"What?" she said. "They're here twice a week."

It was nice to know how successful I had been in warning them off. I wondered why they did this at the hotel. Why did they need a room? Coach was single. True, he was twice her age, and he was a public figure, but he made it out to be no big deal. Two consenting adults. But if that was true, why the pricey hotel room?

Michelle wouldn't let me think on that much longer.

"I get off at two," she said. Crookedly she grinned at me.

11

The next morning I woke in a strange bed, with a slightly less strange woman shape beside me, her back turned to me with covers pulled tight to her neck. Her side rose and fell with each breath. Surprising in synch with the same cadence coming from my own chest. Her dark, mocha hair gathered in a pile on her pillow. A digital clock read 11:30 on a nightstand just beyond her.

Sometime between climax, and us collapsing to sleep in a sweaty embrace, I had decided that I was through with Coach Tom Cain and Marisol and Jandro Rodriguez. And, once I dropped his pictures off to him today, Billy "Sample" Smith.

I ran my hand through the silky strands of her hair.

She stirred and turned bleary eyed to me. She covered her mouth with the back of her hand, either to stifle a yawn or to barricade morning breath. "Hey, you," escaped from behind the hand.

"Hey," I said. "I guess we really tired ourselves out." I nodded to the clock.

She looked at it over her shoulder and waved it off. "That's what time I usually get up."

Bartender hours. So the night games had only affected me then. "I have to see someone today. Preferably as early as possible. But what d'ya say to some breakfast first?"

She sat up in bed. She clutched the cover to her chest, covering all the nudity I had seen up close and personal last night. She nodded her head in the affirmative.

She reached up with her other hand, and lightly scratched her head beneath her thick, heavy locks. There was something undeniably feminine about the scene.

I resisted the temptation to provide the masculine half and scratch my ass. "I have a buddy who owns one of those pancake houses. How does that sound?"

"Yum, I could go for some pancakes."

If I didn't get us out of there soon, we would spend the whole day in bed. I play tackled her and nuzzled my head at the base of her neck. I grew stiff against her thigh.

She limply slapped my shoulder. "Stop it. There was enough of that last, night. You old dog. I'm hungry," she said. "Feed the lady."

I rolled away and stood and stretched. Bare-ass naked. My member saluting our efforts from last night and boldly suggesting a repeat performance.

She shook her head, but I did catch her eyes hungrily settle on my erection for a moment. She stood and let the covers slide down her curves. She had many. She was a lot of woman. More than I typically enjoyed. She was tan. She was smooth. She was sexy as hell.

Her place was a small 2 bedroom house. It was well kept, and I remember recalling last night, that the neighborhood was a nice, middle-class, and much more expensive than I could afford. Yet, her she was on a barkeep's pay.

She stepped out of the room, and the raging pulse of my blood eased below the waist.

She returned in a gray sweatshirt, with the collar cut out,

so it could easily slide off one shoulder. She had on yellow runner's shorts that were probably two sizes too small for her. Yellow striped tube socks were pulled up to just below her knees. The shoes were the high-top, white Reeboks with the strap. If she had weighed thirty pounds less, she would be the picture of any horny, 1980s, teenaged boy's pornographic fantasy. As it turned out, she was just mine.

She tossed me my jeans. Held out my old, threadbare whitey tighties pinched in her index finger and thumb, and said, "You are not wearing these."

I stepped into the jeans, commando-style. Pulled my Drive By-Truckers T-shirt back on. Gave the pits a quick, sniff test. And we were gone.

THE REPORT CAME over the radio just as we pulled into Jimmy's flapjack house. Coach Tom Cain had not been seen yet this morning. Kick-off for the big game was less than an hour away.

Michelle, not paying attention to the news at all, reached for the handle to let herself out.

I reached over to stop her. I turned up the volume. "Listen," I said.

"The news has reached the stands, now, Tom,", the reporter explained. "And I've talked to some of the Gold and Teal faithful, and the consensus opinion seems to be just more of the same typical, misfortune for the Manatees. That, of course, and a few choice, colorful words for their missing leader."

I could almost hear the reporter's smile.

"Had Coach been drinking when you saw him last night?" I said.

"No, well I don't know. I actually only saw Marisol. She

was only at the bar for a few minutes. She hadn't even ordered. I think she was waiting for one of the snowbirds to buy her one. She was touching up her make-up, and she must have seen him, because she got up and said, 'Daddy calls.'"

I couldn't think of anyway Michelle could have drawn a different conclusion than she had. "You say he always stays in the same room?"

There was a dazed look on her face. She nodded.

I snapped my fingers in front of her face. She shook her face, like a dog who had just had cold water tossed on it. "Stay with me."

"Whenever he can he stays in 315. All Fall, except for one time. Early in the fall, they checked out the room to someone else."

I started my truck back up. "Do you have a discreet way of finding out if 315 has checked out this morning?"

"I can call and ask the front desk?

"Discreet, Michelle, Discreet."

The dazed and confused look was returning. "Oh, God. Fuzzy you don't think something's happened to Coach? Do you?"

I couldn't tell her I thought something stunk. She already looked like she'd seen a body. I thought there was probably some other explanation than a body, but whatever it was, it would not be good. NCAA coaches on the brink of taking their team to their first ever bowl game, do not suddenly decide they have something better to do on the morning of the game. I backed out. "I'm sure there's some explanation, but if we want Coach to keep his job, we have to find him. And find him quick."

———

I SPED DOWN KINGS, took a quick left on 8th South, just as

the light on 9th turned red. I tooled the Ranger down the curves of 8th as it wound around the perimeter of the Family Kingdom Amusement park. The streets were dead like the park. I don't think I passed a single car, until I took a right on Ocean Boulevard, and pulled behind some old, blue hair crawling down the street in a red Chevy Cruze, pointing out all the pretty hotels to the crumbling Octogenarian in the passenger seat. He sat, hunched over like a stroke victim, ignorant of the tour guide act his wife provided him. I was able to observe all of this because the old bat was speeding down the Boulevard at the lightning fast speed of 10 MPH.

Proudly, the Coral Beach stood erect about its $50 a night brethren in all of its pastel green glory. It was only a block a way, but I couldn't take the cruising couple anymore. I whipped out into the opposite lane. There was no oncoming traffic as far as I could see. I floored it, and resisted the temptation to wag my middle finger at Mrs. Blue Hair, as I passed her by. I peeked at Michelle as I pulled off this maneuver. There was no reaction. Primly, she sat upright, as if we were headed to Sunday Mass.

I coaxed the little 4-cylinder up to about 45, just as I approached the entrance to the resort, and laid some rubber down to hit the turn in without having to double it back. I pulled my car between two vans inscribed with the Coral Beach logo. I scanned the parking lot. There were a few white sedans. There always are, but none of them appeared to be Michaels.

"Michelle reach into the glove box," I said. "There is a leather case in there. Grab it for me."

I realized the error of my ways after it was too late.

She swung open the glove compartment, and her breath caught. Both hands went to side of her face like in the Edvard Munch painting. My Glock impotently sat there a top paperwork and random other shit and the case of lock tools in the leather case, which had worked its way to the bottom of the totem pole.

I slid it out from beneath the pile without dumping anything on Michelle's lap. I hesitated as I reached for the Glock. Decided against it and swatted the compartment shut.

Michelle still looked like a shock victim.

"Babe, I'm gonna leave you, here. Okay?"

She nodded like an obedient toddler who wasn't quite sure of her words yet.

"But I'm gonna need you to snap out of this. There's a chance I may need you, and if that chance comes I can't be slapping you silly every minute. Got it?"

She nodded again.

My palms were slick with sweat, I noticed as I gave her thigh a squeeze. I leaned into kiss her.

She death gripped the wrist at her thigh. Looked deep into my eyes. And not the "kiss me" eyes. They were the don't you fuck around with me eyes. "Is Coach gonna be alright?"

I don't know, Michelle came to mind. I pecked her on the cheek and I went with, "Sure everything is cool."

I resisted my impulse to sprint across the lot and into the lobby and settled on the walk/run of a man who has been holding it in for a 5-hour road trip.

When I hit the lobby, I slowed it down to a determined stroll. I waved to the smiling receptionist and patiently waited as the numbers teased me with their slow descent in the elevator lobby. I had the car to myself when it finally arrived, but it even more slowly ascended to floor three. When the doors finally opened to floor three, I jogged to room 315.

I stood before the door and released a breath I hadn't known I was holding. Silence behind the door.

I knocked.

More silence.

I knocked again.

Nothing.

I opened the leather case. It was complete with the typical thieves' tools - pins, hooks, files, and slide. But the pies de resistance that I was seeking was a contraption tucked into an empty Lifesavers roll. It was an electronics do-hicky devised by another punk criminal I knew named Bennie Blades, far as I know that was his real name. I shit you not. Anyway it looked sort of like the earbuds set that comes with your iPhone, except black, and they didn't go in your ears. In fact, I didn't do anything with them. I think the brains of the operation resided in those two things.

I ran my finger along the bottom end of the card reader door lock. On the left end, I felt the recess of the AC jack, and slid the connector of my buds into place. Waited the space of one breath.

Click.

The lock opened.

Ha. Modern security. Easier to break than the simple key lock.

Like Benny says, "And they think I'm fucking stupid."

I opened the door and smelled freshly sheared copper.

I stood at the open doorway. Took a deep breath to build my resolve.

A painting of a sunset with palm trees hung askew on the wall. Its protective pane of glass was shattered, and a shard had fallen from the frame to the ground.

I looked down the empty corridor, before stepping into the room, quietly closing the door behind me. I had forgotten my gloves, so I hit the light switch with my elbow.

The toilet room was open on my right. Two sodden, otherwise clean, white towels lay like dead animals on the tile floor.

No blood in there.

Another deep breath. I grabbed a clean towel off the rack and lightly wrapped it around my left hand.

The sink was clean. The vanity was littered with men's shaving kit items. Razors, cream, toothbrush unused, after-shave. An opened bar of soap looked unused. If I didn't know what the metallic smell meant, I would think nothing of what I found in the toilet room.

Breathe.

I stepped back into the room, and out into the sleeping area.

He lay on the floor, face-down. He wore nothing but one of those white towels around his waist. A pool of dark, blood, like dark chocolate syrup, stained the beige carpet above his head. A fallen, bedside lamp rested beside the stain.

I scratched my chin.

The place was a wreck. Obviously an altercation had occurred. The bed was unmade. Its mattress had slid at an angle, cock-eyed of the box springs. Another picture, this of a conch and sand dollar resting on beach sand, was tilted but not broken on the wall above the bed. The plaster wall was crushed beside it, as if a blunt object had been thrown or slammed into it.

I took a closer look. The cracked plaster seemed to be caused by an oblong shape. The wood of the bed's head-board was splintered as if it had been smacked, too. I had an image of Coach juking and jiving as the killer took swings at him.

On the same wall, there was a light spray of blood. I looked down at coach. The swings eventually had caught up to him.

I sat on the bed. Reached in my pocket for my cell, then thought better of it. Where was the room phone?

It wasn't on either nightstand.

I crawled across the bed.

It lay in the corner of the room. The receiver was off the cradle, and the cable had been yanked out of the wall. It seemed to be in one piece - a minor miracle if it had been swatted by the same thing as Coach.

I plugged the cable back in the wall, pressed the plunger down with my towel wrapped hand, and listened as the dial tone sang in my ear. I dialed 911.

"Myrtle Beach Emergency Services," the dispatcher said.

"I'd like to report a body found in room 315 of the Coral Beach Resort on Ocean Boulevard."

"May I ask who I am speaking with..."

I dropped the phone back down on its cradle and walked out of there as calmly as possible.

The corridor was still empty. I took the stairs. The same ones I had taken pictures of Coach and Marisol from 3 nights ago. I picked up the pace a little going down the stairs. The sunlight blinded me as I hit the ground floor and shouldered my way out the door.

I got my bearings, dropped the towel behind some shrubs, and repeated my slow stroll to my truck. It seems so simple, but when you've just seen a body, called it in, and had no interest in talking to the cops, it took all the willpower in the world to keep from hightailing it out of there, but that would have caught the attention of someone.

I made it to my truck in what seemed like twenty minutes later. I crawled in, started her up and slowly backed out.

Something was missing. Actually, more accurately, someone was missing.

Michelle.

I'd have to figure that one out later. I pulled away. As I turned onto 9th Ave, and disappeared in the shadows of the Swamp Fox roller coaster, I thought I heard sirens. Though I may have just imagined those.

12

I ended up on a barstool at a biker bar two blocks east of Molly Maguire's, trying to numb my already numb mind with flat, domestic beer at a dollar a glass. The bartender was a peroxide blonde, riddled with tattoos, and otherwise bad skin. She tried friendly banter, but soon realized I wasn't in the mood, and wisely left me to my beer.

We were the only people in the place until two denim jacketed bikers entered. One of them had a prosthetic leg from the knee down that he proudly displayed by wearing jeans cut-off at the knee. He introduced himself as, "Gimp", as he and his buddy, a stereotypical, overweight, bearded guy that looked like he came from central casting, sat down beside me.

A full bar of empty stools, and these guys decide it's a good idea to sit down right beside me. It was that kind of day.

"Say, buddy," Gimp draped his arm over my shoulders. "How about we play some darts?"

I leaned away from him enough, so he got the idea about my thoughts of his arm wrapped around my like old war buddies. "I don't play," I said.

He removed his arm. "Hey Carla, How about two Buds? And one of whatever our friend is drinking here?"

I got up, and stepped towards the back door.

Gimp called, "What? A beer bought by me ain't good enough for you?"

I pulled out my cell, pointed to it. "Gotta make a call. I'll be right back."

In the lot,I admired their Harleys, all polished chrome and pastels with oiled leather saddle bags. They didn't look like they could gather twenty bucks between them, but they had forty grand of polished chrome sitting there. I remembered Rod, and his wardrobe and studio. Gimp and his buddy probably shared the cost at some single-wide trailer. Then, I remembered where I lived.

I tried Jimmy's number with no success. I recalled that in all of last night's festivities that I had forgotten to get Michelle's number. She had been shocked, thinking the worse, which ended up coming true, but I still wasn't sure what had led her to leave the truck.

When I returned, Gimp and buddy, had moved their beers to a high top table over by the dart boards on the other side of the bar. A TV mounted on the wall above their heads, displayed a still image of Coach, with subtitles scrolling beneath. I couldn't read them. It didn't matter, I knew what they said. The media insanity had started.

Three beers and three fruitless calls to Jimmy later, my mind was foggy, so I decided a trip to see Veronica would be a good idea.

I paid Carla and left her probably the best tip she'd seen that week.

THE SHORT DRIVE to Maguire's was uneventful, but I noted

the fuzzy edges to the striping on the road and realized that I had no business being behind the wheel of the car. I pulled into the lot and pulled in between two Cadillacs.

Big Paddy Meibaum stared me down a little more than I was used to.

I asked,"Is she in?"

He smiled, "She's in. She walked out of here with more lettuce than I've ever seen a girl pull down in the off season last night."

"Good for her", I said. I got the impression Paddy knew the current Veronica- Fuzzy situation.

"Yeah, I bet she took home a G."

If that was true, Paddy was right. That had to be a November record.

I paid the $5 cover to a smiling 19-year-old blonde wearing a black body suit and black panty hose and black choker necklace. All the black offset her golden hair and a brilliant smile. I found myself, not for the first time in my strip club visiting history, wishing I could see the front door girl on stage. I tossed a dollar in the plastic pitcher on the desk. My bill had a lot of company. Maybe she'd break a November record for front door tips.

"You carrying, Fuzzy?", Paddy asked from behind me.

"Not tonight, Big P."

"Good," he said. "We've got some pissed off football fans in here tonight. Don't need anything escalating."

I'd lost his trust with the Veronica break-up. Two days ago, he would have welcomed my piece as something that could keep things from getting out of control.

I shoved my way through the doors. Much like the parking lot, the place was only half full. There were a lot of teal and gold jerseys on both middle-aged men and college aged kids. There were even more college aged couples than normal in Maguire's. Couples coming to strip bars became a thing about a decade ago, but Maguire's had mostly avoided this trend, because it looked like such an arm pit from the outside. It was the appeal of Maguire's for Veronica. She claimed guys were tighter with the money with their girl-friend by their side. Also, she said there was a tendency for these couples to get shitty with each other during the night, and could take the fun right out of the room. I didn't know how much I believed either of those reasons. I've been in clubs where the girl is buying dances for her man, so she could watch.

And vice versa.

That kind of action doesn't suck the life out of the room, either.

Tonight's crowd, though, just seemed depressed.

There was one exception. A bald guy with wire-framed glasses, and a #1 jersey pulled over an enormous girth, was flashing a wide smile, his shoulder rolling to the pulse of "Darling Nikki" by Prince playing over the house system. A girl was grinding her hips in his lap. She was bent over at the waist, her head hung low, as she held on to his pale, chubby ankles for support.

Even with her face out of view I knew it was Veronica.

A cute waitress, manufactured from the same plans as the front door girl, stood by my side. She carried a tray with test tubes filled with fluorescent liquors. "Wanna shot?". Her smile glowed as brightly as her drinks.

It was impossible to look at her drinks without taking in the cleavage provided by her low-cut top. It was as if her assets presided over the stock she was trying to sell. Or, more likely, they were her best marketing tool.

"What do you have there?" I said.

"Brain drains," she seemed to be able to carry on a conversation without the smile ever leaving her face.

This girl was going places.

"What's in it?"

Her breasts jiggled as she shrugged. "I don't know," she said. She slid a test tube between her breasts. "But you get to take the shot from between them."

I gave her a $10. She put her tray down on a high top and took my head in her hands. She lowered my head to her bust.

I took the tube between my teeth and slid it from its carriage. Tilted my head back and took the shot down in one swallow. It had some fruity flavor and wasn't much on the liquor. Like the girl alluded to, you didn't pay for the booze. You paid for the boobs.

"Keep the change," I said, as she sifted through a stack of bills on her tray.

She bounced off to another mark. I resisted the temptation to smack her on the ass and give her an "Atta girl."

The last chords of "Nikki" were fading. Veronica rose, flipped her hair over her shoulder like Rita Hayworth in Gilda. And stepped away from her customer's lap. Her eyes settled on me. She turned and lowered her chest to baldy's face. Her knee was up against his khaki shorts covered crotch.

I noticed the tent Veronica had propped there. I seldom got jealous of Veronica's work, but I couldn't watch anymore.

I turned to the stage, and watched the lithe black dancer that had been dancing there gather her stuff, and climb down the steps.

The DJ must have had the night off, because no words came over the system, as the girl from the other day, Raven, took the stage.

Some hip-hop song took Nikki's place. Raven's eyes found mine like they had last time, but I couldn't get the image of Veronica servicing the bald guy out of my mind.

I went to the john.

Baldy stood before a urinal, masturbating to finish the job Veronica had started.

I entered a stall, and couldn't produce a drop. All I could think was, get the hell out of there. I waited until I heard Mr. Five Knuckle Shuffle leave, and then I hit the door.

Of course, the first person I ran into before I could make it to the front door was Veronica.

Her smile was as authentic as a politician's hand shake. "Wanna dance?"

I've never wanted to hit a girl in my life, but so help me god I wanted to slap that smirk from her face. "We need to talk Veronica."

"Sure," she said. "But I only talk in VIP."

"Really, V? That's how it's going to be?"

Her face went flat. "My time is money, Fuzzy."

"Yeah, I saw." I could taste the acid dripping from my tongue.

It seemed to have little effect on her. "What's that supposed to mean?"

"Nothing," I said. "Look, I don't have the cash for VIP. Can we maybe just have a seat at one of those tables?" I pointed to a corner of the room which had fewer customers.

She pointed to the other side of the room. "We have an ATM right over there."

I felt the cold slither into my insides. I couldn't believe how quickly we had gotten to this. Pissed. I stomped off to the ATM. I couldn't feel her presence behind me.

Taking money out of an ATM at a strip club is an almost universal no-no. Not only do they charge exorbitant fees, ten dollars the machine asked me to agree to, but there are endless cases of the machine scanning the card info, storing it, and draining the account later.

I withdrew $200 from my gasping for air checking account. Paid the ten buck fee, and said a quick prayer, to whom I don't know, that this was all that this trip would cost me.

Veronica wasn't behind me, and she wasn't where I left her.

Good God, woman.

I scanned the room and saw her flirting with a couple college aged kids. She leaned over their table, elbows resting there, chatting like it was the most interesting conversation.

Dumbfounded, I walked over to within earshot, and cleared my throat.

She looked up at me, and held up a finger, asking for a second.

When her boys finished their story. She said something to them in explanation, frowned, and tucked a few locks behind her ear.

Jesus, she was good. No wonder she was pulling a grand a night, even in the offseason.

She left them there wanting more.

She hurried over. "Ready?" she smiled.

Somehow this smile didn't look fake.

You might think the VIP room at a strip club is a plush space, a step above the decor and environment found on the main floor. In most cases, and certainly at Molly Maguire's you'd be wrong. You paid you're $150 bucks, and the bouncer, a greasy haired meatball with a pock-marked face, dropped the velvet rope. You stepped into more of the same. Same worn carpet. Same red vinyl upholstery. Same black painted ceiling.

If anything the space seemed seedier. I'm convinced that when this space was vacant, the girls used it for a smoking room. South Carolina outlawed smoking in bars, but there was a haze of smoke clinging to the ceiling in the VIP, and it emanated from the curtains that hung in front of each dance booth. The only other distinguishing feature was a gloss, display cooler filled with cheap champagne that the club would sell you for $60 a bottle.

Veronica and I appeared to be the only VIPs at the moment. She waved her arm at the open booths, like a game show hostess showing off all the fine prizes you could win on their show. "Pick your poison," she said.

The feelings I was having were foreign to me. I was somewhere between punching my hand through a wall and finding a sink to throw up in. We walked to a random empty booth and took a seat.

The booth had a low, cushioned seat back designed to coax you into an almost laid back position. The position most guys preferred to be in when a stripper, who was thinner and more willing than the wife they had at home, crawled onto their lap. I sat up, at attention, like a kid in the front of the class. Veronica sat beside me. She crossed her legs, such that her knee rested on my thigh.

"You know the deal, Fuzzy, twenty dollars a song. Three songs for $50. Tipping your dancer is always appreciated."

Most of the $150 I handed the bouncer went to the house. Only forty bucks went to Veronica, which covered her tip-out to the house that night. Other than the benefit of getting the tip-out of the way for the night, the girls made the same for dances back here as they did on the floor. The club pushed VIP both through the DJ and the girls because it could be a good take for them. They tried to convince the girls that the guys willing to pay for the VIP were the high-rollers that could bank a whole night for them. Any girl that had danced for more than a week saw through this bullshit. $150 was a big hit to all but the most wealthy of poor losers, and it took a sizable chunk of the available spend out of the girls' garters, and it put it in the sleazy owner's greedy hands. The only way to make the VIP a winning position is to succumb to the true allure of the VIP room - a little more privacy than the floor.

That meant offering extras. I'd heard a lot of stories about wild stuff happening in VIP rooms, but I had witnessed none of the that.

"I only have fifty on me Veronica."

"Ok," she shrugged. "So three songs. We'll wait this one out."

This one was an old Whitesnake song. The one that featured Tawny Kitaen rolling around on the hood of a sports car, dressed to fit right in at Molly Maguire's.

"Look, V, I'm just wanting to talk," I said.

"Still costs the same."

"Why this cold shoulder stuff, V?"

"Fuzzy, I already apologized for the way I reacted the other night," she said. "This isn't the cold shoulder. I realize that you're hurting, and you're a good guy. You are. It hurts me, because what I really, really want is to be with you."

"But..."

She stopped with the press of lacquered finger nail to the tip of my nose. "This isn't cold shoulder treatment. This is me showing a little self-respect and getting paid to do my job."

David Coverdale sang the last chorus, and the guitars faded. Veronica reached behind her back and released her brassiere.

I grabbed her shoulder.

She shrugged it away, like I was any poor loser, the typical client. No better than Baldy. Worse, because I wasn't carrying as much bank.

"You don't have to do that, V?"

She stopped. "Suit yourself." She pointed up to indicate a new song had started, some non-descript hip-hop / pop mash-up. "But the clock is running."

"I'm sorry," I said.

She looked at me like I was simple, but her eyes also got

glassy. "You didn't have to come in here, and pay a hundred fifty bucks to the door to tell me that, Fuzzy."

"I know," I said. "There's more, and I know the clock is running, but I needed you to know that first."

"Oh brother," she said.

"What?"

"You're sweet. But now you got me scared what else is coming?"

"You heard about Coach?"

"Who?"

"Coach," I said. "You remember the job I was working?"

She searched me while her mind dug through the files stored back there in her memory.

Two things occurred to me. One, Veronica had not heard the news. Two, if she had thought of me at all the last couple of days it had not been about my fucked up case. It had been about my fucked up life, and the shit hand I had been dealt. That was my Veronica, always focused on the important stuff. Her first priority was her job and making a living. The second was my internal struggle and pain, not the external issues of my job. I wasn't there to talk about either of those two. I wasn't as good as her at prioritizing. I was here to talk about that external stuff.

She was still turning it over, and the first song was a minute, thirty seconds in, halfway, so I hurried things along.

"You remember Sample hired me to peek on the call girl, and the Coach of the CAU football team ended up in my pictures?"

She snapped her fingers. I couldn't tell if she was fucking with me.

"Right, so what about Coach was I supposed to hear?"

"They found him dead today."

She had the bitter beer taste look. She said nothing.

"I know," I said. "It gets worse..."

"Oh... My... God, Fuzzy," she said. "When did this happen?"

"Right around kick-off time they found him."

"All the people in the jerseys," she said. "I'm sure some of these guys have mentioned it but I tune almost all of their bullshit out."

I knew that, she had shared it with me before. It was the only way to survive in the clubs as long as she had. You couldn't care about the losers. There was not a small amount of pride in the realization she was listening to me.

"I found the body, V," I said.

She stood up. Looking down on me, I couldn't tell if she was pissed at me, afraid for me, or confused. Or some combination of the three.

"Shit, Fuzzy. What'd the cops say? How deep in this are you?"

"I'd say I'm deep into it, but I didn't talk to the cops."

"But you found the body..."

I shook my head, and her voice trailed off. She sat back down beside. She rested her head on my shoulder.

"I called it in anonymously, and high-tailed it out of there," I said. "You know I was this close." I had my index finger and thumb an inch apart. "This close to handing my pictures off to Sample and being done with this."

"Oh, so now you want to make me an accessory?"

I lied, "I have done nothing illegal. I need someone to talk it out with."

The second song, "Copperhead Road" by Steve Earle, came on. It was an interesting track for the strip club crowd. "Am I still on the clock?"

She slapped me on the wrist like I was a disobedient child.

"Good," I said. Then I told all of it to her, except that part about spending the night with Michelle and her disappearing from my truck while I broke into Coach's hotel room. I didn't leave out the part about me breaking into the hotel room, just the part about Michelle.

She was quick to point out, "Isn't breaking into his room illegal?"

"Keep your eyes on the ball, V," I said. "I'm fairly certain I went unseen there. What I'm concerned about are my trips to see Coach and Marisol. Her brother saw me at both places the night Coach was murdered. They have put people away on less circumstantial evidence."

She changed it to a reassuring pat on my arm now.

There, there soon it will be okay.

"Fuzzy, you're innocent. Try to remember that."

"You're right," I said. "I guess I should go to the station, show my Uncle the pictures. Just come clean."

She chewed on the corner of her lip like it was chewing gum. "But there's Liza..."

"Marisol," I corrected.

"I know, I know, I can't think of her as anything but Liza, the girl afraid to have her brother find out she was an exotic dancer." I chewed on the lip a little more. "Let's not forget her, Fuzzy. She's just a kid, and if those pictures get out, it will wreck her."

"Let's not forget that we can't be sure she's not behind this."

"What? Coach's death? You can't be serious?" A look of disappointment came over her now.

I didn't know what Marisol Rodriguez was capable of except trapping men in her spell with some deadly mixture of looks and above her age sex appeal. I did, however, know I had Veronica back on team Fuzzy, and if I wanted to keep her I couldn't continue down the line of questioning Marisol's innocence. This stripper protected her own. "Nah, you're right."

She seemed pleased and gave a quick nod of the head with

a down turned smile. She hopped to her feet, giving my thigh a squeeze in the process. She faced me, and leaned over, and placed both hands on my knees and pulled them apart. One of her knees slid up and nestled into a comfortable place. "Don't worry, old bear, it's gonna be okay," she leaned forward, and whispered in my ear. The twin nubs of her cloth covered nipples prodded my chest.

I focused myself to concentrate. It was hard. Very hard. "So maybe, I drop the stack of photos off with Sample like I promised."

She shoved herself off of me, her knee giving me a not so subtle nudge in the groin. She stood with both fists at her hips. "You will not give those pictures to the drug dealer."

"V, I promised them to him, right before I found Coach's body."

"Yeah," she said. "And you promised them to him when you took the job, Fuzzy. But that didn't keep you from holding them back and sharing them with Coach and Marisol. What's so different now?"

I do not think my knowledge of women has improved with age. If anything, it has gotten worse. However, my self-awareness has gotten better. And looking at Veronica now, with fuzzy fluorescent light haloing her angelic face, I knew she would always get her way.

"I just want to be through with all of this," I said.

Again with the hands on my knees, running up to my thighs. "I know baby," she said. "But isn't handing these pictures over just going to complicate things?"

I didn't know about that. The third song ended. I had my mind made up. So, I sat back and enjoyed the next three songs on the house.

That I always took the opposing view of any advice given by my best friend for life, Jimmy Alou, a man with a Bachelor's in Sociology and an MBA from some esteemed Midwest business school, yet accepted the advice from my stripper, ex-girlfriend, with a degree from the school of hard knocks, was not lost on me.

As I watched, Veronica get dressed, probably my favorite part of the show, my phone buzzed against my thigh.

It was a text from Sample.

"Meet me at the Kingdom in front of the Fox. 8 pm. Don't fuck with me."

It was Sample code for bring my pictures to the Swamp Fox roller coaster at the closed Family Kingdom amusement park.

I'd already decided that Sample wasn't getting the pictures, at least not yet. But I had been stringing him along. So I owed him an explanation. Plus, I wanted to hear what his thoughts were on Coach's death. The fact that he had hired me to take those pictures, and Coach ended up dead, made Sample a suspect. Me not turning them over to the cops put me in deep shit with them, but kept them out of Sample's hair. It would be nice to see if this was really worth it. None of that could be ascertained from text messages, or even a phone call.

Nope, I owed Sample a face-to-face. And he owed it to me even if he didn't realize it.

"What is it?" Veronica said. She was sliding into some nylons that she did not have on before. I had no idea where they came from, but I'd learned not ask such things. She knew I had a thing for nylons though.

I was losing my mind watching her roll the upper edge of them up her thigh.

She giggled. Snapped her fingers in front of my face.

"Huh?" I said.

"The text, Fuzzy. What is it?"

I shook myself clear headed, noted the time as 7:15 on the phone and tucked the phone into my jeans' pocket. "Nothing."

"You sure it's nothing? The look on your face doesn't say nothing."

I climbed to my feet. "Positive," I said. "Just an old friend wants to meet at the Kingdom. I have to run."

She did a Groucho Marx thing with her eyebrows. She cradled her breasts in each of her hands. "The old friend got these or not."

"It's a guy," I laughed. "Veronica, thanks for everything."

She looked down at the lap dance couch. "Everything is what I do best."

I left her there with a kiss on the corner of her mouth, and two twenties and a ten in her garter. I got out of there before we ended up back in the booth.

My feelings for Veronica had somehow gotten more complicated. I hadn't thought that possible.

13

For as long as I could remember, the Family Kingdom amusement part had been the red-headed stepson of amusement parks on Ocean Boulevard. Most of my life, it was the less popular of Myrtle Beach's two amusement parks. The Pavilion was the main attraction for tourists looking for thrill rides, deadly carnival food, and Main Street fair games designed to con you out of all of your money in hopes of winning that big stuffed Pink Panther for your sweetheart. It was most popular because of a slightly better location and a more thrilling, wooden roller-coaster. The Kingdom, and its Swamp Fox reigned supreme now. Only because the Pavilion had shut down a decade ago.

The park was a ghost town like the rest of the Strand in late November. The Kingdom during the offseason became a kind of hang-out for never-do-well teenaged kids, the occasional prostitute looking to pick up a quick twenty from an out-of-town golfer astray, and shark-fishing drug dealers peddling dime bags to all of them. It was the kind of haunt that fit Sample to a tee.

I arrived right around eight. The sun was down, and the Kingdom seemed deserted.

The asphalt paths snaking between kiddie rides, ticket booths, and food stands were littered with old cotton candy bags, soiled napkins, and crushed beer cans.

I landed at a plywood ticket booth painted white with faded pink trim just outside the entrance to the Swamp Fox roller coaster, a wooden leviathan which loomed overhead like a huge tinker toy sculpture.

I leaned my back against the wall of the ticket booth. One sneaker on the cracked pavement, the other flat against the sagging plywood wall of the booth. If I smoked, a cigarette would complete the picture.

I leaned my head back against the booth and closed my eyes and thought of Veronica and Michelle. The crunch of a sea shell under a boot heel brought me back to the real world.

As I opened my eyes a flash of steel swung towards me.

I ducked.

The rod crashed into the booth above my head. The plywood splintered and the large, oblong head of a driver clanged to the ground.

Stupid punk, just ruined a three hundred dollar golf club. I hopped forward out of my crouch and turned in the thug's direction.

He looked familiar. He was shirtless and pale-skinned. The waist of his jeans hung low, held in place by bony hips. He shook his right hand in pain.

I stepped in and laid a right hook behind his ear, and he fell like a wet sack of groceries.

It was Casper. The guy who had provided car security services for me at Molly Maguire's the other night.

One of his friends hopped on my back and wrapped the shaft of another golf club underneath my chin. I could feel rolls of fat pressing against my back. In any other position, I would move too fast, and drop this kid quick as I had Casper, but in the current situation his weight immobilized me.

He pulled the shaft tighter.

My head felt like it was swelling, and I was having a hard time keeping my mind on the current dilemma. I saw Michelle standing across the way, by the kiddie planes ride. She wore her knee-high rainbow striped socks and her tight spandex shorts and tight Coral Beach T-shirt. In one hand, she held a wooden baseball bat over her shoulder. She beckoned me with her other hand. Her smiling lips were moist and full.

Someone hurried to my side and kicked my feet out from under me.

My head smacked the pavement. It sounded the way my father's belt sounded when he would snap it before me, right before giving me a licking. I saw Veronica's concerned face, frowning with glassy eyes, just before the world went black.

I CAME to with a splash of cold water to my face. A flash of gold teeth was the first thing I saw. Sample.

They had bound my wrists in front of me with plastic tie straps. I felt the same bite in my ankles, and I could not separate them.

Sample crouched before me, either scowling or smiling. It was hard to tell with all the moonlight reflecting of his bridgework.

"Fuzzy, how did you come to be so fucking stupid?"

A boot slammed into my side. The pointed toe seemed to bury half a foot into my kidneys.

I had an immediate need to urinate, but somehow saved myself that embarrassment.

"You ain't even got those pictures, now does ya?" Sample said.

I saw Coach's body, the spray of blood on the walls, the cracked glass on the picture frames, the splintered wood on the headboard, and the crushed plaster wallboard. I saw a golf club hurling at my forehead. Sweat was trickling down my sides. Ice cold sweat. "You did it. Didn't you, Sample? You killed him?"

A sarcastic, close-lipped grin took the place of all that sparkling gold. He nodded to his friend, who promptly planted a boot in my side again. This one landed a little higher in the ribs.

"You are fucking stupid, Fuzzy." He stood up from his crouch, turned away from me, and began pacing back and forth, like a feral animal in a cage, or like an old friend trying to decide what to do about the buddy who let him down. He wiped sweat from his brow with his forearm. A semi-automatic pistol was in that hand.

The pistol worried me. I'd known Sample a long time. He'd gotten involved in some shady stuff, but somehow, I'd never seen him carrying a piece. I always assumed that was a line he wasn't willing to cross, the line that separated those crimes that could involve you firing a weapon at someone and those that would not. I had assumed wrong, and if I was wrong about that assumption, I could be wrong about another assumption. The one that involved what he would do if I double-crossed him.

"Look Samp, I'm not trying to screw you over. I came here tonight to talk it over with you."

"Talk it over? Please. You already done talked it over with her."

Marisol?

I was sure I hadn't vocalized that, but he said, "Yeah Marisol. What did you think she was just gonna shrug her shoulders about somebody paying to have her spied on?"

Sample wasn't pissed at me for holding out the pictures on

125

him. Well, he was, but that's not why I was fending off swinging golf clubs and stomping cowboy boots. He was mad because he got caught. He was mad because he had fallen for Marisol Rodriguez, too. He lost all hope now that she knew he was spying on her. It was irrational thinking. What did he expect her reaction to be if he ever confronted her with the evidence I had discovered? Irrational, yes, but typical Billy Smith.

"Samp, trust me. We have bigger problems than Marisol finding out about you hiring me to follow her around, and your feelings. If the law finds out about any of this." I paused for effect. "Especially, if they find out about those pictures, we become their two biggest suspects."

"Marisol, ain't gonna go to the law," he said.

I wasn't so sure. In less than 24 hours, she had gone to Sample. "What did she tell you, Samp?"

"She was pissed, Fuzz. I didn't catch much of it outside all the cussin'. But I got the important stuff, she was pissed, and she wanted me to step the fuck back and outta her life."

"Samp, she was with Coach last night. Do you think she could have done this?"

He leaned in close and looked my face over like a jeweler appraising a diamond. He hadn't shaved in a couple of days, and his stubble was splotchy on his face. His body smelled like spoiled milk. I cowered from him, but there was nowhere to go, tied up as I was with the ticket booth's plywood rough, like sand paper against my neck.

He hit me, up close like that, with a straight right and extended right through as if he were trying to punch a hole in the ticket booth's wall with the back of my head.

I felt blood pour from my nose straight up into my eyeballs. My head bounced like a tennis ball off the wall, snapping back into place with such force I felt the vertebrae in my neck crack like arthritic knuckles. "You about as stupid as they come, Fuzzy. And I was stupider to fuckin' hire you. You get that shit out of your mind about Marisol. Ain't no way she beat up Coach like they sayin' he was beat up. You got that, dummy?"

He lashed me with his left this time, the hand with the gun in it. The nubby sight tore open a gash on my cheek. Warm blood spilled down my face. It saturated my shirt collar.

Before I could respond, a voice seemed to come from somewhere behind me, and it seemed to come from the mouth of someone who'd had about ten too many shots of bourbon. I couldn't make out what it said, and it didn't matter, because I faded out of conscious, again.

14

I woke up in a bed adjusted thirty degrees above flat. Bright fluorescents hummed, and a beeping apparatus at my right shoulder gave me stabbing pains in my head. The pillow case had the same texture as the plywood booths at the Family Kingdom. I'd have to ask the billing office if they used the same supplier.

Two shadowy figures rose to their feet at the same side as the torturous, beeping Nazi.

I blinked a few times. Realized, I had a patch over my right eye. It made it difficult to focus on them. I rotated my neck and felt the tooth of the sandpapery pillow case gouge at tender spots at the back of my head. But the picture became clear.

Jimmy Alou and Veronica.

Their voices came to me in stereo. "Fuzzy, what happened?"

I ignored the question and hit them with one of my own. "How did I end up here?"

Here had to be Grand Strand Medical Center.

"Anonymous caller to 911, said you needed help at the

Family Kingdom. They found you tied up and beaten like a dog," Jimmy said.

Now it was Veronica's turn, "Who did this to you, Fuzzy?"

As much as I wanted to return the favor to Sample, I also felt I deserved my punishment. I had a cardinal rule. I cited it all the time. Never reveal the client. I'd breeched that contract with Sample, and with myself. The cops would be by soon, if they weren't already waiting outside my door now, asking the same question. Who did this to me? If I shared the answer with Jimmy and Veronica, it would end up with the cops before they even had the chance to ask the question.

"I don't know," I said. "I remember getting jumped, getting blindsided, but I never saw who did it."

Veronica wasn't buying it. She tapped Jimmy on the shoulder, and they both left me there. A cute, dirty blonde nurse in royal blue scrubs replaced them. She had a cheerleader's figure and smile. I dubbed her Nurse Ra Ra. "Mr. Koella, it's so nice to make your acquaintance."

I tried to sit up, but my ribs screamed at me and I collapsed back in the bed. "Ugh," I grimaced.

"You have broken ribs, and you're passing blood in your urine. Doctor doesn't think you'll have any lasting effects, but the next couple of days you will wish whoever did this to you had finished the job," she said.

The way she smiled, I wondered if she found humor in what she said or if she was trying to be reassuring. I didn't care. The smile was pretty.

She jotted something down on the metal clipboard in her hands, hung it from the bar at the base of my bed, and left me to my beeping torture.

Veronica returned with a purposeful look on your face. "Who were you meeting at the Family Kingdom, Fuzzy?"

"Nobody," I said. "I don't know how I ended up there."

She frowned and sat down on the side of the bed. Her flank pressed against me and shot pain up my side.

"Fuzzy, last night, when you left me. You were going to see an 'old friend,' at the Kingdom."

Shit. I'd forgotten about that. I tried giving her the heavy eyelids.

She pinched my chin. It may have been the only square inch of my face that wasn't an open wound. "Don't play dumb with me, Fuzzy. Not about this."

"I don't know, V. I don't even remember being at the park," I said.

"Unbelievable," she said. "Was it that drug dealer, Fuzzy? Was that who you were meeting?"

I shrugged and let my eyes droop closed.

Her weight left the side of the bed, and I heard her mutter, "Fuck you, Fuzzy Koella."

The door slammed, and I must have fallen asleep not long after.

I didn't wake again until Nurse Ra Ra came back to check on the beeping stuff, and various bags hanging from various hooks, all with plastic tubes terminating somewhere inside my body.

"When will I be able to get out of here?"

She lifted a bag from beneath my bed and examined the pinkish, brown liquid it contained. "Doctor says he wants to hold you overnight for observation, and release you in the morning, but from the look of this," she held the nephrostomy bag up for inspection, "I'd say you have a little longer stay. How is the pain on a scale of 1 to 10? Five being a kick to the gonads."

Ha, this one had a sense of humor. It was somewhere near my gonads being tightened down in a vise grip. "Maybe a two," I lied.

She nodded and looked at me sideways while she jotted

away on her clip board.

Before she had finished, my Uncle Rod appeared beside her, dressed in a lavender, silky shirt with a stiff collar. He was tie-less, which was a sartorial look he'd been trying on for size. His shark-skin slacks were tailored to the perfect fit and ironed to a crisp crease running up the front of them you could lose a finger on if you weren't careful. The brand-named gold watch on his left wrist went for a grand. If it were any other copper, I would question whether he was on the up and up. I knew better with my Uncle Rod. Some people liked fishing boats, some liked tee times every weekend morning and once during the week. My Uncle Rod? He liked to dress nice. He otherwise lived humbly in a small studio apartment. He drove a 10-year-old American mid-size, and he cooked for himself most nights, since he and my aunt had parted ways. Rod spent all of his extra dough on his wardrobe. From the way Nurse Ra Ra looked him up and down before leaving us, the investment was a worthy one.

He waited until the door clicked shut with her departure. "Fuzzy, what the fuck have you gotten yourself into this time?"

I admired my Uncle Rod, he was an honorable, well-dressed man, who'd progressed well in a tough, competitive environment at the job, despite being an African-American male in the Deep South. However, subtlety was not one of his virtues.

I grimaced in pain and added a little method acting to make the pain his question caused me more believable. "I don't know what you are talking about."

He scanned the room. All the beeping equipment, the IV drips, the plastic tubing in arms and midsection. He laughed. "You are a walking train wreck, man. You know that?"

He stared me down, waiting for a response.

I faked heavy eyelids and a droopy lower lip.

"Your name came up in the Cain investigation."

I could not hide my interest on that one.

"Oh, now I have your attention. Do I?" He said. "That's right. I hear you visited Coach Friday night. The night before the big game. The night before his body was found. The night he was killed. If the coroner's office is to be believed, just a few hours before he was beaten to death. Probably with a baseball bat." He delivered that last bit with an accusatory finger jabbed at me, aimed right between the eyes.

It was a cheap implication, and he knew it. The conversation was in danger of going in the direction most of our's went, with him in lecture mode. I wasn't in the mood for stupid accusations or lectures. "I'm a pitcher, Rod. A bat isn't a tool of the trade." I added, "And I went to Coach to wish him luck on the big game. I'm a booster. One of the few perks is that it allows me an ear to say things like, 'Go get 'em, Coach.'"

It was so much bullshit, and he knew it. It showed in his face, but he let it pass.

"So you did see him?"

Shit. Maybe I should have just denied it. I grunted, "Yeah, I saw him, but he didn't have much time for me. He seemed preoccupied."

"Preoccupied? How so?"

"Rod, he had the biggest game of his career on his mind," I reminded him.

"Right," he said.

"Look, Rod. This morphine is some heavy shit. I'm not trying to be dismissive, but is there anything else you need, right now? Or can it wait until I'm back on my feet?"

"Fuzzy, this ain't checkin' up on Mom. I can't protect you on this one. I ain't lookin' at you, but I can't run defense if my colleagues look your way. Is there anything else you want to tell me? You know, before they uncover anything?"

I didn't like the comment about checking up on Mom, and I didn't like the smile he was flashing now. It was the same smile, he flashed at the Nurse when she was checking him out. It was predatory, a shark's smile. I gave his question the proper pause as if I were digging my memory for some piece of information that would be crucial to solving his case. Then I gave him an empty shake of the head, "Can't think of anything."

"None of this ties back to that Marisol Rodriguez. Does it?"

That hit me like a short hook to my bruised kidneys. And it wasn't until, I saw the knowing look on Rod's face, that I realized that I had bunched my sheet up in both fists. I let go, and tried to act calm, but it was too late. "I don't see how," I said. "I told you that was nothing. Just an easy money inquiry for me."

He patted me on my side.

Hot pain stabbed deep inside me as if he had slid a fire-place poker between my ribs. I held my breath.

"Hey, I'm glad the pain is only a 2," he said, still with that smile. "Like I said, I'm not looking at you for this Fuzzy, but not everyone in the department sees your follies for the humor they are. Keep your head on a swivel," he said. "You never know who might be watching."

He left me there, conflicted. Did I want to slap that silly smile off his face? Or did I want to clap him on the back and thank him for informing me of the tail I would pick up?

Sometime in the night, a visitor woke me. I didn't hear him, it was almost as if I felt his presence. He sat in the dark corner of my room. I wouldn't have even noticed him there, he was so shrouded in darkness, if I hadn't smelled the cigarette smoke that emanated from his clothes, his hair, hell, probably even his skin.

I felt an uneasiness I had not felt in our previous

encounter. He visiting in the middle of the night when I was laid up in a hospital gave him an upper hand I didn't allow when he had slipped in the passenger's seat of my truck. "Visiting hours are over, Michaels."

He leaned forward into the faint light entering the room from the slightly opened door. He had as serious a look on his face as he could manage. Alfred E. Neuman was tough to take seriously, but he was giving it a go.

"I'm a private eye, Koella. You know how it goes. Sneaking in and out of places is kind of my thing."

"You need to give up the cigs. They are blowing your cover."

"Is that right?"

I sat up in bed and felt the sear of a hundred matches being lit on my rib cage. "You smell like an ashtray that hasn't been dumped for a month."

"I love you, too."

"Right, now what do I owe the pleasure of your visit?"

"You've fucked me over, Koella. With Coach dead, there isn't any appetite for continuing the case. At least, not in the immediate future."

"Any violations had to run deeper than Cain," I said. "Hell, most of them he probably didn't know about. That's the way they like to operate. The less the head of the snake knows the better."

He nodded. "NCAA, Indianapolis, says we need to be sensitive to the current situation. I think they're concerned that some of our digging may have led to this."

He was still leaning forward in his seat, like a cat ready to leap.

"Them's the breaks," I said.

And he leapt and landed right beside my bed. He leaned in so close I could taste the stale smoke and coffee on his breath. "Look here you dumb ass. You want to fuck around and play detective with a heart, so you can get a closer look at the little Puerto Rican sweetheart? I could give a shit until it takes money out of my wallet. And that's what has happened now, you've stirred shit into the pot, and now I'm down a case, one with legs and deep pockets."

I still didn't like him with the upper hand, and I didn't see a way around it, sitting in a hospital bed connected to all the devices. But I also didn't see what he expected me to say. I went with, "Well, sorry."

He plopped back down in his chair and rubbed his forehead. "What happened the other night? I saw you pull in to the Coral Beach and leave with that fat bartender. The same one you had visit Coach and Marisol the night before."

Jesus, he and Rod and Marisol had my balls in a sling. If I didn't end up behind bars, it would be a small miracle.

"She isn't fat," I said.

"Whatever, far be it from me to stop you defending a girl's honor, but what happened?"

"Nothing," I said. "Well, nothing, I saw! What about you? You were obviously there."

"I was watching you."

"Me? What the fuck do I have to do with the NCAA?"

"Nothing, I was trying to get a read on where you fit into all of this. Like maybe you had Marisol working for you now. And, if so, why? You said she was looking for a better offer. Why do you have this girl still on your mind after you pretty much already delivered what you were asked to do?"

All good questions, but I felt no compulsion to answer any of them. "I saw nothing."

"And you didn't kill him?"

"Get out of my room," I said between clenched teeth.

"Where the girl? The bartender? She didn't show up to work tonight."

Michelle? God, she'd better be okay. My conscience

couldn't take another body bag draped from it. "I don't know." I looked around the room. "I've been predisposed."

"I see that," he said. "And who's responsible for this."

The heat in my kidneys and ribs reached the point of no return. I laid back. "I don't know. You tell me. You've been following me, haven't you?"

He stood. I notice he had a hat in his hand. A fedora. Jesus, what was this 1952? "Last night I was busy getting drunk, drowning my sorrows for this recent turn of events. So I didn't see what happened to you, but it has to be whoever did Coach in doesn't it?"

That would probably be my conclusion if I were in Michaels's shoes. As much as I liked to think, he was the lesser detective, I was no brighter. "They got the drop on me so I didn't see them, but maybe you're right."

"They? You said you didn't see 'them', but you know there was more than one?"

"There would kind of have to be," I said. "I don't know if you've noticed, but I'm a big guy. To kick my ass, the way they did, I'd think there was more than one."

"So maybe there's more than one in on the Coach job?"

I didn't think there was. I was trying hard not to care. "Beats me, why do you care? You're off the case, aren't you?"

With that, he turned to walk away. "Good point, Fuzzy. Probably the only sense you've made tonight."

As he stepped to the door, I notice the glint of steel at the small of his back. "I hope you get caught carrying that piece in here. Not even open carry permits are allowed to bring weapons in here."

"I'll slip out of here without notice, just like I slipped in," he said.

Not if anyone out there has a nose, I thought.

"And Fuzzy, stay away from Marisol, huh? I'd hate to see

the kid end up like Coach, and everything you touch is turning to shit."

If I wasn't hooked up to IVs and other contraptions, I would have crawled out of bed and beaten him senseless. Instead, I closed my eyes and dreamed of Michelle and Veronica both looking over me. Both holding weapons. Neither with looks of mercy on their faces.

I CHECKED myself out of the hospital against my physician's advice. A physician I never spoke to, mind you, and one I never remember seeing, at least not in a lucid state. I decided that there was no case. I had done my job, sort of. All the collateral damage was none of my concern. I stopped by my branch of Carolina First and dumped the photos in my safe deposit box. Then decided there was one stop I needed to make, before I could retire back to my shanty in Murrells Inlet and get some of that rest Nurse Ra Ra had advised, but had been impossible amongst all the racket at the hospital.

The Carlton Arms seemed somehow less depressing today. It had more to do with the overall beautiful weather we were having than anything else, but it seemed less oppressive. Less like the communist stronghold. I had not seen a tail on me on my drive over. So I had either checked out before anyone at police headquarters expected me too or I had picked up the world's greatest police tail. I had been looking that close.

I decided it was the latter and had no fear climbing the steps to the Rodriguez apartment. Again, the Salsa Meringue played behind the door. The sound was faint, but pleasant.

Papi answered my knock.

"You," he said.

"I need to talk to Marisol, Mr. Rodriguez."

"She no here," he said. "She no come home last night."

"Does she often do that?"

His lower lip trembled. "No, Mari come home late often, but she always come home."

"Mr. Rodriguez, maybe you can let me in? I can see you are concerned. Maybe we can talk and figure this out together."

He held his chin up in defiance. "It was after you come talk to her she act funny and disappear."

Despite the puffed out chest, he stood aside and let me enter his home. The living room was about what I expected. Beige carpet, white walls scarred with marks from moving furniture, scuffles, life, second hand, brown sofa, sagging in the middle, old tube-type 19-inch TV set on a red plastic milk crate turned on its side. A video game console was hooked to it. Mr. Rodriguez pointed to the sofa.

I took a seat on one end, thinking he would take the other end.

But he grabbed a scarred wooden chair from the dining set that shared space with the living room and set it before me. He took a seat and asked, "Tell me, Señor, who are you?"

The morphine must have been lingering in my veins, because before I knew it I had blurted out, "I'm a Private Investigator."

"What like a police?"

"Kind of," I said. "But I am private, I don't work for the police."

"Then," he said. "Who do you work for?"

"I really shouldn't say, Mr. Rodriguez. It's kind of against the rules for me to tell people who I work for."

He stood up. "Ah, so you no care. It's okay, I let you in my home. But you no can say why you are here. You no can say why you talked to my Mari. This always the way it work, no?"

He was right. I wasn't being fair, and I could see the

disappointment in his face. Disappointment, yes. Surprise, no. I didn't know how long Mr. Rodriguez had lived here, but I knew the lack of respect I had just shown him. He expected from my kind. I gave him some of the truth. "A gentleman hired me to check in on Marisol." Calling Sample a gentleman tasted bitter. That kind of lie felt almost as dishonorable as telling Papi Rodriquez that I couldn't say who I worked for.

"How this man know my Mari?"

"I don't know." The truth tasted much better.

"But he thought she might get in trouble?"

I nodded.

"Last time you came. You had envelope. What was in it? Something to do with trouble?"

Papi was an observant guy, and a protective father. I respected him more than any of the others I had come across in this case. "Pictures." I let that sit for a moment and then continued. "Marisol and an older man."

His lip trembled again. I wasn't sure if it was anger, fear, or sadness which caused it. I wasn't sure I wanted to find out. It stopped. He had another question. "Why the guy you work for care about Mari and this old man?"

Papi Rodriguez was illustrating just how much of a fool I was. "I don't know," I said. "But who the old man was, is why I am here today, Mr. Rodriguez. It is why I am concerned about Marisol."

"Who?"

I caught myself before I answered him. Another thought ocurred to me, "Where is your son?"

"He at school, why?"

"Is it possible Marisol is with him?"

"Why would Mari be with Jandro?"

I remembered Sample telling me how Marisol liked to hang out at the college. I remembered how Michaels told me how she joined up as a recruiting girl on her own when she found out about it.

"Sometime younger siblings like to spend time with their older siblings on a college campus," I explained.

Papi frowned. "Younger? Mari isn't younger than Jandro."

"She's Jandro's big sister?" I asked.

"They are twins," Papi said.

I'm not sure what that meant about anything, but it was interesting. "They get along, don't they?"

He looked at me like I had ants crawling out of my eye sockets. "They are at each other's throats every minute of every day."

"Mr. Rodriguez were you aware that Marisol was helping recruit football players over at the university?"

"I know something," he said. "She very proud, say no girl ever do it who not student. She a special case. Jandro hate. I think he jealous. Like she is trying to take the spotlight off him and what he do at school. I try to show pride in both my kids."

"They seem worthy of your pride, Mr. Rodriguez."

"How could you know," he asked. When I didn't answer he continued, "What you know about my Mari and the old man? The Coach?"

It was time to protect the truth. "Let's just say that Coach was taking advantage of a position of power, and Marisol was his victim."

That lip began full-out jumping. "He rape?"

I waved that one off. "No. It was consensual. I meant to say Coach should know better."

"So should my Mari," he said. By the look on his face he said it more to himself as if I were no longer in the room.

"Mr. Rodriguez, I came today to tell Marisol that I would not be turning over the pictures of her with Coach to the police. I feel that should be her choice. I do not think she did this to Coach."

"Jandro very angry," he said.

"Huh?"

"Yes," he said. "Very angry about what happen to Coach. He blame Coach for loss."

Papi's broken English confused me, but I didn't want to push it too much.

"His anger is good for that sport he chose," he said. "Me, I told him all his life. Baseball is the game he should play." Papi pointed at his temple. "In baseball, most times you get to keep this. His game? They all lose their head."

"Did you play ball," I asked.

He nodded his head and stood. "You wait," he said. He left the room and came back holding an old wooden bat like it was a prized artifact. He held it out to me.

I turned it over in my hands. There was a signature in black ink just below the branding on the sweet spot. I didn't look closely because I was busy checking it for fresh cracks or stains.

He stopped me rotating the bat in my hands and pointed to the autograph. "You see? Marichal."

"No kidding," I said. "You got Juan Marichal to sign it, when you were a kid?"

"Kid? Maybe I was in my twenties, and Marichal no more pitch for Giants. He old like me now. But I hit homerun, he pitch. In Venezuela."

"Wow, thanks for showing me Mr. Rodriguez."

He took the bat and held it back and over his right shoulder like he was stepping into the box against Juan Marichal again. "I always say Jandro you go very far in baseball. But he never listen. He choose loco game."

Mr. Rodriguez and I shared brief histories of careers in baseball. His ended with stints two summers in a row in

Venezuelan summer leagues. Mine was still dying a slow death in the Carolina Independent League. It seemed to earn his respect. I didn't return the conversation to Marisol other than to ask that he notify me when she returned home. I gave him one of my cards. I left him waving his bat with a gleam in his eye.

IT OCCURRED to me that I now had two missing women on my hands. I stopped by the Coral Beach resort. It was mid-day, and the place was deader than road kill, and the bar keep looked no better than road kill. She was a bottle blonde with dark roots where she parted her hair down the middle, like it was 1984 all over again. She had a teenager's acne riddled face, but still looked ten years older than me. She wore light blue jeans and a black Coral Beach T-shirt. Both were two sizes too small, and she didn't wear them as nicely as Michelle. Every piece of exposed skin had some homemade tattoo ink, including her face which had a small blue heart the size of the end of a pencil eraser on her jawline. I wondered how one decided on that location for a tattoo. I didn't wonder on it long though. By the looks of her, I'm sure crystal meth figured into that decision.

She smiled, and said, "Well look at you, tall and handsome. What can I get ya?"

I sat at a stool. "Shot of jack," I said.

"Now we're talkin'" she said and set about pouring me my drink.

I tossed it back and felt its warmth throughout my extremities. "Another one," I said.

While she worked on number two, I asked, "Is Michelle around?"

She looked up from the pour and overflowed the shot

glass. "That's not a pretty topic around these parts," she laughed. "They had to call me back in, because she ain't showed in two days. Not that I'm complaining."

Her smile was missing two front teeth, and her breath wasn't much better than Shane Michaels's. She placed the shot glass before me and tucked her hair behind an ear. "So how do you know Michelle?"

I tossed back the shot, and put the glass down, upside down on the bar top. "We're old friends."

"I bet," she said. "With benefits?"

I ignored that. "How much do I owe ya?"

"Aw, c'mon you don't scare off that easily do ya?"

I pulled out my wallet and waited.

"10 bucks," she said. "You're no fun."

I dropped a ten and a five on the bar and got up to leave.

As I turned my back on her, she said, "You see Michelle, you tell her you ain't the only one's been in looking for her. Them cops that been around here because of the coach, they's wanting to talk to her, too."

That got my attention. I looked at her back over my shoulder. "What's that you said?"

"Pigs are looking for Ms. Michelle. Couldn't have happened to a better girl if you ask me?"

"What did you tell them?"

"Same thing I told you. Little Miss. Perfect hasn't shown for two days."

"Why do they want to talk to her?" I wondered out loud.

She held out both hands, palms out and shrugged her shoulders. Her t-shirt hitched up and exposed pale roll of fat along with a barbell stud in her navel. "Beats me. Probably has something to do with her disappearing right around the time we pull a stiff out of our rooms though. Wouldn't you think?"

I turned on my heels and hurried out of there.

I still did not understand why Michelle disappeared on me the day I found Coach's body, but she had the best alibi of any of the people involved in this case. She was in bed with me. I wasn't ready to share that with the cops yet, but I would if Michelle needed it to stay clean of this nonsense.

As I pulled out of the parking lot of the Coral Beach, I picked up on a silver Chevy Impala pulling in behind me on Ocean Boulevard. When I got to the red light at the intersection with 3rd Avenue South, I stopped and pretended to fool with my phone. I caught the light turn green in the corner of my eye, but I continue to play with the phone.

The Impala remained stopped behind me, without hitting the horn or moving to pass me. Just as the light turned amber, I sat up, looked in the rearview, smiled, and waved at my tail.

His eyes dilated, but that was about all I could say about him, because I floored it through the intersection, as the light turned red. It put him in a no-win situation. He could chase me down, even give me a ticket, but it would mean losing his cover. Or he could do what any upstanding citizen would do, sit at the light and wait for the green. He went with upstanding citizen.

I sped down two blocks and took the left onto 5th Avenue without braking. I swerved just out of the way of an African-American woman and the toddler son which held her hand. He was shirtless and wore floaties on his arms and was dragging momma in the direction of the beach. She gave me the finger as I sped past them.

I'd feel bad about nearly killing the little kid later. I ran a red light at King's Highway, and two blocks later I was in a middle class neighborhood. I weaved through streets with names like Elmwood Lane and felt comfortable I had lost my tail by the time I emptied onto Executive Avenue. I pointed my truck toward North Myrtle Beach. I hoped it remembered how to get to Micelle's little 2 bedroom cottage, because I was having a hard time with it.

———

I ARRIVED at her place twenty minutes later. A black Hyundai Elantra sat under the aluminum carport. It seemed familiar. It must have been the car I followed Michelle home in the other night. Again, I admired her little stucco house. The yard was well kept and the flag stones leading from the driveway to her front stoop were all properly aligned. The flower beds were a little sparse, but you couldn't expect everything. She was a single working girl.

I skipped over the flagstone, like I was playing hopscotch, and arrived at her screen door. There was a button for the doorbell housed in a metallic seashell, but I passed on it and opened the screen door and pounded on the wooden door.

Sometime before sunset, the door creaked open and Michelle stood there in a baggy t-shirt and sweatpants with holes in the knees. She wore no make-up, and she needed it to look presentable. She had gathered her hair in a nest on top of her head. When she recognized me, her sleepy eyes went wild. She went to close the door.

I slid my foot in between the door and the frame. "Come on, Michelle. Let me in."

She swung the door open and turned her back on me and walked back into the house.

I followed like an obedient puppy, closing the door behind me. She sat down at her dining table which sat in a nook on the other side of a bar which separated it from the kitchen. She propped her elbows up on the table and dropped her face into her hands. "Fuzzy, I told them everything," she said.

I eased back a seat from the table opposite her. "Who?" I'm not sure why I asked. I knew exactly who she had told everything to, but I needed sometime to process the information. So I needed to stall to give me time to arrive at the right questions.

"The police," she said. "They just left fifteen minutes ago."

I had to swallow my laughter. I was fifteen minutes away from losing one cop just to land into the lap of some other. I decided not to ask her what 'everything' was, and instead ask her what I had been wondering for the last few days. "Michelle, where did you disappear to the other day?"

She lifted her head from her hands and searched my face. Then she remembered. "You found his body, didn't you?"

"Yup," I said. "But why did you leave?"

"I knew it, Fuzzy. I knew you would find him. Have you ever been in a car wreck?"

"This wasn't a car wreck..."

"I know, but you know that feeling you have when you slam on the brakes. Every time, I've gotten into a wreck, I've known it before it happened. Like I know the brakes weren't going stop in time. And then you hear the crush of metal. On the close calls, when the brakes held, I never had that feeling."

"What are you saying Michelle?"

"When you jumped out of the truck, and hurried to the hotel, I felt it. I didn't have to hear the crushing metal. I knew."

Tears welled in her eyes.

She didn't deserve this. I had brought this into the life of a smiling, confident girl. A girl who had bought herself a small piece of the American dream, with bartender's tips. I reached for one of her hands.

She yanked the hand out of my reach. "I got scared, Fuzzy. I didn't want to be part of it, anymore. When you had me knock on their door, so you could get a picture, that was fun. I liked all the cloak and dagger stuff, then. It seemed harmless. But, my God, Fuzzy, what have you gotten me into?"

She collapsed face first on the table.

I reached over and patted her on the shoulder. I expected her to pull away, but she sat there whimpering into the table-top. I left my hand there. "I'm sorry. I expected none of this, either. And I'm scared too. There isn't anything wrong with that, Michelle." I stopped, hoping for some response. Some reprieve, that would allow me some time to figure out what next to ask her.

She didn't do me that favor. She choked on her sobs.

I stood and came around to her and lifted her back up to a seated position.

Her head lolled to one side as if she were drunk.

Guilt was probably my least favorite emotions. Was it any wonder I was a non-practicing Catholic? "Honey, you said you told the cops everything? You weren't with me when I discovered the body, what do you mean by everything?"

"Oh, you pat me on the back. Tell me it will be okay. But all you really care about it how much trouble you're in." She shook her wobbly head and laughed. "You're such a guy, Fuzzy. What? Are you going to try to get me in bed again, now?"

"Honey, I'm trying to figure out how to keep both of us out of trouble."

She lunged forward and spat, "I did nothing. It was you. All you."

I knew I had to calm her down, but short of smacking her across the face like they did in the old movies, I wasn't sure how. Not to mention, who really believes smacking a woman across the face did anything but piss her off more? I pressed forward. "Just tell me what you told them, Michelle."

She crossed her arms across her chest. "I told them every-thing. I told them you were the anonymous caller."

"How did you know that?"

She scoffed at that. "C'mon Fuzzy. You broke into his room."

I didn't argue the point. It was a guess but she was right. "Ok," I said. "What else?"

"I told them how you sweet-talked me into the little job with the room service, and how you were taking pictures of Coach and Mari."

It felt like the ship was sinking. "And did you use Mari's name?"

"Huh?" She tilted her head and looked up at me. "I don't know her name. Just Mari and no I just said some hooker."

"You called her a hooker?"

"I said what she was. Don't be stupid."

"Okay, so you didn't say the girl's name was Marisol."

"I did not know her name was Mari-sol," she said it like I was a small child just learning to speak.

"What else?"

"I told them how you knew they had been in the room the night before the game, and how you had taken me to the hotel and tried to get me to let you into the room. And how I said, 'no'."

There was more than a little bullshit in all of that, but I let it slide. "Anything else?"

"I told them you went up to break into the room, and that I was sure it was you who had put in the anonymous call."

My stomach felt like it was doing somersaults. I went into the kitchen and helped myself to a glass of water.

When I came back to her, her head lolled to the side again, and she appeared to be sleeping. Maybe she'd been on a bender the last couple of days. Or taking pills for anxiety. I recalled her demeanor when we drove over to the Coral Beach that day. It was possible Michelle suffered from anxiety disorders. This did not make me feel any less guilty of my actions. Who knew what to do in a situation like this?

While I stood there trying to decide if I should just leave her there or carry her onto the couch, it occurred to me that there was one more question I needed to ask her. Because I was such a guy, I put my hand into my glass of water, and flicked drops of water at her face.

Her nose twitched a few times as if she had to sneeze.

I hit her with a little more water.

Her eyes opened. "Asshole."

"I was afraid you passed out on me."

"Look, Fuzzy, you're not a bad guy, but I can't help you. And I can't be around you anymore."

"The cops that came to see you, did they give you their names?"

"They gave me their cards, but I don't know what I did with them. I said I can't help you, Fuzzy. I think you should go."

"Ok, forget their names. What did they look like?" I said.

Her eyes narrowed, and she frowned.

"Was one of the black, and a sharp dresser?"

"They were both white."

It was only a matter of time until word got back to Rod. I believed him when he said he wasn't looking at me. I also believed him when he said he wouldn't run interference. I also wasn't sure he would continue 'not looking' at me, when he heard Michelle's story.

I leaned over and kissed Michelle on the cheek.

She didn't pull away.

"I didn't mean for any of this to happen to you," I said.

"I know," she sobbed. "But I need you to leave."

And I did.

As soon as I took a seat behind the wheel, my phone buzzed.

It was my Uncle Rod's personal number.

I probably owed it to him to pick up, but I had been letting people down all week and I didn't see any reason to turn over a new leaf now.

The sun was setting over the rooftops of the houses in Michelle's neighborhood. The streetlights flickered on. The street was quiet except for the song of a lonesome bird. It was also empty of silver Chevy Impalas. I figured I had done enough damage that day and decided to take the forty minute drive home.

I spent that time trying to figure out what I was doing. Michelle had done me no favors but despite some convenient half-truths and omissions, I really couldn't blame her. Plus, she still had a rock solid alibi, her problem was that I wasn't sure the Myrtle Beach Police Department would view spending the night with me as an innocent act.

Fortunately, I had found half of my duet of missing women. I was worried about Marisol, and I had no doubt that Rod would put two and two together soon, and they would be looking for her. I just hoped that she was still breathing the clean ocean air and not laying in some hotel room like Coach. I wasn't sure why she should be, but then I hadn't made sense of anything yet. For all intents and purposes, Marisol was probably the best suspect for Coach's murder, not named Fuzzy Koella, but I couldn't come around to thinking of her as a murderer.

Like most of the dilemmas I found myself in, there appeared to be no good answer. Unlike baseball, I couldn't pitch myself out of trouble. After forty minutes of not paying attention to the driving, I had not come any closer to a solution. I was still convinced that my pictures were best suited for my safe deposit box. I would wait to hear from Papi about

Marisol. Most importantly, I would get a good night's sleep, and hope tomorrow would be a better day. I'd like to think it couldn't get any worse, but I knew better.

I SAW the cruiser parked beside the boathouse, as soon as I turned into the marina, and figured it shot holes in my idea of getting a good night's sleep. I gave doing a U-turn and hauling it out of there, about half a second's thought before realizing I was worn out by the day and didn't have the motivation. Instead, I pulled in right beside them. They were closer to the front of the boathouse, so it was a short walk to my front door, but I figured I would try to get it over with. A silver Impala sat just outside the halo of light provided by the boathouse, alongside the curb in front of the sidewalk running along the slips.

In the driver's side of the cruiser, a beefy guy with a Beetle Bailey style flat-top turned to look at me as I parked my truck. His arm was propped in the open window of his door. A tattoo of barbed wire circled his flabby bicep, a good reminder as why I should never get a tattoo. Beside him, in the passenger's seat sat a lanky black kid, who reminded me of a young Doc Gooden.

I got out of the car, and tried on my goofiest smile, and came around to Beetle Bailey's side with my hand held out like an insurance salesman's. "Hey, fellas. How's it going?"

Bailey, who's name, if his tag was to be believed, was ironically enough, Bailey (Officer H. Bailey) said, "Are you Francis Koella?"

I held my hands out in front of me in mock surrender, maintaining the goofy smile. "Guilty as charged," I said. "But you can call me Fuzzy. What can I do for you officers?"

Bailey's face hadn't change expression one bit. "Need you

to come into the station," he said. "Detective Gilbreath wants to speak to you."

I waved that off. "Rod? He has my number. He can call."

"Yeah, he's tried that."

Right, I'd forgotten that my phone had been buzzing pretty much the entire drive to Murrells Inlet. "Huh, I must not be getting a good connection. I'll just give him a call tomorrow. It's been a long day." I kept the stupid look on my face by maintaining a mental image of Shane Michaels. I turned to scan the marina, half expecting the cop in the Impale to be walking my way. "Some beautiful night, we're having. Huh, fellas?"

With that Bailey lost his patience, he swung his door open, and pried himself out from behind the wheel. Doc got out on his side with an amused look on his face. I preferred Doc over Bailey, but he looked fresh out of the Academy. I knew Bailey would do all the talking. When he finally unfolded himself, he was about my height, and with all the donuts and exercise from writing tickets he went about three hundred pounds. He tried to hide it by sucking in his gut, when he stood in front of me, but it made him look like more of a fat slob. Jesus, didn't they require regular physicals on the job anymore?

Doc came around the front of the car and stood beside Bailey like an obedient mentor. His tag said, J. Johnstone.

I thought of the old outfielder from the 70s. Phillies, wasn't it? He was white though. So I stuck with Doc.

"Officer Bailey. Doc." I said nodding to each of them in turn.

"Doc?", Bailey said.

"Sorry, Johnstone." I said, turning up the stupid smile a notch.

"Cut the shit, Koella," he said. "We need you in the car now. You can make it easy." He opened the back door to the cruiser. "Or we can do it the hard way." He patted the handcuffs hanging from his belt.

I looked from Bailey to Doc to back to Bailey. "Sure thing, fellas. Just show me a warrant for my arrest, and I will be happy to hop in the back there. No need for the cuffs."

Blood pooled in Bailey's cheeks.

Doc's smile left his face, and I was only left with the whites of his eyes. They nearly glowed in the dark.

"Look here, Koella," he said. "Stop with the fun and games. Get in the car. Gilbreath needs to talk to you and we aren't coming back empty handed."

I shrugged. "Show me the paper," I said. "Otherwise, I'm heading back to my place, and getting that good night's sleep I talked about."

I saw his hand move to his stick.

"I wouldn't try that, Bailey. You're about fifty pounds of Krispy Kremes past the point of that being a good idea."

Doc clenched his lips trying to stifle a laugh. Bailey looked like he would have a stroke from the blood pressure.

I said, "Tell my Uncle, I'll give him a call in the morning. Y'all are welcome to hang out here in the parking lot. I'm head of security here, but I won't kick you out." I pointed to the Impala. "Your friend over there can stay, too."

Doc and Bailey looked at each other with confused looks on their faces. "Uncle?" they said in unison.

"Come on fellas, you didn't know Detective Gilbreath and I were related?"

I jingled my keys at them. "I'm gonna hit the sack. You get that warrant."

I left them there looking stupid. I felt the same way. Rod would have my ass in his morning cornflakes.

15

I closed the door shutting myself off from the outside world and the three police officers waiting on me, and leaned back against the cold metal door, closed my eyes, and breathed in the familiar air. I hoped that the comfortable smell of my morning coffee still lingering in the air mixed with the Fuzzy smells would ground me, and push back the pending doom I felt bearing down on me. It may have worked for a brief second, but when I opened my eyes, the first thing I did was peer out my little window to the world, and scan the parking lot. All three of them were there. Through the dark windshield of the Impala, the cherry red of a cigarette glowed. Maybe Michaels was out there somewhere, too?

I needed to put all of them out of my mind and get a good night's sleep. I wanted to put all of this behind me as much as any of them would let me. Sleep was the first step.

I swiped a pile of dirty clothes off my sofa onto the floor and dropped onto it. I fished the remote control out of the sofa's cushions and brought my TV to life.

The channel surf landed me on an old episode of the Rockford Files, which saw Jim hired by a lady lawyer, who never payed her bills, to find a missing person who was a witness to a crime allegedly committed by the lawyer's client. Over the next hour, Jim got in three car chases, got himself beaten silly, and dodged the gunshots of a terrible marksman. I compared it to my last few days and wasn't sure what to think. The show ended with a "To Be Continued" flag across the screen.

I tossed my remote into a pile of dirty clothes and closed my eyes. Sleep came in fifteen minute blocks for the next several hours. Something was nibbling at my conscious, but I couldn't set the hook. It was driving me insane.

In the early morning hours, I stood and walked to the door.

The headlights of a compact car came bouncing into the marina which now appeared to be empty of cops. I wasn't sure whether that meant they had gone to get that warrant, had left for another task, or had given up on me that night and decided they would pick up with me again in the morning. It was probably the latter.

A familiar gray Volkswagen Beetle pulled up to the curb just outside my door. The blonde strung the thin leather strap of a purse, not much bigger than a smartphone, over her bare shoulder, and got out of the car, and hurried to my door, the click-clack of her heels tapping on the pavement.

She stopped with a jolt, when she saw my face in the window, and put her hand to her chest.

It was Marisol Rodriguez. She wore a white peasant's blouse with teal pattern stitched around the collar which she wore off the shoulders. Her jeans were as tight as yoga pants. The clickety-clackety heels were gold, strappy, open-toed sandals. I wasn't sure what occasion the look was appropriate for, but like every time I had seen her, I approved.

Outside admiring her, one other thought bothered me. I wasn't sure how Marisol Rodriguez knew where to find me.

I opened the door.

"Geez, Fuzzy. You almost gave me a heart attack, staring back at me like that. Who is up at this hour looking out their window?"

I stood back from the door, so she could pass. Her hip brushed against my thigh and carried with her the sweet smell of girlish perfume.

"I'm sleeping light these days," I said. "And I heard you drive up." That wasn't true, but it was less creepy than, yes, I was looking out my window at 2 a.m.

She took in my place. The dirty clothes on the floor, the old newspapers and bills piled on the countertop, the flat pillows stacked on the arm of the couch, where I had been sleeping moments ago. She looked at me over her shoulder, cocking the bare shoulder up by her cheek, like a cover girl pose. "I like what you've done with the place," she said.

I remembered the spartan environment of her father's apartment, where she lived, but decided against pointing it out. "Yes, well, I wasn't expecting company at what?" I looked at my watch-less wrist. "Two in the morning."

That drained the coyishness from her face. "I'm sorry about that, but I need your help."

I wasn't sure my help was such a good idea. I'd been trying to help people, who didn't even ask for it, all week and it wasn't doing them or me any good. That included Marisol. But I had assured Papi that I wanted to help her. "What do you need help with Marisol?" I didn't wait for an answer before hitting her up with another question. "Did you talk to your father?"

Her shoulders dropped, and she hung her head as if resigned to a fate she could not control. She dropped down on my sofa and laid her head sideways on the pillows. "I haven't seen my father. I've been staying with a friend over at the university."

"Okay," I said. I had been partially right, she was over at the university. Just not with her brother. "What do you need my help with?"

"Keeping me alive," she said it as if she were citing the scores of last night's games.

I sat down beside her, keeping a good two inches between our rear ends. The smell of her perfume was seductive. So was the allure of the damsel in distress. I knew of the spider webs Marisol Rodriguez had weaved and lured Sample, Michaels, and Coach (probably countless others) within. She may not even know of it. It didn't matter, she'd done it. I was completely aware of it, too. Yet, I kept my defenses down. There is no other way to explain just how good at it she was. "You can't just say something like that, and leave it in the air, Marisol. Why are you afraid for your life? Is someone threatening you?"

She put a finger to the corner of her eye, both eyes looked up to the ceiling, and swiped a clump of mascara from her lashes. It was as if I had questioned why she arrived without bringing a housewarming gift. She examined the a black speck on the tip of her fingernail and said, "I've nearly been run over twice in the last two days."

"On campus?" I said. "Did you report it?"

She wiped her finger clean on a pillow.

Nice, I thought. And, the girl sure wore a lot make-up for two in the morning.

She sat up and patted her knees. "So," she found the right words. "Do you have any idea who is doing this?"

"Trying to run you over? I didn't know it was happening until 10 seconds ago. How would I know who is doing it?"

She crawled out of the sofa and looked down at me. "Coach, Fuzzy. Who did that to him? Do you know?"

"Marisol, I'm not even trying to find out. All I'm trying to do is keep the police who are best suited for figuring that out, from wasting their time looking at me and you." And Michelle, I thought.

She paced around the place, looking things over.

I wasn't sure why she did it. You could tell everything you needed to know from the front door.

She picked up a newspaper. Still folded up of the counter. It was from before all this happened. "Why do you read the paper?" she wondered aloud. "Pretty much all of it is available online. How new can the news be in print?"

I wasn't interested in discussing my idiosyncrasies. I stood up and crossed over to her side in one step. Standing there beside her, I was conscious of just how petite she was. Jandro and her were twins, but about as unidentical as you could get. She seemed fragile, vulnerable standing there beside me.

I took the paper from her hand. I regretted my talk with her father. I now felt on the hook for helping her. Who was I kidding? Even without my little talk with Mr. Rodriquez, I was in. That brush of the hip and smell of the perfume had set the hook. I, too, had been snared in her web. "What do you know about all this, Marisol?"

She frowned and studied my face. Foundation bunched in the burrows on her forehead. It was like learning the Easter Bunny was my dad sneaking around the house with plastic eggs before sunrise. "I know nothing. It is so confusing."

I believed her.

She rested her head against my chest. "I need you to protect me, Fuzzy. I have nowhere to go. Whoever did this to Coach is now after me. I go home, they will find me, and kill me."

I didn't believe that, but I ran my fingers in her blonde hair. There were no dark roots. "You can stay here," I said. "But I'm not so sure it's a good idea. Cops will crawl all over this place in the morning."

She stepped back and looked up at me. "I can stay?"

"You missed the part where I said the cops will be all over this place?"

"Maybe talking to the police would not be so bad an idea," she said.

"There's something to be said for coming clean," I said. "Just realize that they will plaster all of this in the papers. I haven't handed over the pictures I took to either the authorities or my client for just that reason."

She chewed on a thumbnail. Somehow it was the most human thing I'd seen her do. Almost as if she read my thoughts, she stopped. "I appreciate that," she said. "To be honest, that's why I'm here. You're the only one that seems to be thinking about me." She thought on that for a second. "Except maybe Jandro."

Jandro had done nothing but the mention of his name flared hot new pain in my sides.

On cue, she noted the bandage on my face. She laid a hand on it. "What happened to you, Fuzzy?"

"I have people trying to send a message, too."

She removed her hand from my face and put it to her lips. "Coach's killer is after you, too?"

"No, this is Sample's work," I said.

"Why would Billy do this to you?"

I stepped away from her. The perfume and her presence was just a little too overwhelming. I went to the fridge and fished around for a beer. There were two on the bottom shelf behind a week's worth of takeout cartons. "Billy is just trying to force my hand on giving him the pictures," I said. "You want a beer?"

"Sure."

I twisted off the top on two bottles.

She reached for one.

I held it back, as I remembered she was under-aged. I decided I didn't care and handed it to her.

We both enjoyed the first pull. They had sat in the back of my fridge for a while. It was painfully cold as it slid down my throat. For cheap, domestic beer, it tasted wonderful.

Marisol's eyes closed in sensual pleasure, as she took down half of her beer. When she opened her eyes, she said, "No one can ever accuse you of serving warm beer."

I tapped the neck of her beer with mine. "And no one can ever accuse you of nursing a beer."

She laughed. When she remembered the predicament we were in, the amusement slid from her face.

"I deserved it," I said.

The furrowed brow look, that I came to recognize as confusion, came over her.

"Billy, and what he did. He hired me to do a job. It turned out to not be as simple as it originally looked." I shrugged my shoulders and took a quick swig of beer. "I didn't play straight with him. I deserved it."

She put her hand on my gouged cheek again.

It felt warm. There was almost a motherly gesture to it. The hum of hundreds of insect wings kick-started in my midsection, replacing the burn of my bruised ribs and kidney.

"Nobody deserves this," she said. "And nobody deserves to be run over in the street, either."

I took her wrist in my hand and held it there close to my cheek. "Sample would never try to run you over, Marisol."

"A week ago, do you think he would have had the shit kicked out of you like this?"

Touche.

"If he killed Coach," she said, sliding her hand out of my grasp. "We need to find out, and talk to the cops."

I didn't believe Sample killed Coach.

"Marisol, if you think Sample is behind this, maybe it is worth sharing the whole thing with the police? I can be there with you."

"Why do people call him Sample? You always call him that, and I've heard others."

"Forget that, I'd no more share that, than I'd share your pictures without your permission."

That got her attention. She sat on the couch, tucked her legs underneath her and leaned forward for juicy details.

"Pictures? Cops? Billy?" I snapped my fingers. "Let's stay on topic."

"That's what I need you for, baby." She said.

I didn't like her referring to me as baby. I'd seen too many films in the noir cycle. I snapped my fingers again. "I'm not your baby," I said. "Stop flirting, Marisol. We have to sort this out."

"If you find out Billy did it, then we offer the whole story, including pictures, to the police."

"I thought you wanted me to protect you from drive-bys," I said.

She stretched out on the sofa. Her whole figure fitting snuggly between both arms. She grabbed the pillows and tucked them under her head. She smiled and swiped a few strands of hair from her eyes. "You are," she said.

"You can stay as long as you like," I said. "But remember the cops will crawl all over this place. Try to stay out of sight as much as possible."

"I'm good at keeping myself hidden."

I didn't remind her I was just one of two private investigators with photographic evidence otherwise.

She placed her empty beer bottle on the floor at the foot of the couch, and yawned.

I took a seat on one of my barstools. "That folds out into a bed," I said.

She didn't open her eyes. "I'm okay. Where will you sleep baby?" The words came out slurred, like she'd had more than the one beer. She was already half asleep.

"I get little sleep," I muttered.

She shifted her shoulders and adjusted her head on the pillow. I'd lost her. She was gone.

And that is the story of how I came to investigate my own client for a murder I was certain he did not commit.

16

As the clock turned to five, I decided I was best served getting out of there, before sunset. Bailey, Doc, and the gang hadn't returned yet, but it was only a matter of time. I left a note to Marisol to stay out of sight and not answer the door. Then I pulled out a small curtain system I had put together last year.

It was a small curtain rod, maybe 24" wide with opaque curtains that were also 24" long. I sized the whole system to cover the small window to the world in my door. The curtain rods turned 90 degrees on each end, and I had outfitted the feet of each end with adhesive magnets. It was a poor man's engineering, but when I set those magnetic feet on either side of the window, it blacked out the rest of the world.

I did just that, and looked back on Marisol sleeping on the couch, before closing the door quietly behind me.

I realized that in the night, watching her sleep, the temptation faded, and it left me with big brother feelings toward her. Did Coach experience that inner conflict before his death?

The pre-dawn air was crisp and silent, but you could feel

it forfeiting its grasp to the pending sunrise. Any time now, birdsong would replace the pre-dawn silence. I had enjoyed this time of day, many times in the past. It is one of the few pleasantries for the chronic insomniac. Often, I had used it as a good time to wet a line by the pilings of an unoccupied slip. By sunset, I would pull a few sheepshead out of the water and onto my hot-plate, which would suitably fry their filets in butter to make a nice, fresh fish sandwich.

But I wasn't fishing this morning. At least not the kind that involved a hook and line.

I pulled out of the marina and found the parking lot of a seafood restaurant called the Crabby Clam.

My tires crunched on the seashell and gravel parking lot as I pulled out front. The restaurant was abandoned at this hour. But that was fine, I only needed a safe spot to send a text without the police pulling me over.

I texted Veronica. "Awake?"

I sat, waiting with breath held for a response. The breath beat around at the insides of my lungs as time passed.

"Yes, why?"

The breath escaped my nostrils. Veronica was awake, and she responded to me. There was something in my need to see her respond to me, but I couldn't investigate that now. Or, I didn't want to, I should say.

"Breakfast?" I punched out on the phone and went back to holding my breath.

Again she tortured me with a slow response. "Sure. Where?"

FIFTEEN MINUTES LATER, I sat at a booth at a Waffle King off Kings Highway just south of Myrtle Beach.

I fended off the old lady wielding her yellow pad for the

next twenty minutes, waiting on Veronica. Sunrise on the ocean with a fishing rod in your hands was much better than watching it rise over piney woods through the sooty windows of a greasy spoon. I caught myself checking my phone for text messages. I knew Veronica would take time to get fixed up. Not for me, but for the rest of the world.

I was just about ready to give up, figuring she had stood me up, when I saw her Miata pull up beside my truck.

She had on a white, unbuttoned cardigan pulled-over a black form fitting tank top, and skinny jeans that ended just above the ankle bone. Her right ankle sported a hair-thin, gold anklet, that I had purchased for her last birthday. She wore flat sandals with straps that matched the anklet. Her face was clean of the heavy make-up she wore to work. She had bird's feet at the corners of her her eyes, and the beginnings of some hairline wrinkles at the corners of her lips, which deepened when she smiled. If I ever pointed any of this out to her, she would kill me with dagger eyes, but this was the way I preferred her. It was my Veronica, not the fantasy put on display on stage at Molly Maguire's.

Her approach was direct, no hip sway. There was a certain business-like manner to the way she walked up with no smile, and slid into the booth before me.

"Thanks for coming, V." It seemed a silly thing to say given our history, but it was true. I was thankful.

"You left the hospital early," she said nonchalantly, but I could see the concern in her eyes, as she examined the wounds on my face. "You didn't even let me know. I came to visit you again. I knew I shouldn't. Somehow I knew. And yep, I ended up there looking like an idiot, walking into your empty room. That nurse, the cute one, she told me to tell you you're a dumb ass. Her words, not mine. Mine are, You're a selfish, fuckin' idiot."

I reached across the table to take her hand. "Veronica."

She yanked her hand out of my reach. "Don't Veronica, me," she said. "You know it took me 30 minutes to back down my driveway. I sat in the car for 30 minutes to decide if I should come see you this morning."

The guilt I felt had nothing to do with any of the stuff she was mentioning. At least not at the moment, I felt bad about the fact I had called her to meet me at this hour of the morning, not to talk about any of these problems between us. She was right, I'm selfish. I called to talk over the case. For her to be a sounding board. To get her feedback. I tried a smile. "I'm glad you came, even if it took half an hour to come to that conclusion."

Tears leaked from the corner of her eye.

My hand still sat across the table in front of her. I wanted to reach up and wipe the tear away with my thumb and to brush her cheek with the back of my hand. But behind the watery eyes, there was something else besides simple sadness. There was disgust. Or anger. With Veronica, the disgust and anger was inward looking. She was mad at herself for getting into this situation. The situation being me. "It's over, Fuzzy. We're over. I didn't sit in the fucking drive-way deciding whether I should have breakfast with you. Whether I wanted to see you. It took me thirty minutes to get up the courage to do something I should have done a long time ago."

I pulled my hand back across the table. I didn't know what to do with either of them so I folded them together.

I had hurt her, and I hated that. It wasn't just her. I somehow couldn't blame Sample for the blood I was pissing, because I felt like I had hurt him. I also didn't know what to say. Sorry, didn't seem good enough. Or maybe too cliché.

She wiped away her tears with the heal of her hand, and looked over her shoulder to see if the waitress was within earshot.

The waitress wasn't. She had her yellow pad at the ready, but she knew I was in deep shit and she kept her distance on the other side of the diner.

Veronica snapped her head back at me and sneered, "Who the fuck drives the cute little bug, Fuzzy?"

I felt as if my tongue had slid back down my throat. Before I had control of it again, Veronica was back out of the booth. "Don't come looking for me anymore, Fuzzy. Even if you're paying for the dances, I can't afford it."

She hurried out the door, into her car, and out of my life.

Something like a hole opened in my chest. I could feel it there, but I also kicked myself for not bringing up looking into Coach's killer before she sped away.

She knew me better than I knew myself. I would have left my ass, too.

I ATE a big breakfast of sausage, eggs, and hash browns. And drank the Waffle King dry of one pot of coffee. I took my time with it, and with time ole Miss Beehive, whose name turned out to be Sonja, warmed up to me. She assured me that, "She'll be back."

I wasn't so sure of that, but the big breakfast helped with the sour stomach the whole encounter had given me.

I stuck around until the before work breakfast crowd poured in and dumped quarters into the jukebox to play horrible mainstream country songs.

It was a country music kind of morning, but no matter what the stations might want to tell you, that shit was not Country.

I got in my truck and reached under the seat. There was an old CD wallet in there.

I put in an old Townes Van Zandt CD, and skipped to the second track, "You Are Not Needed Now." Townes knew how to twist the knife, like all good songwriters.

I drove around the beach. When I got near the Second Avenue Pier, I parked a block away, in some hotel's lot. The only other vehicle in the lot was an over-sized pick up with tires taller than my waist, and a bumper sticker of the Confederate flag that read, "If You're Offended by this, You Need a History Lesson." On the back window of the cab, there was a sticker of the American flag.

I felt like waiting around to give the pickup owner a history lesson. Instead, I took a path leading between the armpit hotel, and a high dollar resort called The Thunderbird to the beach.

The tide was up, leaving only a thin strip of beach maybe twenty-five yards wide. I liked these kinds of tides, because they limited the number of people on the beach, but in the off-season the beach remained empty.

I started with Sample, because of my two dilemmas, it was the least complicated. I still didn't think Sample had anything to do with Coach's death. I was no longer confident he planned to blackmail Coach, either. Sample, for all of his failings, was a man of pride and honor. The things he took pride in, would leave most of us scratching our heads. And his type of honor is best understood on the streets, piers, and abandoned parks where he demanded respect from punk kids. So yes, he would gang bang me for not handing over the pictures because I wasn't honorable. I didn't live up to my word. But, he would not beat Coach to the death for screwing around with a girl half his age, whom he had an incredible power over, because given the same opportunity Sample would do the same thing, and be proud of it.

That I went to Marisol and informed her of both the pictures and that he had hired me, and then she scolded him for it, was a kick to his pride. I deserved a kick to my kidneys. Coach didn't even know Sample existed. Even when I told him Sample hired me to take the pictures, Sample meant nothing to him. And Sample couldn't care less what happened to Coach. Even now with Coach slain, I suspect Sample felt nothing but indifference.

Did any of this get me any closer?

No. I was pretty much where I started. Sample didn't kill Coach.

Marisol thought he did and thought he was shooting for her next.

What I knew for sure was that I needed to talk to Sample. I needed to know the whole story from his side. I hoped he would talk to me.

I needed the same thing from Marisol.

Half a mile into my walk I came across a mother and child. The tow-headed boy carried a red plastic bucket in one hand and a green plastic hand shovel in the other. He was old enough to walk and talk, but young enough that his legs still bowed from all that time spent in the womb. He hurried around, digging up seashells with his shovel. Every one he found got tossed over his shoulder.

His mother, also blonde sat on a white towel with her knees pulled up and hugged by her arms. She wore a white cardigan unbuttoned over a matching, loose-fitting tank-blouse, khaki Capris, and a mother's smile. Her tan was perfect, even in the cooler season. So were her teeth, brilliantly white and perfectly straight. Her eyes were the color of cornflowers and were free of smile lines. She was the beauty you expected to find on your TV screen, but never out in the wild.

I stopped short, and took a seat on the cold, moist sand. I was close enough to hear the little boy's cries of exasperation, every time he tossed another shell with clinging sand over his shoulder.

Mom looked over at me. I thought I saw the beginnings of a frown.

I waved and flashed a smile. I was going for the, "Hi don't mind me. I'm not a budding pedophile" message.

I must have pulled it off, because she went back to ignoring me and watching her son.

I couldn't blame her. He was cuter than me.

The boy examined his latest dig. His shoulders sagged. "Momma, they're all broken," he cried. "Every time I think I've found a pretty one, it's cracked. Everything is broken."

You have no idea, kid.

But mom was less cynical than me. "Braden, just keep at it. You'll find one, and it will be the most beautiful one you've ever seen. And all of this digging, will make it even more beautiful. You just keep digging. They're not all broken."

I looked at her and wondered if she was talking about herself, and her flawless beauty, or the shells. I decided she wasn't so narcissistic to be speaking metaphorically about herself. But only someone who looked like her could optimistically think the perfect shell could be found. I'd given up on shell searching, not much older than Braden. He was right. Everything is broken.

Braden dropped his toy bucket and shovel and trotted down to where the ocean lapped at the wet, packed sand of the beach. As his feet entered the ocean, ankle-high, he shouted in joy and giggled.

"Braden! Not in the water. It's too cold," his mother called to him. There was little fear behind it. It was almost as if she were delivering the lines expected of her.

Braden bent over at the waist, and put his hands in the water, and splashed water onto his pants. The white of his diaper peaked out from the waist of his trousers when he did so. He giggled. He had forgotten the frustration of his impossible search for the Unbroken Shell. "Momma, it's cold, but it feels so good."

Braden had a lesson for me about Sample's case, and my relationship with Veronica. But I couldn't leave the broken pieces alone, and I wasn't idealistic enough to go searching for the unbroken.

No.

Me? I had to try to put the broken pieces back together.

I got up and dusted sand from the seat of my pants. I wanted to walk over to Braden's mother and tell her what an exceptional son she had. Instead, I turned around and began the walk back to my truck.

I had to gather all the broken pieces if I had any hope of putting them all back together.

IT WAS STILL EARLY, and I worried that a trip home would only result in Bailey, Doc, and Mr. Impala gathering me up to take me in to see Uncle Rod and his gang. And it would probably mean Marisol coming along for the ride.

Figuring I could save Marisol some face time with the cops, and control the game a little better, I pointed my truck in the direction of the Ted C. Collins Law Enforcement Center.

I pulled into my Uncle Rod's reserved spot. It wasn't far from the front door, and I knew that he wouldn't need it. Most days, Rod rode his bicycle to work and rode shotgun in his partner's car during the work day. I had never figured out how he managed to continue to look like the front page of GQ while riding his bike to work. But my uncle was a surprising individual.

The police department was an innocuous, ground hugging

brick building with flat roofs and punch windows and doors that were so recessed from the brick veneer that they had the look of cave openings. I entered through the main cave.

It was early enough that the main lobby was not the total chaos you expected during a high profile case. The Maxwell Hammer case had run long enough that the press had pretty much stopped hounding the department about new findings. Their focus would now be on the Cain case. There were a few journalists sitting on the molded plastic chairs in the lobby, but these were youngsters who had not learned that they were going to get nothing from the detectives, who were just starting their day and sitting through morning debriefings, at this hour.

Cricket, the African-American administrative assistant that had manned the front desk for as long as I could remember, had her phone tucked between her shoulder and ear while she wrote something on a pink memo pad. When she noticed me standing there, she smiled and held up one finger.

Cricket's hair was styled differently every time I'd seen her. If I came in tomorrow, she would have it styled differently than the immaculate braids that she had wrapped around and piled high on her head. It was more impressive than the hive Sonja sported at the Waffle King. I had to believe that most African-American women would be happy to keep her current look for at least a month, but no, tomorrow she'd have dreads or straight hair or a brush cut. I got exhausted just thinking about the effort she must go through to keep a different look going.

Fortunately, she cut short my pondering on her personal style, when she hung up the phone. "Fuzzy! What is up? You looking good." She made an act of looking me up and down. She was about 20 years my senior, and any chance we may have ended up together passed years ago. But it was still flattering, and she was good at the mock flirting.

"You too Miss. Cricket," I said. "You look like your turning time backwards." There was some truth in that. Cricket had to be well into her 50s, but she could easily pass for early 40s.

But she swatted my attempt at flattery away with a gesture of her hand. "Your Uncle be looking for you?"

I held my hands out at my sides. "I've been found," I winked.

She leaned forward and whispered, "He in one of them moods he gets about you."

"That's why I'm here," I said. "He ain't got nothing to be moody about with me, but I figured I better come see him, before he starts taking it out on you and the rest of the department."

She picked up the phone and gave me a look of disbelief. "You crazy. You know that?"

"Guilty as charged," I said, and regretted my choice of words.

Cricket's jaw hinged open, too, but the shock was short-lived. "Your nephew is here to see you." She pulled the phone about an inch away from her ear and grimaced.

This was going to be about as pleasant as root canal work.

"Yes, Fuzzy, what other nephew you expecting." She hung up on him while I could still hear his voice chattering on.

"He'll be down shortly," Cricket said. "Good luck."

The phone rang on her desk.

I stepped away to let her do her job and waited on Rod.

It was a short wait.

He strode into the lobby the way I took the hill in the first inning. He wore a starched, blue dress shirt with a button loose at the throat, revealing a thick gold chain. His slacks were casual khakis, which were somewhat of a departure for him. Maybe a nod to the business casual times we lived in. His ox-blood loafers were polished to a blinding shine. Proof that old habits die hard. He held his hand out, his smile as authentic as he could pull off, "Fuzzy, man, how you doing? You healing up okay?"

I knew he was laying the good cop groundwork for the working over he and his partner Kevin Toriani were about give me back behind doors.

I played stupid. "I'm all right, Rod. It only hurts when I breathe."

He laughed a little too much at that. Recognized it and cut it short. "Yeah, so thanks for coming in." He put a hand on my shoulder, still shaking with the other, and directed me back through the door he had just entered through.

"I hope our guys didn't rough handle you too much last night." He let loose the hand to open the door, but kept the other on my shoulder. It was like a doctor comforting the next of kin. "It's just this Cain thing. Your name keeps coming up, and we just want to clear the air. See whether you can help us make sense of some of this."

It was complete bullshit, and my Uncle was smart enough to know I could see through it. "I told them to piss off, Rod. They didn't get a chance to rough handle me. I come in on my terms or with a warrant. You know that."

He nodded his head reassuringly. "Right. Right. So, like I said. We're glad you came in." Then he added, "On your own terms."

We passed through a bullpen of detectives typing away on their computer keyboards or chattering away on their desk phones.

We entered an interrogation room that looked very little like what you saw on TV. This room did have the obligatory table in the center of the room, but it was a varnished wood table, nicer than any dining room table I would own if I ever got around to getting one or a dining room. The walls of the room were lined with waist high book shelves. The books all had titles like, *The Palmetto State : A History* or *The Grand Strand : Throughout the Years*. Above the books, framed posters hung. Beach scenes. Palm trees in silhouette against a sunrise sky. They were all straight out of the Chamber of Commerce playbook.

Kevin Toriani sat at the table. My uncle's greasy and over-weight partner. He wore a short sleeved, white button-down shirt stained by his morning's breakfast. His top button was loose too, revealing a white undershirt faded to gray. Rod Gilbreath and Kevin Toriani were The Odd Couple stepped outside your TV set.

He looked up when we entered, scratched the top of his crewcut head with the end of a yellow pencil, and grunted something I could not understand but took to mean something like, "Hey Fuzzy."

Rod patted my shoulder and finally lightened the load by letting his hand slide free. "Have a seat, Fuzzy." He sat down beside Toriani.

I pulled the chair out across from them. It was the only other available one. I stopped to look the place over. "I like what you've done with the place." I delivered it with a little acid in my tone that I hoped neither of them missed.

Toriani stood, as if he wanted to lay me out. "I see you still have not learned any respect," he said, and then in Rod's direction, he added. "Bailey should have hauled his ass in last night, even if it took the cuffs."

"No, he shouldn't have," I said. "Bailey's smart enough to know I would have had myself out of here with my first phone call. And then he would be seeing a lot of my lawyer. It's a wonder he's still riding a cruiser, and you're the detective."

He scoffed at that.

Uncle Rod gave me a settle down gesture with his hand.

"Take a seat, Fuzzy. Let's get this over with as painlessly, as possible."

Toriani turned away and examined one of the posters on the wall. In the movies, the rooms always had a large mirror, that was actually a two-way. This room didn't have a mirror, just a half glass window in the door.

I resisted the temptation to look over my shoulder at the door to see if we had an audience. Instead, I dropped into the chair, and slumped in a way that let them know this wasn't getting to me. I wasn't sure if the act worked.

Rod leaned forward. He clapped his hands together. "Alright, let's start with the question you're least likely to answer. Who hired you to follow Tom Cain around?"

"No one." I kept my face flat.

Rod sat up in surprise. "No one? So it was the girl?"

I didn't say a word. I tried to keep my poker face.

Rod tilted his head in deep thought.

Before he landed on the girl, I asked him to look into last week, I tried to break his thoughts. "Rod, you know I'm not handing over that confidential information."

Toriani spun quickly back in my direction. His face was the color of fresh sunburn, but it wasn't the season for it. With Toriani, though, it was always the season for hypertension. "Look here you little shit, I'm not related to you. I'm not messing with you with kid's gloves. Start answering questions, or I'll knock you off that chair, and we can start a new method of questioning."

I felt like pointing out that I had 4 inches on him, and wasn't a candidate for a heart attack, and I wasn't cuffed. But I let him have his grandstanding. "I don't share who I'm working for. Rod knows that. If y'all don't have any further questions, I'll just be heading on."

I started to push myself up with my hands flat on the table.

Rod reached over and grabbed my wrist. "Stay in the seat, Fuzzy. We talked to the bartender."

I, of course, knew they had spoken with Michelle, but they didn't need to know that. "Which one?"

They looked at each other. Rod said, "Michelle. The one you were with when you found the body."

"I don't know what you're talking about," I said.

"Dumb ass, we have a recording of you calling it in. Even I can tell it's your voice," Toriani said.

"Take it easy there, Kev. Your eyes look like they're gonna pop out of their sockets, and I don't want you having a stroke."

None of that had the effect of calming him down. He leaned so far across the table, his face so close to me that I could see his morning breakfast lodged between his teeth, and smell the talcum powder he covered himself in to manage the sweat he produced simply by sitting at his desk. Wet rings at his armpits evidenced that the powder was failing him.

Before he could say anything, I turned my face away from him, "All I meant was that I had no one with me when I found the body."

Rod said, "So it was you who found the body, Fuzzy?" Then to Toriani, "Kevin sit down let Fuzzy talk."

Flecks of spittle sprayed the side of my face, "Fuck him, Rod. This little fucker thinks he can get away with anything because you used to lay the pipe to his Aunt. Well, fuck that. He can't get away with this shit anymore. He can't get away with murder."

I wiped the side of my face with the shoulder of my shirt-sleeve. I looked past Toriani to Rod.

His eyes narrowed and lips clenched. He had the look, that said Toriani may have gone too far with the comment about my Aunt, his ex-wife. I almost wanted to sit back and shut up, and just watch if it got to a point that Rod would do my dirty work and kick the fat-fuck's ass. I ignored Toriani and spoke directly to my Uncle, "Rod, you need to keep this animal on a leash. I'm gonna have to send the department the bill for the testing I'm gonna get because this jack ass can't keep his bodily fluids to himself."

Toriani drew close and his breath crawled on the skin of my face.

I put my hand in the center of his chest and pushed him back. He fell back a little harder than he should, like a point guard drawing a charging foul, and landed back in the seat of his chair.

Toriani looked at Rod, "You see this? This fucker just assaulted a police office." He turned to me, "We're haulin' you in on this one, Fuzz-ball."

I continued with Rod, just because I knew it would piss him off, "Will you tell Fatso, here, that I have a better lawyer than y'all have, and if I see two seconds of a cell, not only will I beat those charges but I'll hit him with a lawsuit for exposing me to that syphilis laced spit he just sprayed all over me?"

Rod cracked a grin, but said, "Both of y'all shut up for a minute, and calm your pills."

I shrugged, "I came to you, Rod. I'd like to see at least a little respect for that."

"Respect!" Toriani said.

I kept my eyes on Rod.

He said, "How did you come to find Coach's body?"

I didn't think I could continue with the confidentiality block, I needed to give him some pieces to the puzzle, or Rod would agree with Toriani, and I would spend the night behind bars. I could give him some of the broken pieces I had. "I was working an infidelity case."

Rod butted in, "Whose infidelity? Coach wasn't married."

I wagged a finger at him in the negative. "When I heard

Coach didn't show for the game, I decided I'd check on him at the hotel."

"How'd you know what room to check?" Toriani blurted.

I ignored him. "I didn't think I was going to find what I did. When I saw him there, blood everywhere, all I could think was call the cops and get the hell out of there."

Rod repeated, "How did you know which room to check, Fuzz?"

I flashed a smile at Toriani, then returned to Uncle Rod. "They always booked the same room, at least as long as I was on the case."

"How long was that?" Rod asked.

I shook my head. "I don't know, a while."

"C'mon, Fuzzy, I know you bill by the day. You mean to tell me you don't know how many days you were on this?"

Toriani's seat creaked with his shifting mass. "Rod, let the little fucker think over his station in life tonight in the tank with a bunch of drunks. He'll sing like a canary in the morning."

Rod held my gaze, "No, he won't, Kev."

I knew Rod's next question before he asked it. I saw in the intensity of his stare and the way he grinned on one side of his mouth.

"What about Marisol Rodriguez?"

I wanted to come clean, to just wipe my hands of it all, and if I did, it's possible that nothing would stick to me. If Marisol hadn't come to me looking for help last night, it's possible I would have. If I hadn't talked to her father yesterday, it's certain I would have. Both of those things, happened. "What about her?" I said. "Different case. Though coincidentally she has a brother who played for Coach."

His eyes lingered on mine. It was as if he was trying to determine what card I was holding in the hole. He knew I was bluffing. He was as easy to read as me. He glanced over at Toriani, who had lost interest in the proceedings since they didn't involve throwing me in jail. Now, his partner dug in one of his ears with the end of his pencil. A look of disgust crawled onto Rod's face. When he returned his attention to me, I knew he wasn't going to ask me about the further coincidence of my visit to Coach and my requests regarding Marisol. At least, he wasn't going to crystalize that thought in his inept partner's mind.

"Anything else," I asked.

"Where were you on the night of Cain's murder, Fuzzy?"

I could feel Toriani's eyes piercing through the side of my face. It was almost as disconcerting as his breath. "I was in bed with the bartender. Didn't she tell you that?"

"But she wasn't with you when you found the body? You didn't try to get her to let you into the room Coach was found?"

"That's two separate questions," I said. "No she wasn't with me when I found the body. I guess she had more of a premonition about Coach than I did. She got cold feet. And, yes, of course, I tried to get her to find me a way into Coach's room. She could think of no way to do it without calling attention to us."

"You didn't try to force her?"

"Come on, Rod. How exactly would I do that? And does that sound like me?"

I felt the room shift with the stirring of the fat beast, but Rod stopped him by grabbing his bicep.

He kept his grip on Toriani's sweat slick arm, half on damp shirt sleeve, half on greasy, meaty flesh. It had to turn Rod's stomach. "Maybe not, Fuzzy. But then how did you get in the room?"

I had to be careful here, or I'd give them a reason that could see me behind bars for more questioning, a reason that would make things more difficult for my attorney. "It just so happened that the door was cracked open. The latch bolt was between the door and jamb. When I knocked on the door, it just swung open. When nobody answered, I got concerned and entered."

"So, you didn't break-in?" Rod asked.

"Of course, he did, Rod. Stop letting this fucker pull the wool over your eyes."

We both ignored Toriani, and went about the game of not showing our cards, not showing our tells. "Did you see any indication of breaking and entering?" I asked.

"No," he admitted.

I let a little grin escape. "Like I said, the door was open."

"You got anything you want to ask him, Kev?"

Again with the creaking chair, and the table sagged as he leaned onto it with his elbows. "Yeah," he said. "How did you know Tom Cain?"

I kept my eyes on Rod. I could hear Toriani huffing like a rhino. I answered, as if it were Rod, who asked the question. "I didn't. I've only spoken to him one time."

"And remind me again what you talked about." Toriani scoffed like he was getting ready to hear a good one-liner.

"I told Rod, already. Didn't he put it in the report?"

The table slid toward me. Its sides pressed into my midsection. It felt like getting kicked there all over again. I grunted in pain. It was a concession I hadn't wanted Toriani to see.

He stood over me now. His hands flat on the table. "I'm the one's asking the questions, Fuzz ball. And you'll answer them, or I'll have you tossed."

I was too busy fighting back the pain to argue with him, and the pain had distracted me. I looked up at him when he jumped to his feet. I hated acknowledging his presence in the room. "I'm a Manatees donor. I wanted to wish him luck in the game and pledge my support again for next year."

Softly Rod said, "You know we're able to check that out Fuzzy. We can find out if you're a booster."

"We can? Rod, who's bullshitting who now? We have checked that already!" Toriani was dropping slobber on the table like a mad dog now. He gathered my shirt front in his fist and pulled me half way across the table.

I bit down on my bottom lip, as my sore kidney slammed into the edge of the table.

"You no more gave money to CAU, than I did to Black Lives Matter." He realized that was probably the wrong thing to say and loosened his grip on my shirt.

I pulled free of him and straightened my T-shirt.

Rod nodded his head to the door. I thought it was him telling Kevin to get the hell out of there, but he thumbed the door. "Fuzzy, let's go."

Slowly, I stood. My insides screamed, but I kept as calm a face as I could manage.

Toriani tried to step in behind me. Rod placed his palm on his chest.

"Not this time, Rod", he said, trying to force his way past.

Rod stood firm. I prayed Kevin would push him just a little further, and Rod would knock him on his ass. "I need to talk to Fuzzy," he said.

"Rod you're gonna get us taken off this case for conflict of interest."

"I gotta talk to him, Kevin."

"Then we can finish up right here."

I opened the door and paused before I stepped out.

"No we can't Kevin. This is family stuff." Rod pulled Toriani close and whispered something into his ear. Toriani's face perpetually looked like someone had forgotten to flush the toilet, and while Rod whispered to him, he kept his eyes on me. His expression never changed, and his eyes never left me, but when Rod stepped away, he let the two of us leave the room without his escort.

When we got out of his earshot, I asked, "What did you tell him?"

"Just said I wanted some time to talk to you about your mom."

"And that worked, huh?"

His face remained deadpan, and he kept walking us out of the bullpen. "We all got mothers, Fuzzy. How's yours doing?"

We passed Cricket at the front desk, and I waited until we were outside until I answered his question. The sun was baking the morning cold away. It was turning out to be the nicest day we'd had in weeks. "Come on, Rod. You don't really want to talk about my mom."

He smacked me in the back of the head. "First, I wanna hear how your mom is doing. Then I'll talk about why I'm trying to knock some sense into you."

"She's in jail, Rod. How do you think she's doing?"

"How you think she'll be doing if you join her there?"

I didn't bother pointing out that the prison system wasn't co-ed. I also didn't educate him on how my mom would feel about me if I ended up behind bars. She'd think it was a riot. "Rod, you can't think I had anything to do with this."

"I don't, Fuzzy. I don't. I just think you're being fucking stupid again. When you do that shit starts sticking to everyone. I'm stupid, too, and I'm gonna let you take off. But we gonna have to talk about this little fling Marisol Rodriguez and Coach had at some time. And God help me, Fuzzy, if I find out she had something to do with his murder, I will beat you so bad, you'll wish I'd put you in the stir to be someone's bitch." He thought something over, play punched by broken ribs, and said, "Give your momma my best, next time you see her."

I'm pretty sure it was blood I tasted in my mouth from his

little love tap. "She asked about you last time I saw her. You should go see her," I lied.

He turned and walked away. Then, stopped and looked back at me. "And Fuzzy. Don't lose them pictures."

Fuck.

17

By the time I had completed the short drive from the Beach to Murrells Inlet, I had gone from a sense of imminent doom at how much Uncle Rod had already known to relief he already knew everything I was trying to keep hidden from him. I still had no intention of volunteering any of my evidence, but I felt the weight of playing the dishonesty game lifted from my shoulders. That weight rested on Rod's shoulders now, until he reported it. I'd worry about that if it ever happened.

The day continued to look like a late summer day with clear skies and a light breeze off the coast. I drove with the window down, and I could feel the bake of a light sunburn on the arm I propped on the door.

The inlet wasn't bustling with activity, but there was a promising number of girls strolling the streets dressed comfortably in loose fitting blouses and Capris for the light chill.

Which also meant there was a disproportionate number of boys for the season, strutting like cocks with chests puffed, all trying to catch the eye of the hens, more interested in what was in the shop windows.

I laughed at the duality of life. Twenty minutes ago, I was sweating getting thrown in jail by family. Now, I was girl watching in the off-season. As I pulled into the Marina, I noted that the Kingfisher, too, was reaping the benefit of the good weather. Passengers de-boarded from one of their half-day fishing trips, and the mates were tossing stringers full of short, fat sea bass to the waiting patrons. I also noted, Marisol's Beetle, as had Veronica, parked before my front door. Across the drive, in the spot reserved for The Royal Flush, a large sailing yacht away on one of its many long excursions, was Michaels in his simple white sedan. I could see his shock of red hair in the driver's side window. I wondered why he bothered with the games. Why not just hang out with Marisol in my place?

I decided to not bother with the games and backed in beside him.

I rolled down the passenger side window.

He did the same with his driver's side.

"What's up Michaels?"

He lifted his chin toward my place and Marisol's bug. "Your friends left shortly after Mari arrived. I didn't realize you had moved on from strippers and plump, but cute, bartenders to jailbait."

"Shut up, Michaels. I asked what's up."

A middle-aged blonde, who wore the years well, walked by. She wore a peach windbreaker over a white blouse knotted above her waistline to flaunt a tanned belly paid for at a local salon. Her hips swayed in cream colored flared slacks. Michaels admired her all the way down to the crowd breaking up at the Kingfisher. She took pictures of two teen-aged boys wielding a stringer of about half a dozen sea bass. It was a light catch for the $80 bucks she'd spent to send them out on the boat, but they were all smiling, and mom got pictures to put in the albums back home. So, in that regard, it was money well spent.

We both stopped our leering and returned to the matter at hand.

"You ever wonder about the similarities between the beating you took, and the one that killed Coach?" Michaels said.

His face showed no concern, no amusement. It was a neat trick with a face like Alfred E. Neuman.

I decided I didn't like it. It was all business. I preferred him looking like a fool. His question, though, was something I had felt peek its head up from the covers of my consciousness from time to time, but I kept throwing another blanket over it. Not wanting to examine the possibility.

Now with Michaels yanking the covers off, it was there naked, exposed, and shivering. The image of Sample beating the shark over the head with a little leaguer's baseball bat played in my mind like it was in Technicolor. The way he leaped into the air and chopped the bat down on the already dead fish was like the pride a lumberjack took in his performance in one of those wood splitting contests. I remember a similar look of amusement in Sample's face, when he watched his goons pound on me with golf clubs and pointed, leather cowboy boots. "Why are you here, Michaels? I thought the case was dead for you? Why aren't you back at MAD headquarters waiting for your next assignment?"

His lips curled in confusion for a moment. When it passed, he let goofy Neuman take residence on his face. "Just trying to help a brother in the profession." He pointed to my apartment. "Another piece of advice. Keep it zipped up with that one. I'd hate to see you and Mr. Johnson caught up in that Venus Fly-trap." With that he rolled away, his window sliding back in place, shutting out any retort I might come up with.

I had none.

WHEN I ENTERED MY APARTMENT, I found Marisol sprawled out on my couch, clicking through channels on the TV. She wore a loose fitting teal CAU Manatees T-shirt and white boxers pinstriped in teal. They nicely contrasted her tan legs. It reminded me of how Veronica dressed on the rare occasions when she had two nights off in a row, and she could spend a day lounging around my place with me. The thought gave me uncomfortable thoughts.

She hopped to her feet, and the bounce of her bust made me realize that she was going for the complete comfort get-up. No bra.

I took a deep breath. If nothing else, I didn't smell the perfume. I let that thought anchor me. "You left, Marisol?"

She smiled, "Yes, as much of a palace this place is, I still was getting the cabin fever. Besides, I had to get some of my things." She held her hands out, and a cocked a hip to display some of the things she had to get.

"I told you, Marisol. It's dangerous if you're seen here with me." I almost couldn't believe I bothered saying it. Bailey, Doc, and Michaels all now knew she was at my place. Not to mention Veronica, who knew someone with a cute Beetle, was shacking there. Rod knew I was holding pictures of her getting with Coach, right before his death. Yet, I still mocked concern that she took a trip into town to gather her things.

She waved away my suggestion of danger and walked past me to the door.

Marisol slid the curtain back to scan the outdoors. "Oh

you mean the cops? Fat dude with the military hairdo?" She did a gesture with her hand circling the top of her head to illustrate. "And skinny black dude following him around like an obedient puppy? I got rid of them easy."

"Yeah, how'd you do that?"

"I told them they had just missed you." She snapped her fingers. "You know the craziest thing. Sergeant Dickface called in, right after that. And then the two of them drove off. It was almost like they checked it out and you were over there talking to the cops."

Concern replaced her nonchalant look as she thought over what she just said.

I chuckled, "Sergeant Dickface?" I had to admit it was more catchy than Beetle Bailey.

SHE CONTINUED to stare out the window.

"Marisol, we need to talk about Michaels, and his investigation."

"What is there to tell? He wanted me to pose as a Lady Tee. Work the program, so I could set them up. I said screw that."

"But you became a Tee, anyway?"

Still she stared out the window. "That's right," she said. "Because fuck them."

I wasn't sure who "them" were.

She continued, "Did you know you have to be a student to be a Lady Tee? I'd come around to see Jandro. Coach saw me. I told him I would help him recruit, and I would do my best to the point where the recruits expected me to spread my legs, but I was no prostitute." She rested the crown of her head on the door. "Then I ended up spreading them for him."

Marisol Rodriguez was a sad, if not uncommon, case. She

had learned early on that she could get her way with men using sex, either actual or implied, and now she felt handcuffed by that behavior. I wondered if this had started in high school, with the boys or even worse with a teacher. The teacher would fit the pattern. I recalled Terri relating the story of how Marisol had acted with the boys at the gym. She had said boys, but it wasn't a leap to men. I remembered how certain Veronica was that Liza could make a fortune at the strip clubs, if she would break away from the migrant workers and concentrate on the dirty old white dudes. The DOWDs. I suspect Marisol understood that, and part of her inner turmoil was the pull of easy money, and being free of those self-imposed handcuffs. Hustling immigrants wasn't as lucrative, but it also kept those cuffs from tightening on her wrists. "Why did you want to be a Lady Tee anyway, Marisol?"

She slid the little black curtain back into place, shutting off the outside world. When she turned to face me there were tears in her eyes, "It sounded fun." She wiped the tears away with the heels of both hands and laughed, "Not the sleeping for money part. Just the getting to play college co-ed part. Hanging out on campus. Going to parties." She grinned at the thought. "That's how I met Billy. Jandro and some recruits would hunt Billy down for weed. I never touch the stuff myself, but I'd hang with the boys, and that's how I got to know Billy. Once we met, he kind of became like a pet. You know?" She said. "He was around a lot." She stopped to work something out. "I guess it's that way with a lot of men."

I had nothing to say to that. I was around a lot, too.

I didn't ask why she never enrolled. I knew she didn't have the funds. Everything in her story revolved around money. Jandro was in school because he could block and catch the pigskin. He and his teammates put fannies in the seats, wins in the standings, and money in the school's coffers.

Otherwise, he would be on the outside looking in like his sister. The Lady Tees gig was her way of stepping inside that world. I guess I could understand it. I was like Jandro. Maybe I could have worked my way up from Community College or something, bury myself in debt and eventually get a degree, but I was a drafted prospect. I gained entry to the inside because I could throw a ball faster than most kids. Once I got there, I was a consumable resource, like Jandro is today. Like Coach tried to make Marisol. Like he made other Lady Tees. "College life is fun," I admitted, as much to myself as to her.

"Right, and you know, I got to feel like I was part of something. The other girls were sweet. They all assumed I was doing recruits, too, and I never corrected them. I also tried not to judge them. They didn't act like whores."

I couldn't make that leap of logic. And I could not understand how she was steadfast in not prostituting herself as part of the recruiting program, but she could allow herself to do just that with Coach. But the psychoanalysis of Marisol Rodriguez would take someone with far greater expertise in the human psyche than me. I needed to get her to focus on how this all tied to Sample.

"So, did Sample know about Coach before he hired me?" I remembered how he described Coach when I told him I had the proof he was looking for.

Her face was free of tears now, and she looked her normal sensual and deceitful self. "I don't think so, but I guess it's possible. I think he assumed I was part of the Lady Tees escort service." She chuckled at her little joke, but it didn't seem authentic. "Figured Coach was behind pimping me, and that pissed him off."

"And when I found out about the relationship with Coach, he..."

Before I could finish, she blurted out, "Snapped."

I couldn't wipe the image of Sample and the shark from my mind. Now, the jowly face of Tom Cain was superimposed over the shark.

"My God, Fuzzy. He killed coach. Didn't he?"

I took out my phone and began to text Sample.

"What are you doing?"

"Texting Sample," I said. "Finding out where we can talk."

"He'll be at that stupid pier," she said.

I sent the message asking for a meet.

"Sample got protective of you didn't he?"

"I think he wanted in my pants, but he couldn't bring himself to make a move. Then, he got it in his mind I was putting out to college kids for money, and it drove him crazy."

"Did he say anything to make you think he could murder anyone, though?"

"He told me to stop doing what I was doing. What he thought I was doing," She lifted her shirt to expose her navel, and scratched a pink splotch right beside it. It humanized her in a way the forgotten tears had not. "He said he would take care of whoever was behind it. I got pissed at him for suggesting I had a pimp. It's so stereotypical of you white boys, you want a taste of Puerto Rico, but if you can't have it you assume we're all whores."

"So Sample sounds like a jealous dick. How do we come around to him killing coach?"

Her look painted me as a naïve school boy. "They kill people for a lot less. Don't they?" She stepped the three steps to my kitchenette, put two fingers down on the countertop there. Thought of something then returned to the front door. "What if Sample came to the same conclusion as Michaels?" She walked back to the kitchen. Back to the door. Nervous pacing wasn't a good look for her. "What if he thought on top of sleeping with recruits as part of Coach's plan I was also sleeping with Coach? Don't you think he could kill him?"

"Was it actually Coach's plan? Not some booster's?"

Her chin lifted and then dropped. "He never came out and told me. 'Hey, sleep with these recruits, and you'll get paid.' But I always figured that's because I told him upfront, that I wasn't there to prostitute myself." She had walked behind the counter now.

I hated that she could see my dirty dishes. It was silly. Those dirty dishes had sat there all morning in my absence. "How did he take that?"

"Fine. How else could he take it? He wanted me to himself, anyway."

I walked into the kitchenette, leaned a hip against the bar top.

She stood in front of the kitchen sink. She spoke to the wall. "They all want me to themselves."

The resignation, the matter of fact way she said it, saddened me.

I wanted to take her in my arms and comfort her, but I knew it would make me one of those guys who wanted her all to themselves. "How did it come to be with Coach?"

"I slept with Coach before I ever hosted a recruit," she said. "He tried to use an excuse about me not being eligible to be a Lady Tee because I wasn't a student. After I slept with him that was never an issue again."

She studied my face waiting for a reaction. "You have the most unexpressive face I've ever seen. Are you a machine? Do you have no emotion?" She went on studying, but she must have learned nothing, because she changed the subject. "I stopped talking to Billy after he pushed me on the prostitution stuff. Until I confronted him with this shit." She waved her hand up and down in front of me to let me know I, or my case, was "this shit."

"I accused him of attempting a blackmail scheme with Coach," it was a thought spoken aloud. "I'm not sure why that would make him want to kill the guy. If anything it should be one more reason for him to kick my ass." My finger went to the bandage on my cheek. "But I suppose, if you pile enough on a guy, he breaks." Again, I recalled the mindlessness of the shark beating.

WE SAT on my couch with paper plates on our laps, eating greasy New York-style pizza from a shop at the mouth of the marina. Marisol spent more time chewing on her finger nails than the pizza. Our little talk had died down and been replaced with a silence like quarreling lovers. The calm after the storm.

My phone buzzed.

The text was from Sample.

"I'm fishing tonight," it said.

I tossed the phone on the counter and took a deep breath.

Marisol chomped on her pinky nail between two incisors. "It was him, wasn't it?"

"Yep."

"You're going to meet him?"

"I am."

We stood. She on her toes. She draped her arms around my shoulders. All that pleasant girl flesh had stiffened with fear. It was still hard to beat. She laid her head against my chest. Her hair smelled like a bowl of strawberries and whipped cream.

I drew a breath deep down into the lower caverns of my lungs hoping to clear my mind of shameful thoughts. It only gave me a more powerful whiff of her.

"Oh God. Fuzzy, be careful," she said.

18

The sun painted beautiful light on the ocean and pastels in the sky as it kissed the horizon.

I paid my walker's fee to different help and made my way to the end of the pier.

Sample wasn't there.

It meant nothing. Maybe he hadn't made it there yet. He said he was fishing tonight. It was only just now sunset. Still, it didn't feel right.

A teenaged kid was draping a cast net over his shoulder. He put a piece of the outer edge of the net in his mouth, biting down on the rope between two lead weights. He spun a full 360 degrees, spraying flecks of cold sea water onto my t-shirt. Just as he completed the rotation, he released the net from one hand and his mouth. It launched into the air and opened in a perfect circle. Tethered by a loop around the kid's other wrist, when it reach the extent of the length of the rope, it hung for a fraction of a second and dropped straight down. The sinkers took it quickly to the sea bottom, and the kid leaned over the pier's railing and began the labor of pulling up the net, heavy with its own weight, seaweed, and baitfish. As I watched the strain build in the jaws on the side of his face, and cords of his arm muscles flex, I realized that I knew the face.

He was the kid that reeled up the shark the other night. The shark that's image I could not get out of my mind. The one Sample tortured with the baseball bat.

The kid hauled the net over the rail and onto the deck. The net flashed with the silver sides of jumping bait fish fighting for air. The kid began the process of filling his bait bucket with his catch.

When he had a bucket full of bait, I stepped closer. "Hey have you seen Sample around?"

"Sample?"

"Sorry. Billy. Billy Smith."

He searched my face. "Do I know you, mister?"

"We didn't meet," I held my hand out. "Fuzzy Koella. I was here the other night when you caught that big shark."

He took my hand cautiously.

"Obviously, you were preoccupied with other things." I flashed my best, "hey I'm one of the boys," smiles.

"Fuzzy? You know I kinda remember the name, but I don't remember the face. You were talking to Billy about something. It got him a little worked up."

Don't paint me a picture, kid.

I took my hand back because the kid had a cold fish handshake that was creeping me out. "I didn't catch your name the other night," I said.

"Dickie," he said. "Dickie Stern."

This kid probably caught, as much shit for his name, as Sample caught for his nickname. "Nice to meet you Dickie. That sure was a nice fish you caught the other night."

"Thanks." He looked anxiously at his bait bucket and rods he had lined up on the railing.

"Yeah, well, I won't take up your time. I'm just looking for Billy. He said he'd meet me here."

"You just missed him. He got some text, said he had some business he had to go to." He looked out to the gleaming, colorful beach resorts lined down the coast. He didn't want to look me in the eye when he mentioned Sample's business.

"I know he deals, Dickie. It's cool. But it is kind of important that I see him. Do you know where he was headed?"

He thought it over, doing a little shuffle with his feet, like he was kid needing to pee. "Most of his deliveries this time a year, are down by Yaupon. Down by the Kingdom."

Yaupon made its way into the papers for its supposed trade in prostitution and drugs, but you wouldn't know it by day and most of the night during the season. It ran right along the amusement park and emptied onto Ocean Boulevard. I don't think I'd seen anything but tourists walking that street before midnight. It was comforting to know that the papers got it right, and there was some drug trade down there. Even if it was a low-life punk like Billy Smith.

"Thanks, Dickie. Good luck, tonight."

He frowned at the that. "I'm gonna need it. I've been skunked ever since that shark. I tell Billy it's on account of what he did to that shark. Like, what is it they call it?"

"Bad karma?"

"That's it."

"Don't sweat it, kid. I bet your luck changes tonight."

He let me know the conversation was over by reaching into his bucket and fishing out a squirming greenback minnow.

They were a good all-around baitfish, I suspected his luck would be just fine.

Mine on the other hand? Even with the information Dickie shared, I still had a bad feeling about Sample. I could use a change in luck, too.

EVEN AFTER ALL THESE YEARS, a drive down Ocean Boulevard in November was a sobering experience. Only two to three months removed from bumper-to-bumper traffic, this felt like shifting from 10th gear to 1st on your ten-speed bike. I kept the needle under the 35 miles per hour speed limit, and I still made it to my destination in a swift ten minutes.

I pulled into the abandoned parking lot of the Friendly's Ice Cream stand on the southeast corner of the Family Kingdom. It was open but the kids working inside sat at booths scrolling their thumbs over the surface of their smartphones. Even at minimum wage, they were overpaid, but it balanced out if they had also worked the summer, when they worked as hard as most construction workers feeding the fat, sunburned faces of middle America down from the Midwest states. I still had something turning in my stomach, and I remembered that I was walking into some drug business. So, I grabbed my piece from the glove box. Checked the safety and stuffed it in my waist band above the crack of my ass.

I stepped to the sidewalk on Yaupon. It seemed stranded. For some reason, I hurried in a jog-run back across the Friendly's parking lot, behind the restaurant, and slowed to a walk once I crossed over into the park.

It was so quiet that I could hear each of my footsteps echo off the structure of the log flume ride. I scanned the full 180 degrees constantly as I walked deeper into the park. Every so often, I stopped and turned around to scan the area I had just walked through.

By the time I got to the other side of the park, I felt reasonably comfortable that I had the place cased, and no one was tailing me.

Then underneath the trusses of the Swamp Fox in the crushed stone gravel I saw a fracas.

A young blond guy, who looked straight from Muscle Beach, wrenched back the arms of a thin bald man kneeling in the gravel. The bald guy's head was slung low. Two men, built like Mr. Muscle Beach stood, in front of him.

Even in the dark of the Swamp Fox's shadows I recognized the pale bald head, as belonging to Sample. A mumbled voice came from one of the two captors in front of Sample. Then, a foot shot out from the one on the right, landing a side-kick that so violently snapped Sample's neck back that I could hear the pop of cartilage in his neck even at fifty yards.

I froze for a second. Wiped my damp palm on my pants leg.

Long enough for another kick to Sample's face. This time from the other. His whole body displaced on the force of the kick, but the blond guy held firmly onto his arms and dragged him back into place before the kicking duo.

I'd seen enough. I yanked my rod, thumbed the safety off, and sprinted in Sample's direction.

Muscle Beach caught my sprinting shape almost immediately.

I skidded to a stop just as I entered the gravel base below the rollercoaster.

"What the fuck?" Muscle Beach dropped one of Sample's arms, and pointed at me.

I held the gun in the air and squeezed a round off. Despite the ringing of the shot in my ears, and the sound of the round ricocheting off the structure above, I heard footsteps hurrying in the stones to my left.

I turned.

And was hit by a blow that felt like a diesel truck running over me. I didn't lose conscious, but I did lose my gun. It flew loose of my grip on contact, and my assailant scurried after it.

I expected him to turn and level my own piece on me but he picked it up and kept on. Hardly slowing his sprint in reaching down to pick up the gun. His level of dexterity at his size and power was impressive. I turned to look in Sample's direction and saw his three assailants speeding off in a similar fashion. They entered the empty street adjacent to the Fox. It was too dark to make out anything but their massive forms as they turned the corner and out of sight.

Sample lay like a sack of garbage in the shadows of the Fox.

19

Unfortunately, I couldn't check on Sample, and I couldn't stick around and wait for the ambulance to get there. I didn't need to call it in, either. The approach of police cruisers bleated out in the night. Shots fired in a small town had that effect.

I didn't run, and I didn't toss the gun, because I had done nothing illegal. I made my way to the west end of the park, bordering on Kings Highway, and exited the park onto the sidewalk, four flashing cruisers screamed to a halt in the parking lot where my truck sat. Cops of varying sizes and shapes gathered outside their cars.

Predictably, their strategy involved four groups of partners entering at the perimeter four corners and working their way towards the center.

I skipped across the street and watched from the west corner of Kings and Yaupon. I shared my viewing corner with a plump black woman in a too short, silver dress with matching dollar store pumps. She may have been one of those working girls, I had said I'd never seen in the area.

I watched as two cops, a tall, beefy male and short, fit female, arrived at the corner across the street from us.

They stood for a short time. The female, a red-head with a stern, all-business face, held her radio at the ready in one hand. Her partner had his automatic pistol drawn. She nodded her head, and they both entered the park.

"Did you see what happened?" I said out of the side of my mouth.

She stepped forward into my peripheral vision. She dropped a cigarette, and stomped it out with one of her stems. "You tell me, sugar?"

I realized I didn't want to know what she'd seen, and I didn't want to be around when the police got around to asking her, either. When Myrtle Beach's finest disappeared into the bowels of the Kingdom, I trotted across King's and down Yaupon to my truck.

The cop cars were on the other side of the lot. My truck was still the only other vehicle. A small gathering of tourists taking advantage of the $50 per night rates the offseason brought, stood on the corner of Ocean and Yaupon watching the show. I slipped into my truck and out of the lot drawing no attention. They were all busy watching, listening to the guts of the amusement park, hoping for more hell to break loose.

WHEN I GOT home that night, there was no Marisol Rodriguez.

I set the alarm on my phone for 5 a.m., and set out to get a good night's sleep, but images of Sample taking a beating made sleep impossible.

Marisol Rodriguez had convinced me that Sample could have killed Coach, and I wasn't even able to look into it before someone beat Sample within seconds of his life. I knew if I had not fired that shot, had not arrived when I did, Sample would be another dead body reported in the paper. Now Marisol was gone.

Michaels's opinion of Marisol aligned with mine before she had convinced me she needed help. Maybe I was back to seeing her as bad news, but I couldn't quite get there, either.

I kept coming back to baseball bats. Sample swung one at the pier. Mr. Rodriguez wielded one in his home with pride. I don't know why, but I was sure a baseball bat was the weapon used to kill Tom Cain.

I texted my Uncle Rod, "Any idea on weapon?"

It was 3 a.m. I didn't expect a response until sunrise, at least, when mortals without a guilty conscience awake.

I was wrong.

"Baseball bat. Wood. We're going with."

Wood.

Both bats were wood. Sample's and Papi Rodriguez's.

Another text from Rod, "Why?"

I turned off my phone and crawled out of bed. I pulled on a pair of well-worn jeans, a black concert T-shirt from some band called Rumor Jenkins, that I had no recollection of ever seeing, and slid my feet into a pair of leather, soft-soled moccasins. I looked like I was just getting dressed to step outside for a smoke. I got in my truck and drove to Grand Strand Medical Center.

I PULLED in to a spot on the first level of a stacked, covered garage. Much like the season, the hospital was bare at 4 a.m. I went through the sliding doors into the bright, sterile light, and I could feel cold fingers tickle my bruised ribs. The cold gripped my bludgeoned kidney. Even my healing cheek felt the scrape of an icy finger nail. One sleepy woman with blue gray hair and bags under her eyes that could carry my entire wardrobe tried to smile. She should have given it a rest, she had the teeth of a lifelong coffee drinker.

I kept my distance at the reception desk, as to not enter the aura of her breath.

"How may I help you?"

"I was hoping to see Billy Smith," I said.

She tapped away on her keyboard. The clickety-clack was so fast I assumed she was doing it for show, and the monitor was off, and she knew all the room assignments by heart. The keyboard went silent. She frowned. He's on floor three. Visiting hours do not start back up again until 8 a.m, She made a show of looking at her watch, and frowning again. "Sorry."

"It's okay," I said. "It was a long shot. I'm meeting someone for breakfast at sunrise, and I sometimes forget how easy it is to get around in the offseason. I'm a little early."

Deadpan face on blue hair now. The name plate on the desk tagged her as Mrs. M. K. Morris. M. K. short for Mary Kay? I hated that name. Every Mary Kay I'd known had a personality like this one, friendly, but fake. A crab waiting behind the facade. "Our cafe doesn't open until 9 a.m.," she said.

"Oh no, I'm not meeting my friend here. I would never subject her to hospital food."

That turned her face sour. I half expected her adroit keyboard fingers to fuse into hard-shelled crab pinchers.

I continued, "I gave this a try figuring I could kill two birds with one stone, while I wait on meeting my friend over at the Waffle King. It's okay though, after breakfast I have meetings for work out this way, so I can still swing by during visiting hours."

Her eyes crawled up and down me. At first, I thought she

was checking me out. Then I remembered my attire and realized I didn't look like someone going to business meetings. I should never make that mistake as I am never dressed for business meetings. I stopped her inspection and judgement by asking where the men's room was.

She pointed off to the left. "Down that way, on the left right before you reach the cafe."

"Thanks."

As I walked off, I heard the keyboard come to life again.

Further down the hall, beyond the cafe, I saw the illuminated exit sign. I looked at Mrs. Blue Hair, the keyboard warrior, still preoccupied with her computer screen.

Through the exit door, I found myself in a stairwell that also had an egress door that emptied into the world. I took the stairs up to the third floor.

The door spilled me out into a dimly lit hospital floor like any other. I realized Mrs. Blue Hair never gave me Sample's room number, making the chore more difficult.

A halo of light half down the hall gave me a clear idea of where the nurse's station was, and the elevator lobby, too.

I had the hallway to myself, and there were plenty of carts and medical equipment on rollers to give me cover as I began my process of elimination. I'd figure out what to do about the other side, once I got close to the nurse's beacon of light.

I nudged open the doorway to 331, the room was lit by a small task light mounted above a narrow desk opposite an empty bed. Beyond the bed there was a curtain bifurcating the room. I stepped to the curtain, my soft soled moccasins serving their purpose.

I peered around the curtain, and saw a skeleton of a man, his skin stretched tight over his bones, and a hospital gown draped over him. Wires and tubes radiated from his arms and chest. He slept atop the covers. His head tilted back at such an angle and his chin thrusted to the ceiling that he looked like he was struggling for his last breath. His cheeks were hollow and puckered. The image was a reminder of why I tried, unsuccessfully, to stay away from hospitals.

An old sculpture of sleeping death opened her eyes as I stepped into another room. Spooked, I nearly slipped on the slick, polished vinyl floor. But I noticed her eyes had gone a ghostly, blue gray with cataracts, and realized she could not see me. I regained my footing and snuck back out without checking her roommate behind the curtain.

It was a calculated risk, not to check. It paid off. The next room I checked was Sample's.

He had the room all to himself. He didn't look much better than all the old dying folks he shared the floor with, and he had no less equipment hooked to him.

I closed the door behind me and lifted one of the visitor's chairs as quietly as I could and placed it down close to his bedside.

I took a seat.

And waited.

He had lacerations like mine on both sides of his face, and yellowish-brown half-moons were forming under his eyes. He had a gauze bandage taped across the top of his head, leading me to believe he'd received a lot of stitches up there. He grimaced with the slightest movement. He was worse off than I was, but neither of us were the picture of health.

Time crawled, and I feared a nurse would catch me before I could talk to Sample. Just as dawn light seeped into the room through the gauzy curtains in the window, Sample opened his eyes, and licked his lips with a pasty tongue.

A dry glass sat on his tray pushed away to the other side of his bed. I walked to the other side of the bed and grabbed the glass.

Sample followed my motions with wide, if sleepy, eyes.

I filled the glass from a faucet in the room's toilet room.

I handed it to Sample.

He drank ravenously.

I took my seat.

"It was you who fired that shot?" he rasped.

I nodded.

His glass was empty again, and he handed it to me.

"You want more?"

He frowned and shook his head. "You saved my life, Fuzzy."

I said nothing.

He grunted like a caught fish gasping for air. He swiped his lips with his tongue again, making a sandpaper-like sound.

"Thanks," he said. "You're a good friend, Fuzzy."

I let it hang there in the air. Sample wasn't my friend anymore, but there was no use in making that correction. I was feeling guilty about making him carry the conversation though.

But carry it he did, his eyes settled on the bandage on my face. He reached up and patted his much larger bandage on his head. "How are you healing up?"

"Not so good," I admitted. "I suggest you stick around and take your doctor's advice."

There was a slight shake of his head, and the corners of his mouth upturned a millimeter.

"You're as stubborn as me," I said.

"It's the Seahawk way."

He referred to our mascot for Myrtle Beach High, back when we were friends.

"Who did this to you, Samp?"

He looked to the pale light seeping in the window. "Football players. Don't you think?"

They were the size for it. And I remembered the hit I took from the guy after I fired my shot. "It would seem so," I said. "But what would football players want with you?"

"Fuzzy, I ain't come clean with you," he said. "And I hate that the most about the beating we gave you. A football player asked me to hire you to find out about Marisol."

"Jandro Rodriguez?"

Sample nodded.

"He asked you to hire a private eye? How did he get around to asking local weed peddler to hire a private eye? Do y'all typically have private eyes on the hook, waiting on your orders?"

"Nah, it ain't like that. He was going on about his sister a couple of months ago. Worried she was getting into some bad stuff. I mean he was a recruit, too. Last fall. He knows the welcome those Lady Tees give the recruits." Sample's lips shivered at that last revelation.

"So, you're telling me Jandro is the overprotective brother?"

He nodded again. The pained look on his face showed how much it hurt him to do so. "I followed Marisol around for a bit. I got to know her, through Jandro. She's quite a girl. I never caught her in the act with any of those players. I made a couple of passing comments about the rumors of the recruiting girls. She seemed pissed about me sayin' that. In that month, she started gettin' herself nice things. Seemed to have some extra lettuce. And every time she mentioned Coach she seemed kinda sweet on him. That's when I called you. I ain't made for this shit."

"So Jandro is behind this?"

"I can't remember if I saw his face or not. They was big motherfuckers though."

"Come on, Samp. They were standing right in front of you. And you're going to tell me you can't remember if Jandro was there?"

His eyes shifted off me. "You know they say they had to bring me back? I think I glimpsed heaven, too."

"Yeah, heaven, huh? They let the likes of you in there."

"Ain't that something", he said, still keeping his eyes off me.

"What was that like? Heaven that is."

"It ain't bad," he turned to me and smiled a gap-tooth smile, his bridgework removed. His lips cracked at the healing wounds left by Janro's lackeys. Fresh blood seeped from them. "Nah, Heaven ain't bad, at all. But what's a guy like me gonna do in heaven?" He laughed, and it was the most pitiful sight. His hands - one went to his bandaged head, and one to his side. The laughter mixed with groans of pain, but he couldn't help himself the more he tried not to laugh, the more he carried on.

I couldn't help myself. I laughed too. The funniest jokes were the one's grounded in truth, and there was a lot of truth in his observation on heaven. If they ever had me, I'd hold the same position as Sample. "But why would Jandro want to send you to heaven?"

"He asked for the pictures. The ones you took. I said I ain't had 'em."

"Jesus Christ, Sample. How come you didn't tell me?"

His eyes widened. "I didn't know. He said 'Meet me.' So I did. But it ain't only the pictures. I think he could tell I'd takin' a likin' to his sister." He frowned at that thought. "I know guys like me, ain't gettin' a girl like Marisol."

"Samp, you're like ten years older than her."

He waved that off, and his face tensed with pain. "She ain't gettin' with a guy like me. But you know when we were together, sometimes, and we would talk. I dunno, she made me feel special. 'Fore I knew it I was thinkin', maybe. You know, just maybe."

It was a sad confession from Sample. He was right. I'd never seen him land a girl like Marisol. In fact, I hadn't seen him land many girls at all. "And you think Jandro, did this to you because you had a crush on his sister?"

"He was talkin' crazy shit."

I realized he had given up acting like he couldn't remember if Jandro had been there. Sample's inability to lie was legendary. I let him continue.

"Like somehow I killed Coach. Or maybe his sister. And I was holding back the pictures to protect her."

"Wait a minute, Jandro did this to you? And he is saying he had nothing to do with Coach?"

"I dunno, Fuzzy. Jandro's always had a crazy ass temper. Maybe he forgets shit. It wouldn't surprise me. I once saw him beat some boy from Conway High with a baseball bat, just 'cause the cat said they was gonna beat the Seahawks ass and wax his sister's."

Baseball bat again. This shit was getting confusing.

"I would think he'd remember beating his Coach to death, though. So, either he didn't do it or he's acting like he didn't."

He lifted his eyes. His eyelids were red, which gave the tears growing there the look of blood. "He knows it's you who took those pictures, Fuzzy."

My phoned buzzed. A text from Veronica.

"Breakfast?"

Only maybe an hour past sunrise. Could this day get any stranger?

I texted back to meet me at the Waffle King near the hospital in about an hour.

See? I hadn't lied to Mrs. Blue Hair, the Keyboard Warrior.

I turned my attention back to Sample. "Don't sweat it, Sample. I'm sure Marisol already shared that with him. That isn't your fault."

"I think he thinks you is gettin' with his sister, too."

Great, now I had an over-protective tight-end brother

with roid-raid issues thinking I was sleeping with his 19-year-old sister. I kept my concern off my face. I stood up, and patted Sample on his foot, "Don't sweat it buddy."

I left through the door just as a cute black nurse in magenta scrubs arrived. She looked at me funny.

"He's all yours," I said, and walked down the hall to the exit. I could feel her watching me.

She didn't call security because I made it out without incident. The morning sun was a false sense of optimism, on what had already been a turbulent stormy morning.

20

I pulled into the Waffle King. It was a new one, so the door, tabletops, the vinyl bench seats - none of them stuck to me.

I waited for Veronica.

This time she was only 15 minutes late.

Her hair was disheveled. No make-up hid the bags under her eyes. She wore a My Morning Jacket t-shirt I had lent her over a year ago and had never seen since, and a pair of nylon soccer shorts, a nod to the pleasant weather.

I stood as she approached the booth.

She smiled at that, but it was a weary one. "Don't be silly," she said. "Sit back down."

We both slid into the booth.

"Didn't work last night?"

"Huh?" she said. "I worked. What makes you think I didn't?"

She looked like she had just woken up from a full night's sleep, but I knew better than to step in to that one. "No reason, I guess," I stumbled on my words before landing on,

"When we have breakfast after work nights it's at 2 a.m., not after sunrise."

She didn't acknowledge my explanation. Instead, she scanned the menu.

"What's up, V?"

She peered up at me. "It's probably nothing, Fuzzy. But it's gotten weird at work."

Occupational hazard, I would think. "How so?"

"Um, I'm getting a lot of propositions the last two nights."

She emphasized "a lot" to make sure I didn't miss it, but I'm dense. So, I asked about the propositions.

She gave me an "are you serious" stare.

"What? You're a stripper. A beautiful stripper. I'll add. I would think you get guys asking you out a lot."

This time, I punctuated it.

"I mean 'takeout'. Guys wanting to pay me for out of club extras. I probably wouldn't think anything, except they aren't the type."

"What is the type?"

"Dirty old men. They aren't that. DOWDs have the money to afford that stuff."

"Okay so what type are these customers."

"Kids," she said. "College-aged. If it was only one, no big deal. But I've gotten about ten propositions in the last couple of days. All from young kids. Jock-types."

That last part got my attention. "Jocks?"

She patted my hand. "Don't worry, Fuzzy. I'm not passing judgement on your kind."

That stung a little and was a good reminder that this woman had just told me she wanted nothing to do with me.

"I'm simply trying to understand what the problem is, V."

"It's like the college football team is ganging up on me, Fuzzy. They even have these looks on their faces, when they're doing this. Like they're in on some secret joke."

Football players. I was trying to figure out how they'd connected me and Veronica. Then I remembered, again, this woman wanted nothing to do with me. "You tell Paddy? Or the owner?"

"No," she said. "For all I know they'd encourage this."

I shrugged. "What do you want me to do?"

Her jaw hinged open. "Unbelievable. You're trying the dick ex-boyfriend on for size, are you?"

"No, but I will not sit here and catch punches, V. Keep it up and I punch back."

She looked over her shoulder to make sure neither of the waitresses were within earshot. She leaned forward and whispered, "Is that some kind of threat? Punch back, what the fuck, Fuzzy."

"I was speaking metaphorically." I watched as a rail thin waitress, who must have been at least six foot tall approached. She was pretty in an understated way. Her name plate said, "Emelia". She asked what we'd like to drink with a thick Latina accent.

We both ordered coffee.

I waited until she walked away. She didn't have much to look at from behind, but I let my eyes hover there, anyway.

When I returned my attention to Veronica, she stared at me with pure hatred. "You called me here," I said. "Now what is it you want me to do?"

She got up and tossed two bucks on the table. "Nothing," she said. "I want you to do absolutely nothing."

I felt proud of myself for not letting myself get all walked over until she pulled away, then I felt like shit.

21

I ate a light breakfast of poached eggs and grits. I drank three mugs of coffee in the process to keep the cobwebs of sleep deprivation at bay.

Still in the parking lot of the Waffle King, I dialed my uncle's personal cell phone. I expected to leave a voicemail, but he surprised me and picked up during work hours.

"Fuzzy, where the hell are you?"

"And good morning to you, too."

"You're gonna have to come clean with the pictures, Fuzzy. Toriani has a wild hair up his ass, and he's putting my nuts in a vice, because he thinks I'm holding info back from him. And the hell of it is, I am!"

"I don't know what you're talking about." I said it with a complete lack of emotion. "Look, the reason I called..."

He didn't let me finish. "Fuzzy, I know you have pictures of Coach and Marisol. Don't make me get a warrant."

"Since I don't know what you're talking about I suggest you get that warrant." My hands shook, and I suddenly had the urge to urinate, but somehow I kept my voice steady. "I need you to make sure you put an officer on William Smith's room over at Grand Strand Medical."

"Say what?"

"William Smith. Y'all brought him there last night. Assault victim, found over at the Kingdom."

"Oh. My. God. You fired the shot?"

"Well, now that you mention it. I need to file a report on my missing piece."

"Oh, so, what you're saying is someone stole your gun and then used it to fire a shot over at the Fox last night."

"Not what I'm saying at all. I fired the shot to keep them from killing Billy. But someone knocked it out of my hands and then ran off with it."

There was a prolonged pause, then his breath exhaled in my ear. "Get your ass to the station, Fuzzy. I will meet you there."

I started to protest, but he wasn't there.

Two cruisers, and my Uncle Rod's Chrysler 300 sat in front of my place at the marina. Across the lot, in front of The Royal Flush's mooring, Michaels's boring white sedan was parallel parked.

Missing was Marisol's Beetle.

I backed in beside Rod's waxed car. It was black, and like the feathers of a raven shined so bright it was almost blue.

As I threw the gear shift into park, Beetle Bailey, excuse me Sergeant Dickface, and Doc crawled out of their cruiser. Two kids, with crewcuts clipped to the scalp, followed suit. Rod remained in his car.

I got out.

"Time to stop fooling around, Koella. You're coming with us," Dickface said.

I walked around the front of my truck, and around to the driver's side of Rod's car.

Dickface stepped in my path. "Hey numb nuts, Koella."

I tried to swerve around him, but he was more dextrous than he looked and he sidestepped in front of me. "Outta the way, Bailey."

A look of confusion came over him, but he didn't dwell on the Bailey comment for long. He reached for my arm. "Can't do it, Koella. This time you come with us."

I tried to break my arm free, but doing so unleashed fresh pain in my ribcage. I continued to struggle, but I got nowhere.

Doc put his hand on my arm.

The two kids, straight out of the academy, grinned. I'm sure if I looked at Michaels I'd see a similar dumb look staring back at me.

When I gave up the struggle, Rod swung open the door of his car. He stepped out with all the aplomb of a Mafioso Don. His brilliant smile was missing, and the deadly stare of the pitcher carrying a no-hitter into the ninth replaced it. He nodded to Bailey and Doc.

I yanked my arms free, when I felt their grips loosen. "I thought we were meeting at the station."

"We decided to wait on you here. I figured you would stop by here first."

"Wait?" I said. "You were here when I called?"

"You're a popular guy, Fuzz. Everyone wants to talk to you, and we're losing our patience."

"Did you get a man on my friends hotel room, like I asked?"

He waved me over. "Let's go inside and have a word about that, too."

I knew it was all a ploy to get a look inside my place

without a warrant. With Marisol gone, I didn't care. I walked past him.

He tried to put an arm around my shoulder.

I slipped it.

I could hear the Keystone Cops shuffling there feet behind us.

"I'm gonna take care of this, boys. Y'all can head on back to the station."

Dickface started, "But ...."

Rod stopped him short, "I can handle this one. Trust me."

Inside, my place smelled like girlish perfume. Marisol had left her t-shirt, boxers, and a pair of white cotton panties piled on the arm of the sofa.

"Still dating strippers, Fuzz?"

I let that go, and tossed Marisol's things in a small plastic laundry basket. "What's this all about, now, Rod?"

He held his palms out. "You tell me."

"What do you want me to tell you?"

He scanned my tiny place, looking for obvious hidey holes. "What happened to your friend last night?"

"How the hell should I know? I was just going to see him, and I show up as he's getting his face beat in."

"Fuzzy, your friend is a known dealer. Only reason he hasn't done time is he otherwise stays out of trouble. The Fox this time a year, is where guys like him peddle their weed. Now over a few days, we find you and your friend there and ship both of you to Grand Strand Medical with ass beatings. With all due respect, Fuzzy. You tell me what the hell is going on."

My Uncle was a patient person. It's one of his best qualities as a human, and certainly as a detective. I could tell he was losing his patience, and I suspected that, as with most patient men, when he lost his patience it would be like the boiling over of a long dormant volcano. Nobody, least of all me, would want to be around for that.

So I laid it all on him. How Sample had hired me to catch Marisol in the act. How when I had, I suspected him of blackmail. How I had tried to make things right by approaching Coach and Marisol. How all hell had broken loose after that. I even told him my suspicions of Jandro Rodriguez and why. The only thing I left out was that those were Marisol Rodriguez's panties on my sofa. If I had recalled the drive-bys, I would have told him that, too. But I had forgotten about them.

By the time I finished, Rod paced the room like an anxious tiger in a cage at meal time. "So you have these pictures?"

"I can't give them to you, Rod. She's a good kid, and if they get out now, the press will just paint her as a whore."

"Right, and when they get out later, she'll be a madonna?"

"You know they exist, Rod. Is having them in hand going to increase your odds of finding a killer in any way?"

"Goddamnit, Fuzzy. This is how you're going to get me kicked off the force," he said.

I could see he was looking it over from all angles in his mind. "The pictures are in my safe deposit box, Rod. It's a Saturday morning. On Monday, I will drop them off."

He frowned, but nodded his head. "Fair enough," he said, but he jabbed his index finger at me. "You know I could have the bank opened for this."

"I know," I said. "Rod, I hope we can manage this. So the spin doesn't go out of control and ruin a nineteen-year-old girl's life."

"Bring her in to see me, and we'll see what we can do. She ain't been home for two days."

I thought of the panties wadded up on my floor. "I don't know where she is."

They say the truth will set you free. God, I hope so.
It had at least kept me out of jail for the moment.

22

A fter Rod and his entourage left empty-handed, I scanned the lot only to find that Michaels had disappeared on me again. The dude was a mystery inside this mystery.

I was at a loss for things to do. I suspected the police would visit Jandro Rodriguez, and when they didn't arrest him (and they wouldn't), he would be even more pissed off. If he put two and two together, I'd need some home remodeling. Or a plot, at the cemetery.

I couldn't stand the thought of waiting around. So, I went to Molly Maguire's.

IT WAS ten a.m. on a Saturday morning, when I pulled into Molly Maguire's. Maybe if it had been July, there would be activity at the club. But it wasn't July, so there were only two vehicles in the lot. One was a twenty-year-old, maroon Jag in need of a paint job. The other was a primer gray, 70s model pickup that had not moved in at least two years. The Jag belonged to the owner, Donnie Stratavini, an Italian who looked British. He got the cold shoulder treatment from the Italians. He hated it.

I walked in the back door of the club without knocking, and found myself in a dingy, nicotine-smelling corridor. The girls dressing room was on my right through an open door. Mirrors and vanity tops lined the walls and the haze of last night's cigarette smoke clung to the ceiling. On my left, was a flimsy looking white, turning brown door with the word Office written on it in black Sharpie marker. Coming into the corridor from the club and right at me was Donnie Stratavini.

He stood maybe five-seven and had Sample's build. His face was absent any wrinkles despite his age of greater than sixty years, but if you looked closely, you could see the scars his vanity had placed there. He wore a satiny, gray shirt open at the collar to reveal a hairless chest and a gold rope chain the thickness of a school pencil. He had on white slacks after Labor Day, which painted him as the Yankee he was.

"What the hell are you doing there? We're closed, and this place is off limits!"

"Need to talk to you Donnie."

As he stepped closer, a look of recognition came over his face. "You?" He shook his pointer finger at me. "You're the one with Veronica."

I stepped forward to him and held my hand out, "Fuzzy Koella."

He ignored the offered hand. "What the fuck kind of name is that? Koella?"

I was taken back by him questioning the last name and not the first.

"Don't sound Italian, but I don't know, maybe?"

"French on my dad's side," I confessed.

He gave me a suspicious look. "Don't sound French

either. But hey, you can't be in here. I can't have no guys snooping around the girl's dressing room. I run a tight ship."

I must not have kept a straight face.

"Look, I'll have you thrown out on your ass. Wipe that smile off your face."

He was a clown. It took all of my effort not to laugh my ass off at this little man, thinking he's the next Don Corleone, and going to muscle me around. "I'm here for Veronica. She's nervous and doesn't feel safe here."

"She don't feel safe, huh? How come she don't talk to me?"

"That's what I asked her Donnie? I don't know why, she just gave me that look. You know that look?"

He flashed a crooked grin. He opened the door to the office and stood aside so I could enter. "I know the look."

It was an eight foot-by-eight foot-by-eight foot cube with stained acoustical ceiling tiles, stained vinyl floors, and stained sheetrock walls. Two black metal filing cabinets were jammed in a corner. A fold-out card table pretended to be a desk in the center of the room.

Stratavini gestured at a metal folding chair with a blue vinyl seat cushion.

I took a seat in it.

He sat in a Wal-Mart special, rolling office chair. He took a metal cash box sitting on the table and placed it on the floor at his feet.

"Sometimes these girls get spooked easy," he said. "What's bothering Veronica?"

He held that crooked grin trying to make light of the situation.

I kept it serious. "Veronica's been working the clubs long enough to know when something stinks."

"You'd think so, but..."

I cut him off mid-sentence, and by the look on his face he

wasn't used to it. I didn't care. He was still a joke. "She knows when something stinks, Stratavini. She knows better than you or I."

"Okay, okay. So what's going on?"

I sighed, because I knew it wouldn't sound as serious as I was making it out to be. "She's having problems with football players. College kids over from the university."

"We get our fair share. The girls hate it, because they don't bring a lot of cash, and the kids expect the girls to fall all over them. If the girls would learn not to do that... fall all over them, then the problem would correct itself."

"Veronica isn't falling all over them."

Again with the smile. "I'm just telling you like it is," he said.

I could feel a hot wire wrapping around my brain. I closed my eyes hoping it would go away. When I opened them, it was still there. "She says they're all looking for takeout."

"We have a strict policy against that."

"I know..."

"We keep the girls safe when they are working here. What happens outside the club, we can't control. That's why we insist that they not date customers."

The wire twisted tighter. Its temperature rose.

He sensed something and looked away from me.

"I want to see surveillance tapes," I said.

"What?" He scoffed. "Absolutely not. That shit would end up on the internet, and every one of my girls would sic lawyers on me."

I stood up and shoved the table into him. "I want to see those tapes, Stratavini. It can happen right here. I just wanna see what the score is. It's like you say, maybe she's imagined things worse than they are, but I have to see."

He rubbed his mid-section, where he caught the edge of the table. "Look, I tried to be cool about this, but I draw the line at assault. Now haul your ass out of here or I'll have it hauled out for you."

The wire snapped.

I reached across the table and grabbed Stratavini by the throat and lifted him out of his seat.

I felt his little feet kicking at my shins. His eyes bulged and his tongue stuck out of his mouth like a fish reeled up out of the deep waters.

"Are you ready to show me the video?"

He shook his head. His eyes shifted to something over my shoulder.

I tossed him like a sack of dirty laundry to the floor, his head and upper back hitting the wall with such force the sheetrock caved in leaving a crushed dent in the wall. I spun around just before Big Paddy could grab me. He was attempting a bear hug, which left an opening I exploited with a short right to the solar plexus. When he bent over in pain, I draped an arm around the back of his neck, and drove another right so deep into his mid-section that both of his feet left the ground. I stepped away and watched him drop like falling timber.

I caught Stratavini reaching for his filing cabinet in the corner of my eye, and I realized that this was heading for a tragic ending.

I stepped over Paddy, hit the corridor and then the exit door with my shoulder. When I hit the sunlight, I was a little disoriented by the natural light and my adrenaline. I took a quick breath to steady myself.

Saw my truck sitting beside Donnie's Jag.

I got in it, and peeled out of there just as Stratavini burst through the door with a revolver in his hand. I watched as he aimed at me in the rear-view mirror.

He didn't take the shot.

23

S tratavini wouldn't call the cops because he didn't need the extra attention. My visit hadn't cost him anything, except maybe some re-plastering of the wall in his office.

The bigger concern was my tantrum causing Veronica more harm than good at work. I envied my Uncle for his ability to keep his cool.

It bothered me that Stratavini was so adamant about not showing me the tapes after I shared Veronica's concerns. I wasn't likely to get a look at them now. Then again, what did I expect to see? I was back to my question to V, "What did she want me to do about this?"

A silver Beetle passed by in the oncoming traffic. It wasn't Marisol. It was a brunette who wore clown make-up. The sight of the Beetle gave me an idea of what I could do for V if she would let me. And Marisol didn't show up again. Somehow I didn't think she would.

I did a U-turn and headed South to Murrells Inlet.

IN THE GREENERY between the Beach and my hometown, I got a call from Veronica. I pulled off the road into the shell parking lot of a convenience store advertising $5.99 Miller, School Supplies, and Live Bait.

I answered just before she cut the connection. "V!"

"Fuzzy, where are you?"

I looked up at the bright yellow sign of the store. "I'm at the Whiz. They have 5.99 Miller and school supplies."

"What?" Her voice trembled.

"Forget it," I said. "Look I was thinking, stay at my place, take a few days off. Let this pass."

"They're threatening me," she said.

"What?" I said. "Who's they?"

She sobbed. "I don't know, goddamnit," she said. "But they said they will slice my throat." Her voice reached panic level, she was saying something else, but I couldn't make it out.

"V, calm down."

"Don't tell me to fuckin' calm down, Fuzzy. This is all about you."

"Where are you, V?"

"I'm at your place. Waiting for you."

WE SAT side by side on the couch, like a couple trying to figure out what to do about that positive pregnancy test result, that felt anything but positive. She clutched her iPhone in both hands in her lap. It anchored them, as her shoulders, face, hell, her whole upper body shook. She hadn't said a word since I arrived.

Breaking the silence, I said, "Tell me everything, V. Who threatened you and how?"

She turned her attention to the phone. Illuminated the screen with a press of the button. She handed it to me.

It displayed a text screen. Veronica in green. Her threatener in blue. This is how it went:

"Your boyfriend needs to stay away from the teenagers."

"I don't have a boyfriend. Who's this?"

"He don't keep his nose clean. Im'a kill you."

"Fuck you creep. WHO IS THIS?"

"You tell him to back off. Or Im'a slice your pretty throat open."

My hand trembled holding the phone, now.

"Who is that, Fuzzy?"

I looked back at the messages.

The number on the texts looked familiar.

I took my phone in the other hand and scrolled my text messages. I stopped my thumb on the matching number and opened the message.

Sample.

I must have lost my poker face, because Veronica asked, "Fuzzy, what is it?"

"Nothing. You stay here. I gotta make a call."

I stepped outside and dialed the number. My call went straight to his voice mail. "What's up, this is Billy, leave your number."

I hung up.

I did a quick search on the phone for the number over at Grand Strand Medical. When I found it, I called the front desk.

A voice so pleasant it could not belong to Mrs. Blue Hair answered.

"May I have William Smith's room?"

"Just a moment please."

I looked through the window at Veronica. Her black hair caught the light of my reading lamp, and the luster created almost a bluish halo around her head. But she was crying, big gulping sobs. She looked like a lonesome sparrow grounded with fear. I would set her back to flight.

"Sir, we have more than one William Smith, would you know..."

"The one on the third floor," I cut in.

The line went dead for three crawling seconds.

"'Sup"

"Sample. It's Fuzzy."

"Hey Fuzz, how's it hangin'?"

"Samp, I tried calling you on your cell," I said.

"Yeah, that might be a problem. I think I lost it while I was gettin' the shit kicked out of me."

My hand tightened on the phone. "You sure you had it then?"

"I was checking messages when the big blonde dude got holt of me."

Football players.

Jandro Rodriguez.

"Samp, I gotta run. Sounds like you are doing a little better."

"I..."

I cut the connection.

The phone rang.

Rod.

I considered not answering, but decided I could use him on my side. "Hey, Rod."

"I got your pistola. Someone found it beside a dumpster behind a restaurant down the street from the Fox. I figure, whoever snatched it tried to toss it in the dumpster as they ran by. When they didn't make it in the dumpster, they didn't stop to retrieve it. Why don't you come on in and get it?"

"Can I come by tomorrow morning?"

"Fuzzy come on in and get your gun."

"Tomorrow."

I hung up.

Veronica still cried inside on the couch. I felt as helpless as I had the night of Angel's accident eight years ago. Except, in this case, I had all kinds of uncertainty about my feelings.

That wasn't true. I knew I would not leave Veronica to fend for herself. All we had said the last several days was history.

This was now. The sparrow and I were taking a ride.

24

I took her by her place to pack a small bag. Unlike most women I'd known, Veronica took that to heart. Fifteen minutes later, she hopped back in the cab of my truck wielding a small, ox-blood leather McGregor duffle bag.

I backed down the driveway and headed out of town. "Don't worry, this will be over soon. You'll be back before you know it."

She said nothing.

SHE REMAINED silent for the next two hours. She watched the pines slide by in the side window.

I kept my focus on the black pavement in front of me.

"Where are we going?"

It wasn't until she asked that I realized that I had not told her anything about my plans. I wasn't sure what to make of that. Either she trusted me enough to not ask, or she was in such a state of shock it hadn't occurred to her to ask.

"I have a buddy in Greenville. Another P.I., like me. He's a good guy, don't worry."

"I don't understand."

"I'm going to leave you under his protection, until I settle this shit back at the beach."

She went back to watching the pines, now just shadowy masses in the night. She pulled her feet onto on the dash. They were bare with toes painted a dark red, almost brown.

The color of Coach's blood on the sheets at the Coral Beach.

SAM HORN WAS another old college buddy. He had studied criminal science. While, my police experience began and ended with the mounted patrol on the college campus, Sam had spent just enough time on a real police force to determine he couldn't take following all the orders and political maneuvering involved in moving up the food chain.

I pulled into the parking lot of a strip shopping center with more signs in Spanish than English. We were on the west side of Greenville, the more blue-collared side, which of late had seen a large swell in the Latino population.

Veronica snored like a kitten. She slept with her head against the window at an angle which looked comfortable. Still, I resented waking her.

I shook her shoulder, "Babe, we're here."

Sam stood in the open doorway of the storefront right in front of us. He smiled like a guy who had been forced to put on that face far too many times in his life. To say it was a weary smile, would be an affront to weary smiles everywhere. After four hours of driving through the night with no sleep, however, his face was a welcome site.

Veronica stirred. Mumbled something. Turned her shoulder and went back to snoring.

I slid out of the cab and silently shut the door behind.

Sam greeted me with an abrupt bro hug. "Long time, Fuzzy. What have you gotten yourself into this time?"

I took a deep breath. It must have been telling.

"That bad, huh?" he said.

He stepped aside, and said, "Well come in, and let's talk. She'll be okay out there for now."

"Nah," I said. "Let me get her to bed. She's had a scary day, I don't want her waking up alone in some strange parking lot."

He followed me to the passenger side door.

I opened the door, and she fell into my arms.

She stirred, opened her eyes, noted who held her, and closed her eyes again.

I draped one of her arms over my shoulder and carried her like a bride into Sam's place.

It was a little more furnished than Stratavini's place but not by much. Two old gray formica topped desks. One housed an old putty colored computer that looked like it had seen no action since the Clinton administration. The other had three manila folders, a black laptop, and a pack of smokes.

Sam's desk.

Beyond the desks, a leather sofa was up against one wall. It was split open and bandaged up in places like my face. In front, an old tube television sat on 2-x-4s bridging between two upside down plastic milk crates.

I jutted my chin at the sofa.

Sam said, "No, no. Take her to the back room. There's a twin bed back there."

I carried her back there, and there was a bed. And a dresser. And a TV. And a night stand stacked with detective paperbacks.

I looked over my shoulder at Sam, who had followed me.

He shrugged. "I got tired of paying twice the rent."

I lived in a storage shack. Who was I to judge?

After I tucked V in, we went back into the office. Over mugs of coffee, I gave him the Cliffs Notes version of the events that led me to Greenville.

"You sure you don't need me to line-up a babysitter and come down with you? Sounds like you could use a wingman."

"No I need you to keep her safe. I'm okay down there. I've got Jimmy."

He went slack jawed. "Alou? What is he gonna do? Distract the kid, by putting the moves on his sister?"

Jimmy's way with women was legendary, but it also made people underestimate him. "He's saved my skin more than once. We'll be all right."

Before it turned into a good old days discussion, I stood, patted him on the shoulder, and headed for the door.

"Don't you worry, Fuzzy. She's safe here, and I won't put the moves on her."

I looked at his widening girth. "Yeah, unless you take rejection better than you used to I wouldn't advise on that."

It was a cheap shot you could only pull off with a friend you'd known for over twenty years.

I left him on that note and began the trek back home.

25

The sun had risen above the rooftops of resorts as I crossed over the bridge onto the island that made up the Grand Strand. It was Friday morning, and if I was lucky, I could still catch Jimmy for breakfast.

I pointed the truck to his pancake house and made it there just in time to find him leaving out the front door. I pulled in front of him and rolled down the window.

"You gonna be around?"

"I should ask you that." He looked at his gold watch. "You look like shit, Fuzzy. Where have you been?"

"Greenville. Horn sends his regards"

"What's he weigh three hundred, now?"

He wasn't too far off, but I would not share that. Jimmy and Sam were like oil and water. The two main cogs in our offense twenty years ago. They'd always been competitive, and dismissive of each other's talents. "I dropped Veronica off with him. Things are getting ugly on this case I'm working."

I could tell he was searching for the proper words. Thankfully, they weren't 'I told you so.' He went with, "I heard Sample ended up in the hospital, too."

"Yeah, look Jimmy. I need to know you'll be in town. Things could go down quickly, and if they do, I may need you on wing."

"You got it buddy. I'm there."

It always bothered me how quickly Jimmy answered such inquiries. He had two daughters and a beautiful wife at home. Yet, when I asked him to walk into fire with me, he answered like I'd asked him to join me at Hooters for wings. Like I said, it bothered me. But not enough for me to quit asking. I'm sure his wife hated me for it.

"Well all right," I said, and pulled away.

WHEN I GOT HOME, Marisol's Beetle was there. I almost didn't have it in me to go inside. All I wanted was to crawl in bed and get at least four hours of sleep. But, we needed to talk.

She lay on her back with her head propped on the arm of the couch and her ankles crossed. She was in a T-shirt and shorts again and looked beautiful. Someone on the TV tried to sell her a bracelet inlaid with authentic cubic zirconia stones.

She turned on her side when she noticed I'd entered. She had a more womanly curve to the hip than should be allowed on a nineteen-year-old. "Where ya been?"

The way she said it, almost teasingly, made me want to walk across the room and smack her across the face. But I was too tired for that. "I had to make a quick trip out of town."

She raised her eyebrows. "You're supposed to be protecting me."

"Knock it off Marisol. Half the time I don't know where you've run off to."

She sat up on one side of the couch.

I sat down beside her.

"Have you had any more drive-bys or other threats."

She frowned, as if she missed the attention. "Nope."

"Why are you here?" I said. "What is it you need?"

"I need your help, Fuzzy. You need to keep looking into this. I heard Billy took a bad beating. Do you think someone found out he did Coach in, and took the law into their own hands?"

I noticed her rubbing her hands in her lap. I turned to face her, and took them in my own. "Listen, Marisol. We need to talk about your brother."

"Jandro? What about him?"

"Marisol, who do you think did that to Billy?"

"Jandro? What makes you say that? And why would he beat Billy?"

"I was there," I said.

"What do you mean you were there?"

All the questions irritated me. I was supposed to be the one asking questions. But the only way I would get her to answer mine, would be to let her ask hers. "I mean I was there. I saw the guys beating him up. Two of the guys were Jandro's build."

"But you can't be sure?"

"Not to pick him in a lineup, no. But Jandro was there, Marisol. I know it."

"You were there, and what, just stood by and watched?"

"Of course not," I said.

She stood and looked down at me. Accusation was in her eyes. "So what did you do?"

"I fired a warning shot, and they scattered. It probably saved Sample's life."

She scoffed. "Of course you did. And you never told me why you think Jandro would want to beat on, Sample."

"Jandro is why Sample hired me. You brother worried about what you had gotten yourself into as a recruiting girl."

She dropped back into the sofa and dug fingers from both hands into her golden locks. "Oh Jesus, why can't he let me be?"

"He loves you. Unfortunately, that love makes him the top suspect."

She glared at me, "What did you say?"

"Coach, Marisol. Jandro found out about Coach."

"You don't think it was Billy that did that to Coach?"

"I never did," I said.

Her lower lip trembled, but somehow she managed not to cry. "But it can't be Jandro."

I took one of her hands. It shook like a baby chick. "Marisol, you can't protect him on this. He is making threats on you, on my girlfriend, and to me. He's already killed someone and put another person in the hospital. He is out of control."

"Jandro's never threatened me."

"The drive-bys, Marisol. I know that Jandro himself didn't try to run you over, but he has a posse of football players, who would die for him. One of them tried to scare you."

"But why?"

That was a question I didn't have an answer to.

Marisol must have seen it in my eyes because she took her hand back.

"Look," I said. "Did you ever talk to Jandro about any of this?"

She studied my face. "He pushed me on the Lady Tees thing, both when I first told him. And then every time I hosted a recruit. Sometimes he followed me." She giggled at that.

"What?"

"Jandro is not one for subtlety. CAU may have lost a recruit or two."

I imagined visits he may have made with recruits unbeknownst to Marisol. "What about Coach? Did the two of you ever talk about him?"

She shook her head.

"He knew nothing about it? Until, I took pictures."

Again with the head shake. There was a resigned look on her face as if she was coming around to the possibility of his guilt.

"What about Sample? Did he ever talk to you about Coach?"

"Billy thought I was prostituting myself for Coach with these recruits. We didn't get much further than that because I told him to fuck off."

"But he could have told Jandro," I said, as much to myself, as to her.

I took out my phone to call Sample at the hospital. I had missed a text message coming in.

It said it was from Sample. "You got your titty dancer out of town? Are you staying away from the girl?"

A vein throbbed in my temple, like a small rock hammer tapping away at the side of my head. I looked at Marisol. For the first time since I had met her, she did not look like a sensual trap laid to snare all the men she came within contact. She looked like a nineteen-year-old girl. I had played the whole thing, as if she were that girl, despite her black widow tendencies, because I knew she had a lot of life before her. And she didn't understand what she was doing to her future. "Marisol," I said. "You've got to get out of here."

Now she looked like a kid frightened that her parents would switch the light off at night. "What is it Fuzzy? What came in over the phone?"

"Nothing," I lied. "But if Jandro gets the wrong idea about us. Things could get ugly."

"Us? How would Jandro come to that conclusion? How would he even know I came to see you?"

"How did he know where to find Coach?"

With that she got up and hurried to the door, fishing keys out of her pocket on the way. When she reached the door, she turned and thought of something and came back. She raised up on tip toes, just as far as she could, and kissed me on the corner of my mouth. The smell of her hair was intoxicating. The brush of her breast on my chest, like a light strum on a guitar playing somewhere deep in my insides.

"Be careful, Fuzzy Koella," she said. "I can't figure you out, and you may be the only man I've met that has never tried to get in my pants, but I like you."

Her smile was a sad one.

When she turned to walk away, I turned to look at the flat gray screen of my TV. It wasn't on, but I couldn't watch her sway off. Despite the kiss, the light touch of her on my chest, and the girlish, sweet smell of her, I preferred the nineteen year old girl to the embodiment of a sex pot.

When the door latched shut, I said to no one at all, "I like you, too. Sweet girl."

I SPENT what seemed like half the day, staring at Jandro's text message. Goose bumps formed on the surface of my arms, and I rubbed warmth back into my skin. I had seen the result of Jandro's anger in a room at the Coral Beach Resort. As disturbing as that was, it was not as frightening as the image of his handy work in action.

Even with all the evidence mounting against him, there seemed to be a small hope in Marisol that she held onto. The hope that her brother wasn't a killer. I had no siblings, so I couldn't comprehend the protective instinct Jandro and Marisol had for each other. I had to believe, though, that if Marisol had seen what I'd seen, she wouldn't let down her guard.

Something bothered me. I put a call into Sample at the hospital.

When I made it through the front desk, he answered on the first ring. "'Sup?"

"Samp, It's Fuzzy."

His voice sounded much better than it had just 24 hours ago. "What's up, my man?"

"Quite a bit actually. Samp, in all this stuff with Marisol and whether she was pulling tricks and all that stuff. Did you ever talk to Jandro about the affair with Coach?"

"Are you kidding? No. For one, I wasn't sure about it, until I brought you on. Second, Jandro would fucking kill Coach."

There was an uncomfortable silence on our connection.

"Shit," he said. "Now I feel like a dick."

"Don't Sample. Look did the cops ever put someone at your door?"

"Yeah some fat-fuck," he said. Then in a muffled voice because he must have taken the phone from the mouthpiece. "Yeah, I'm talkin' about you." He returned to the line. "Dude, had a bag of Krispy Kreme donuts delivered to him this morning. Can you believe that? Livin' up to the stereohype."

"Type."

"What's that?"

"Type," I said. "Stereo-type."

"Yeah, whatever. Hype sounds better."

"Right, look, Samp stay in there as long as you can, okay? And if they take the man off your door, call me."

"Whoa, Fuzzy. You freakin' out on me?"

"Just do it, okay?"

"You got it, but you know I ain't got no insurance. I hope they don't kick me out."

"They won't." I wasn't so sure.

"Listen, Fuzzy. Be careful, if you goin' after Jandro. You hear? Dude can be like that crazy motherfucker on Looney Tunes."

"The Tasmanian Devil?"

26

I considered calling Jimmy to run over my options with him. I considered calling Veronica to see how she was doing. I ended up texting Jandro back, because I didn't like him out there holding all the cards in his hand.

"I have something for you. Or should I drop them off with the cops? Or the *Sun News*."

I hit send and had my response before I could even set my phone down.

"What you got? Where's the girl?"

He thought I had his sister. I had a seat at the table. Now, I needed to make him sweat what I had in the hole.

I had a heavy breakfast of eggs, sausage, and home fries at a pancake house, that wasn't Jimmy's. I took my time with it and even ordered an extra order of the fries. They were the kind only cooked right at one of these joints. The potatoes, probably leftover baked potatoes from the night before, were sliced in thick chips and fried up with onions and bell peppers and enough grease to clog up a fire main.

While I enjoyed my breakfast, Jandro texted me like a jealous schoolgirl. All the messages were the same theme,

"Where's Marisol?" The longer I left him hanging, the saltier the language got.

The last one said, "I'm gonna fucking kill you."

That caught my attention.

An hour later, the old waitress who had the jowls of a bulldog and the body of a fire hydrant came to take away my plate and handed me the check.

I figured it was time I got back to Jandro. I skipped the texting though, and direct dialed Sample's number.

He pleasantly answered, "Where the fuck is my sister, dog?"

"I have no clue. And listen, stop the threats or I go straight to the cops. They'll love to see a suspect, and Jandro, they are looking at you... they would love to see that text you just sent me about killing me. That would put the top on an open and shut case."

"What the fuck are you talking about, case?"

"Coach Cain, Jandro. I guess right about now they are making the rounds. Questioning your Papi, teammates, maybe even Marisol, if they can find her."

"Why the fuck would they be looking at me?"

"Forget about that, do you want the pictures?"

"Pictures, of what?"

He was the dumbest person alive, or he was a bad actor. I'd seen him in action. I was betting on the bad actor.

"Marisol with Coach," I said.

I heard him take a deep breath, and sniff and snort to clear his sinuses. "You said something about handing them off to the cops or the Sun News. We can't do that. They will just paint her as a typical Latina whore."

"I agree. They will, but we will have to give them something, Jandro. I know you love your sister, if you come clean, we may keep her out of papers and off the TV."

"Come clean about what!"

"What you did to Coach?"

"I ain't done..." He stopped.

I could almost hear the thoughts churning in his brain. I waited.

"You say you have pictures?"

"I do."

"Okay," he said, "Where can we meet?"

Before I realized what I was saying I said, "The Swamp Fox."

"Okay, like, now?"

It was time to make him twist in the breeze a little, again. "No, I don't carry them around with me. I can do it tonight around eight. But Jandro, we ain't getting no further, unless you agree to come clean."

Silence.

An exhaled breath.

"I know. I need to see what that's buying me."

"Fair enough," I said.

"Just the two of us, Fuzzy."

"Agreed."

"Now where's my sister?"

"I haven't seen your sister."

"Bullshit," he said. "I've got pictures, too."

Goose pimples formed on my forearms. Thick saliva arrived in the back of my mouth, glueing my tongue to the roof of my mouth. I swallowed. It tasted like bitter chemicals. "I don't know what you're talking about now."

"I know she's spent some nights at your place, dude."

Silence again.

My throat felt stuffed with cotton balls.

"Like I said. Just the two of us."

Just like that Jandro Rodriguez had seized the upper-hand again. He cut the connection.

I called Jimmy and told him I'd need him tonight. We went over the details.

———

I HAD a full day to consume myself with worry over the impending meeting with Jandro. I chose to occupy my mind with other things that still bothered me about the case.

The drive to North Myrtle Beach was about forty minutes even without traffic. That gave me a lot of time to worry about Jandro, but I was determined to drive those thoughts out of my mind. I pounded them down by playing a CD by an Alabama band called the Dexateens as loud as I could handle without feeling physical pain in my ears.

The CD began its fade, and I had developed a mild case of tinnitus, when I pulled into the driveway behind Michelle's Elantra.

She opened the door before I could put my knuckles to it.

She looked tired, almost as if she were on the medication they put you on for mourning. Her disheveled, dank hair rested limply on her shoulders.

The image of her beaten like this tied up my insides. I questioned how the vibrant, confident women I'd met working the bar at the Coral Beach could be lessened to this hollow shell of a person who stood before me now.

"Hi." Her voice was a timid whisper, her eyes those of a child who feared the punishment her parents would bring down upon her.

"Can I come in?"

She stepped aside.

Her living room looked like she had leased it out to potheads. Gone was the tidy neatness, and simple decor. Coffee cups from a local shop lined the coffee tabletop. One teetered on the edge of some tabloid magazine it sat upon.

Soiled styrofoam food cartons lay all over the floor. Some contents had spilled out and leaked on to the carpet. Pillows, some without cases, were stacked high on one end of her sofa. The rest was covered with tangled blankets. One of those self-help experts spouted his sermon from the television screen.

As I stood there taking it all in, Michelle crawled in under the covers on the couch. She pulled a blanket with images from a children's film printed upon it, up tight under her chin. She looked like a kid home sick from school.

"Have you been back to work?"

"They called and left a message not to bother to come back in."

I propped a haunch on the arm of the sofa beside her head. "Are you okay, Michelle?"

She stared at the television, but there was no recognition that she was following anything on the screen. "Sure. Couldn't be better."

"Have the police been by to see you again?"

"Nope."

Michelle had her own demons. I wondered if she had ever been treated for a mental illness. I wondered if I should make a call to have her looked at. I wondered if it was any of my business.

"Honey, I need help on this."

She didn't respond.

I continued, "Do you recall if anyone else came in asking about Marisol and Coach? Maybe asking if they stayed there?"

She nodded her head one time, almost as if she were falling off to sleep.

"Was he a big guy? Muscular. Latino?"

"Nope."

"No? So what did he look like?"

Her lips curled up in a smile. "You."

"C'mon Michelle. I mean someone else."

"Oh, he was someone else. And he didn't look like you, but he had your look."

The dumb look on her face irritated me. I couldn't determine if she was pulling my leg or if it was just her mental state. "What look is that?"

"That always snooping in other people's business look."

I remembered my first encounter with Michaels when he was on the far side of the hall from me. When I took the pictures of Marisol and Coach.

"Did he have red hair and look kind of goofy?"

"Yep. You're cuter, but you both have that same look." Her face took on an expression as if she'd touched her tongue to the contacts on a nine volt battery. "The cops had that look, too."

"Michelle, do you remember when he came asking about them? Was it after we took pictures of Coach and Marisol? Did he ask whether they always stay in the same room?"

She pulled her gaze away from the TV and looked at me. "It was before we met. I told him that I didn't give out information on customers." Again, a smile crawled up her face. "Like I said, you're cuter."

"Have you ever seen the guy again?"

"Sure, he comes in and has a drink at a table in the corner of the bar. Always with that look on his face."

I kissed her on the forehead. "Is there anything I can do for you, Michelle?"

"Just leave." She said it with all the interest of voice on the GPS telling you that you've just missed your turn.

I left her there with her spoiled food and self-help programs. Her empty coffee cups and coverless pillows. When I stepped through the door, I looked back and saw her blank face. A tear leaked from the corner of one eye.

I put a call into a psychiatrist friend, who had helped me

through some rough patches after Angel's death, and later the remorse I felt with having my mother imprisoned. I didn't get an answer. I couldn't catch a break.

———

IT WAS A HIGH SKY DAY, a cloudless, baby blue sky, which wreaked havoc on infielders trying to corral towering pop-flies. It made me want to be on a boat wetting a line and reeling in the night's dinner. Instead, I headed back to the Carlton Arm's.

Even the high sky and the bright sun couldn't do anything for the Arms today. There seemed to be more dead spots in the grass. More cracks in the pavement. It was probably my shitty mood after having left Michelle that had me seeing all the flaws on an otherwise beautiful day. That, or the fact, that I was scared to death I would run into Jandro Rodriguez. Or the disgust I felt in going up to drag an admirable man into the ditch his son and daughter had dug.

I got out of the cab and climbed the stairs. When I reached the door to the Rodriguez residence, light seeped out from the edge of the cracked door. Faint meringue music played from somewhere in the bowels of the apartment, but otherwise there were no people sounds coming from the open door. I'd left my piece in the glove compartment, because if Jandro was there I didn't trust myself not to pull it. And I didn't want to do that at all in Papi's home.

I tapped two knuckles on the door, and that swung the door in enough so I could step through. The living room was empty. The glass topped coffee table held only a solitary, white business card. I stepped to the table and took the card in my hand.

It read, "Detective Rod Gilbreath, Myrtle Beach Police Department."

Rod was too detail oriented to have taken Papi in for questioning and left the door open on his exit. I walked down a narrow, unlit hallway, not liking what I expected to find. A door on the right was partially closed as their front door had been. I pushed it open. There was a bare mattress and box spring on the floor shoved in the corner of the wall to my left. The venetian blinds were closed in the window centered on the opposite wall. In the corner of the right wall was a daybed with an intricate wrought iron frame. A mauve and lavender comforter covered the bed. It's corners as tight as a Private's at boot camp.

It had to be Marisol's bed. The toes of a platform sandal peeked out from beneath the bed.

I closed the door behind me and made my way further down the hall to a door that was open but unlit. As I approached, I heard labored breathing. I popped my head into the doorway and saw Papi on the floor on all fours. His chest heaved as he struggled for breath.

I hurried to him and dropped to my knees beside him.

He looked at me. Blood dripped from a nasty gash on his forehead. Desperate eyes searched my face.

"Papi, who did this to you?"

He shook his head and grasped at his chest. He rolled over on his back. "Is tight," he said, patting his chest.

I called 911 and had an ambulance sent.

Papi closed his eyes. "No one did. Policia here to see Marisol. She no here. Jandro be very angry about what? I do not know. But I call." He stopped to catch his breath.

"It's okay Papi take your time. An ambulance is on the way, everything will be okay."

"I call Jandro to ask on Marisol. He get angry. He shout. I do not know what he say. I hang up. My boy will not talk to me as such. That when chest hurt. I come here. Fall. Hit head."

Jesus, this was all I needed. Now, I had people dropping from natural causes.

I patted Papi's arm. "It's okay. We will get you feeling better."

He kept his eyes closed. "This feel better. Like this."

He looked older than I had remembered. I guess that is what kids do to you. I didn't want to further Papi's complications, but I had to push forward.

"Papi, I came to talk about Marisol."

"I am going to lose her." His voice shook on the word "lose".

"You will not lose her, Papi. That is why I'm here. She is not in trouble." I wasn't so sure of that. "But we need to keep it that way."

He opened his eyes and looked suspiciously at me. "Ask."

"Did another man, like me, ever show up asking about or to see, Marisol?"

"Like you?"

"A detective-type," I said.

"Marisol, has lots of men calling on her. This bother me."

"I know, but detectives, like me?"

"Just policia. Just left. One fat. One black."

I'd have to remember to tell Rod, that he was the black and Toriani was the fat. "Okay, and Jandro, why do you think he is so mad?"

"I do not know. He could not say where Marisol. And he seems to get more angry when I say his sister name."

His eyelids fluttered and then shut again.

I couldn't recall much training on such situations, when I was a campus cop, but I'd seen this situation on TV. I patted Papi on the arm. "Come on, Papi. I need you to stay with me until the ambulance gets her."

His chin bobbed, and he open his eyes. "Less tight. I be okay."

"Of course you will be okay. If you could handle the Great Marichal, you can handle this."

He smiled at that memory. "I once play pepper with Tony Perez. You know pepper?"

This was my kind of guy. "I know pepper."

"And Perez?"

"Yes, I know Perez. He led the Big Red Machine."

Color came back to his face. The heaving of his chest slowed. "Yes, Perez. He a good one. They finally put him in Fame Hall, no?"

"Yes they did."

"I have bat from Perez, too," he said.

"You must have quite a bat collection."

He tried to sit up.

I put my hand on his chest. "No Papi, rest." My mention of the bat collection, flashed images of Sample and the shark, and Coach at the hotel. "Say Papi, I would love to see your bats sometime. Are they somewhere I can find or maybe when you feel better you can show me?"

He angled his head toward a closet with slatted, bi-fold doors. "In there. You look."

My knees popped as I got to my feet. I went to the closet.

Inside it held no clothes, no shoes. Just a polished oak and glass display case. The kind gun aficionados and hunters store their rifles in. Papi stored his tools of the trade. Baseball bats. Six beautiful ash specimens, all branded with the Louisville Slugger logo.

I looked back over my shoulder to Papi.

He had turned on his side and propped himself up on one elbow. His smile beamed with pride. "You like?"

"It's a beautiful collection, Papi, but I can't help but notice one bat missing." I pointed to a gap in the display rack between bats five and six.

"Ah yes. This bat is Jandro favorite. A-rod, you know. Like his name. He take with him to university."

My grip tightened on the closet door knob. "I hope he will take good care of it."

The smile remained. "He will. In high school, I had to keep him from using in games with friends. Now, he no play baseball ever. I sometime wish, he would use bat."

I thought of Coach lying on the floor of Room 315. I hoped Jandro hadn't used his father's bat. He would never get it back. He'd lose his son and a part of his collection on that one action. "When did you last see Marisol?"

"Been few days." He shook his head, the smile falling from his face. "I worry her. She think she know men. They like to know her. But I don't think she know as much she think she know. She just a girl."

Papi was the wisest man of the bunch on this case, including myself.

His eyelids drooped again. "Papi!"

On cue, two paramedics entered the room in crisp blue uniforms, carrying large tackle boxes filled with medical devices. Neither of them appeared of legal age to drink. They were pale skinned, fair-haired, and blue-eyed. Both of their hair trimmed tight to the skull on the sides with short shocks of hair on top combed tightly back and to the side. It was the kind of cut you saw on the kids, who marched the streets of Charlottesville. One boy acknowledged my existence with a nod. The other said, "Door was open, sir."

I watched as they treated and examined Papi Rodriguez, with the respect they would give their own fathers. It was a good reminder that first impressions aren't always the best ones, and that things are not always as they seem.

WHEN I LEFT PAPI, he was joking with the paramedics and showing off his collection. He would not need the ambulance. If one positive had come of the case, so far, this was it.

I sat in my truck and searched on my phone for a contact number in Indianapolis. When I found it, I clicked the link.

A cheery, mousy female voice answered my call. She sounded like she was fourteen, but in my experience the voice could easily beong to a 45-year-old woman. "NCAA Headquarters," she squeaked.

"Hi, this is Sergeant Rod Gilbreath with the Myrtle Beach Police department. I am unsure who I need to speak to regarding this, but I need to contact someone you have had investigating possible rules violations down here."

She made a clicking sound with her tongue. "Hm, I guess I'll transfer you to our Rules and Compliance department."

"Fantastic," I said.

She passed me onto some music typically reserved for elevators and funeral homes.

I had about succumbed to the anesthetic noise when a deep, sultry female voice came on the line. "Jennifer Hudspeth, Governance."

"Hi Jennifer. This is Sergeant Rod Gilbreath with the Myrtle Beach Police Department."

"Yes?"

"I wonder if you could help us locate someone. You do not employ him, but I understand you contracted him to investigate possible rules infractions down here at the University."

"We dropped that inquiry."

"Yes, I know. It's just that this Private Investigator..."

"Mr. Gilbreath, is it?" She was trying her best to talk down to me. If I resisted, I'd just end up with a dead line. "Surely, you can find all pertinent contact information for Mr. Michaels by doing a simple web search."

"That's just it," I said. "He's disappeared over the last

couple of days, and we thought maybe if you had heard from him, you might shed some light on where we might find him."

"We have not."

I continued, "We have an unfortunate crime down here that has resulted in the death of the football Coach you were investigating, and we need to discuss this with Mr. Michaels. Understand, we are not accusing him of anything. We simply want to share notes."

"We were investigating the program. Not the Coach. Surely, you can understand the difference."

Bullshit. "Right, right. Nonetheless, we need to speak with Mr. Michaels."

"We have had no contact with Mr. Michaels since we terminated our agreement a month ago."

Michaels had said they cut him off after Coach's death. "A month? Did you replace him with another private detective at the time?"

"We did not."

"Were you using internal personnel, or had you completed your investigation?"

"Mr. Gilbreath, I believe we have shared enough on the subject."

"I could get a warrant. Then your investigation would make the newspapers. That would serve neither of us well."

She sighed. "We cut our investigation short, when we determined that some tactics Mr. Michaels used," she paused. "Or I should say tried to use, were questionable, and put us in a vulnerable situation. Also, we believed no results borne by those tactics would be useful to a case."

"You refer to his attempt to pimp out young girls to prove Coach was doing this as part of recruitment?"

"Good day, Mr. Gilbreath."

I had my answer.

27

I spent the afternoon visiting my mother in prison. It did nothing for the crummy mood I was in, but it did keep the prospects of my meeting with Jandro Rodriguez off my mind.

It was sunset when I found Jimmy Alou sitting at the bar at the Coral Beach Resort. He had the customer side of the bar to himself. A chesty blonde resided over the bar side. She wore a silky black blouse and a gray, sharkskin skirt that came to her knees. Opaque black tights covered her legs. She was one of those smiling blondes, who made it through life on all the things others would do for her because she was a smiling blonde. Her smile and giggles had settled on Jimmy now.

I sat down beside him and clapped him on the shoulder.

He turned to look at me with an olive, speared by a little plastic sword, balanced between his teeth. A dead soldier sat on the bar in front of him, half-filled with ice cubes stained red with the remains of Jimmy's Bloody Mary, the only alcoholic drink he could stomach. Jimmy slid the olive into his mouth and crunched down on it. Between chews, he said, "What's up, Chief?"

"You know the whole story about what's up."

Jimmy wore a black turtle neck and dark blue jeans. Good attire for hiding in shadows at the park. Somehow, though, he made it look like a good outfit for a night out for drinks and picking up ladies. It was one of his many talents. He smiled, raised an eyebrow and said, "Fuzzy, this is Heather. Heather this is my, newly single, best friend since elementary school, Fuzzy Koella."

I said, "It's nice to meet you, Heather."

She still had her eyes on Jimmy. "Likewise, what'll ya have, Fuz-zy."

If we were not meeting a six-four football player, who probably wanted to kill me, wasn't in my future, I would put even money on Jimmy getting Heather in bed that night. "I'll just have an ice water with a wedge of lemon."

She looked at me from the corner of her eye. "Your friend here, sounds like a barrel of fun, Jim."

"Maybe we should get a table," I said, and gestured to all the empty ones out of earshot of the beautiful and distracting Heather.

"We're okay, here. Heather will give us our privacy. Isn't that right, Heather?"

She wiped off a spot on the bar, dropped a coaster on it, and put my water there. Without a word, she walked off to the other side of the bar. Jimmy's eyes glued to her rear end the entire way. She made an act of wiping down the bar there, too.

"So, how should we approach this? We gotta make sure Jandro doesn't see you. And remember, I want nothing to go down, at all, unless he deals the play."

"Relax, I've already scoped it out," Jimmy said.

Two waters for me, and two more Bloody Marys for him later, he had laid the plan on me. I had stuck to water to keep my head clear when I met Jandro. I hoped the three Bloody Marys and however many more Jimmy had drunk before, didn't end up getting me a shot in the back.

28

The Family Kingdom park was just a short walk down Ocean Boulevard from the Coral Beach. Jimmy left about ten minutes before me to get in place before my arrival. I left my truck parked at the resort, and a few minutes later I approached the southeast corner of the park.

A white sedan was parked in the Friendly's lot.

I continued down the sidewalk adjacent to the park rather than weave my way through the vacant booths and the inoperable rides. The sidewalk was more open and clear of any places for people to hide. It also made me more of a sitting duck, but that was the trade-off I accepted.

When I reached the northeast corner of the park, I entered beside an empty ticket booth, which advertised "All-Day Ride Wristbands - $28.00 per Rider". The Swamp Fox loomed above like a treacherous behemoth. I walked in the direction of its entrance.

The park was eerily silent. Apparently even squirrels and birds had checked out for the season. I looked in the direction of the bumper cars. No sign of Jimmy. That was good. He needed to stay clear of sight.

I tapped the gun resting at the small of my back for reassurance.

Just as I laid my hand on the cold steel, I was hit by something similar in force to a semi-truck. His shoulder caught me right in my recovering ribs. An ominous crunch followed, and then another crunch as I hit the black top. My wrist crushed between my ass and the pavement. He was on top of me like a professional wrestler seeking the three count.

I looked up in the face of my assailant. He had a bowling ball for a head topped with tight curly blond hair. The face was familiar. He was the guy who had restrained Sample while others beat on him the other night.

A series of rubber soled tennis shoes slapped the pavement.

The image of the blonde guy's face faded to fuzz. Goddamnit, Jimmy what were you waiting on? I shook my head to clear the fog.

The footsteps stopped at my side. A huddle of them, all cut from the same pattern, formed around me.

Jandro Rodriguez leaned over me. His hands on his knees like a second baseman preparing for the pitch. His teeth were incomparably white in the darkness. There was nothing reassuring in his smile.

"You like fucking teenage girls?"

The blond bowling ball pushed himself up off me.

I jammed my knee up into his crotch.

His breath came like air letting out from a balloon. I hadn't thought the move out well as he collapsed back on me, crushing my damaged ribs and sending a jolt of pain screaming up my arm from my broken wrist.

"Not a good idea, Fuzzy," Jandro said. "You saw how this

played out for Sample. I hope you at least brought the pictures."

The saliva filling my mouth tasted metallic. I spat it into Bowling Ball's face. It covered his face red and sticky.

He still squirmed in pain from the nut shot.

I rolled out from under him.

One of Jandro's other goons (there were three), nudged me with the toe of his shoe.

I looked up to Jandro.

He nodded at his boy.

He lifted a shoe as if he were going to stomp a cockroach.

I bit down on the ankle that remained planted as hard as I was able.

"Fuck."

The sound of a watermelon split open from being dropped from a great height followed. Then the clap of a gunshot.

The kid, who was about to curb stomp me, was thrown off his foot by the impact. His head snapped back like something from the Zapruder film.

Bowling ball's eyes were all whites, and he held himself tight to the ground. The two other goons sprinted to safety behind a plywood booth. Jandro turned to look in the direction of the gunfire.

I used the distraction to sweep his leg. My ankle caught his, and he collapsed face first onto the pavement.

He tried to push himself up on his hands and knees.

I couldn't afford to get into a wrestling match with him. He would over power me, and he would have me beaten before Jimmy could get a good shot. I crawled over to him and dropped my elbow across the back of his neck.

He fell again, but the force wasn't enough to keep him down. He rolled over to face me. He reached behind his back as he turned.

I punched him with a short right. I caught him flush on

the point of the nose and felt it disintegrate into pieces of bone and cartilage. The sound of his head bouncing off the pavement was even more horrific, sounding much like the sound of Jimmy's shot connecting with the curb stomper.

Jandro went motionless.

A stab of searing, white heat hit my shoulder, followed by the snapping pop of a small caliber weapon from the direction of the fleeing thugs.

I collapsed on top of Jandro. My shirt was sopping wet with blood when I touched my shoulder. I could feel a small hole about the size of the tip of a pencil eraser in my shirt and the flesh of my shoulder. It pumped fresh blood.

More feet slapped the pavement, closing in on me.

Jimmy ran head down with his semi-automatic extended before him. He fired off rounds in the direction of the booth. The sky filled with wood splinters and gun smoke.

Bowling ball hurriedly crawled in the direction I had entered the park.

Jimmy put a round in his leg,

He rolled on the ground, clasping his thigh. He cried in pain. "Please. Don't shoot. Don't shoot."

"You move one foot, and I'll put you out of your misery for good," Jimmy shouted.

I hoped Bowling Ball took Jimmy at his word because Jimmy was not one for idle threats.

Jimmy slid to his knees beside me. He kept his pistol trained on Bowling Ball. "How are we doing, Chief?"

"I've been better," I said. "They got me in the same shoulder, as the last one I took."

Jimmy grinned. "At least it ain't the left shoulder."

"At this point, I don't give a shit. I just need to stop getting shot."

Jimmy took out his phone. He tapped in three numbers and held the phone to his ear. "Hi, we have a couple of people down with gun-shot wounds." He looked down at Jandro. "Another one down from a beating." He winked at me. "Family Kingdom." He listened to the dispatcher. "That's right, Family Kingdom, ma'am." Pause. "I don't know what the deal is down here. But if you could get an ambulance down here as soon as possible it would be great."

He tucked the phone in his pocket and reached down and tapped me on my good shoulder. "Okay, Fuzzy. I'm out of here. Give me a call, if you need anything else, that doesn't involve me spending a night in jail."

He jogged off in the direction he had come.

I scooted on my butt over to where Jandro lay motionless. I placed two fingers on his throat. No pulse.

I remembered the little boy searching for sea shells and finding them all broken. When he realized they were all broken, he gave up and went to play in the ocean.

Everything was broken, but for some reason I thought I could fix it.

Now Marisol was out a brother. Papi, a son.

I closed my eyes and waited on the ambulance.

29

I recalled the paramedics coming, and the cops trying to ask me questions. But the memories were all an incoherent mess.

When I awoke at Grand Strand Medical in a darkened room only lit by a door partially opened to the corridor beyond, I noticed another presence in the room. I looked to my right where a shadowy mass stood in the corner of the room.

"You killed him, didn't you?" I asked.

The shadowy figure remained in the corner of the room out of the accusatory light bleeding in from the doorway, but the smell of old tobacco smoke gave him away.

"Why do you say that?" he said.

"You were the only one, besides me, that knew where they met to be together."

The shadowy mass fidgeted. "I don't know if that is true, any more than you."

"You knew they were there the night Coach was killed," I said. "You told me that. You saw me go home with Michelle."

"Why would I kill Coach? His case was my meal ticket."

"That's what I can't figure out," I said. "Why you killed him? But he wasn't your meal ticket. They took you off the case, before I started snooping around."

He stepped from his corner. Into the light. His face, as goofy looking as ever. "I told you the girl was like a Venus-fly trap. Look at you now."

He stood over me. He took the little device that pushed more morphine into my system into his hand.

"That's what happened isn't it? You fell for the girl. Just like Coach, Sample, everyone," I said.

He pressed the button. The machine chirped and bubbled and fed a drip of morphine into my vein. Michaels leaned over me and said in a hushed tone. "I could pump you so full of morphine the only thing they could do for you is announce it as an accidental overdose."

That was complete B.S. They programmed the system to limit the amount of the drug that would be available in a certain timeframe, but I let that pass. "Jesus, Michaels you smell like an ashtray. Your gonna give me cancer just inhaling your fumes. Back the fuck off."

He stepped away from the bed. "You ain't got nothin', Koella."

"You're right," I said. And then I tried something. "I got something you don't though."

"Yeah," he said. In the light from the corridor, his face looked like a garish clown with its makeup scraped off. "What's that?"

"A night with the girl," I said. "She may be a Venus-fly trap like you say, but at least I got a taste of the nectar."

He leapt forward, again hovering over me. His face was inches from my own. "I could fucking kill you right now."

I held up the nurse's call button. "We should have company, soon."

He turned his back on me and walked away. "Fuck you, Koella."

As he opened the door to walk out, I said, "One thing I never understood, Michaels."

He stopped with the knob still in his hand and stood there and waited for me to continue.

"What was it with the drive-bys on Marisol? I get you were pussy-whipped, and she wanted nothing to do with you, but why try to run her over?"

He shook his head. "That was just message sending. She needs to get her act together."

"Michaels, I will get this pinned on you," I said. "You can count on it.

My vision went fuzzy, and I felt the world tilt on its axis. I closed my eyes to settle the effects of the morphine. When I reopened them, he was gone, but the morphine was there seducing me to sleep.

I resisted its allure. Scanned the room for my phone. I couldn't see it, but an old landline room phone sat on the night stand to my right. My wounded shoulder and the broken wrist were both on my right. So I rolled on that side. Searing hot pain screamed in my shoulder. Then my hip rolled up on my cracked wrist, and I understood all new levels of torture.

It took several tries. Each time, I was a little better at avoiding the worst of my injuries, and my reach extended. Finally, I took the phone in one hand. The numbers were not on the receiver, so I tucked it in between my shoulder and jaw, turned over and bit my lip against the pain, and punched in numbers I knew by heart.

"Hel-lo, V?"

"Fuzzy, where are you? Your voice sounds funny."

The bed tilted and rocked like a small craft on the seas. I

looked to the light in the doorway and tried to anchor my equilibrium. "I'm in the hospital. But I'm okay."

"Oh God, what happened?"

"Are you okay?" I asked her.

"Ugh, Fuzzy, talk to me. What happened?"

I imagined her sitting there with panic in her eyes. I wanted to save her from that, but I also knew she would see through any lie. The truth would cause less grief. "I got shot in the same shoulder as before."

There was an audible gasp from her side of the line.

"I'm okay," I said.

The world went black. After what seemed like an hour of emptiness, somewhere in the vast darkness I heard her calling, "Fuzzy."

"Huh," I said. "Veronica?"

"Oh God, Fuzzy."

I opened my eyes and the light above my bed shifted and spun. Nausea grew in my esophagus.

"Fuzzy, you're scaring me."

"Veronica..."

"I'm serious, Fuzzy. Is there a nurse there I can talk to?"

I remembered pressing the nurse call button, but that had to be hours ago. I remembered no one coming. What kind of hospital was this? I forgot about the nurse and tried to focus on what I had to say to Veronica. It was difficult to keep one thought in my head, and whatever needed saying was important. But what was it?

"Veronica..."

"Fuzzy, get me the damn nurse!"

"Veronica, I love you."

Nurse Ra Ra came through the door. Her face came in and out of focus. The expression changed from cheerleader smile to concern. "Is there something I can help you with? I received a call."

"Did you see him? The man, who came to see me? The killer?"

Her eyes dilated, and the whites swam in my vision. "Who? I saw no one..."

I closed my eyes and slept for a season. Veronica's voice echoed in the darkness of my dreamless sleep, "Fuzzy, oh God."

EPILOGUE

On a tip from an anonymous caller, a South Carolina State Trooper pulled Shane Michaels over in Conway, SC, less than a mile away from his office. He searched the white Nissan Maxima. In the trunk, he found a bloodied and splintered Louisville Slugger baseball bat. It bore the signature of Alex Rodriguez on the sweet spot of the bat. I never learned how Michaels came to have Jandro's prized A-rod bat. He awaits trial for the murder of Coach Thomas Michael Cain. Detective Rod Gilbreath was credited with the collar.

Papi Rodriguez never got his bat back, and he never got his son back. Jandro Rodriguez died under Swamp Fox that night from blunt force trauma to the head. Uncle Rod never asked me if the blunt force trauma was my handy work. They listed me as a victim of the attempted assault that ended in Jandro's death. They never identified the shooter from that night. I never corrected the police on the number of shooters.

Papi got his beautiful daughter back if only momentarily. Marisol Rodriguez wasn't implicated in any of the events leading up to and surrounding the murder of Coach Cain. I wiped my phone and computer clean of the pictures I had taken. I dropped the hard copies in an illegal beach bonfire Jimmy, Veronica, and I had on the night of my dismissal from the hospital. Marisol attends Coastal Atlantic University courtesy of funds from the Inaugural Thomas M. Cain Scholarship Fund, sponsored by one Horatio James Alou. Neither Marisol nor Papi will speak to me. I expected that. I suppose. Jandro, despite his faults, loved both of them.

As always, Sample stayed out of trouble with the law. He bides his time at the Second Avenue Fishing Pier where he fishes for sharks and awaits the change of season which will bring a fresh batch of dope heads to the Strand.

I saw Michelle, about a month after the festivities at the Swamp Fox, tending bar at Flattop's. Despite not being named Carol, she fits right in with the rest of the staff. She wants nothing to do with me, either. She looks no better. But I learned from a little boy on the beach one cool morning that not everything can be fixed.

I took Veronica down to Treasure Island on the West Coast of Florida where I booked us on a long-range party boat out of John's Pass. She spent the three days at sea complaining of the smell, trying to keep her hair from getting ruined by the salt air, and beaming with pride when I reeled up a fat snapper. As was always the case with Veronica, she seemed to take her enjoyment from my pleasure. I determined to change that. Everything was broken in the case of Marisol Rodriguez.

I would fix Veronica and me.

ABOUT THE AUTHOR

Anthony DeCastro is a life-long fan of detective fiction. He
has designed religious facilities where thousands of people
worship every weekend, managed the construction of industrial factories for a multi-national corporation, and played
minor league baseball for three weeks. Through all of it he
has written. He figures it's time to let the world read his
stories. *Everything is Broken* is his first novel.

To hear about new releases, interact with the author and
other readers, and preview opening chapters of other entries
in the Fuzzy Koella series visit:

https://www.facebook.com/groups/anthonydecastropulp
or
tonydwritespulp.wordpress.com

75770751R00167

Made in the USA
Columbia, SC
19 September 2019